# The Night of the Virgin

a novel

## Elliott Turner

I0589204

First Edition, 2017

Round Ball Media Publishing

Houston, Texas

Round Ball Media LLC

ISBN-13: 978-0-692-78103-6

# Table of Contents

For Cristhian.
Thanks for believing before seeing.

# PART ONE

Prayer to the Virgin of Guadalupe:

*"Acuérdate, oh misericordiosisima Virgen de Guadalupe, que ninguno de los que han acudido a tu protección, implorando tu asistencia y reclamando tu socorro ha sido abandonado por tí. ¡Animado con esta confianza a tí acudo, Oh Virgen Madre! Y aunque gimiendo bajo el peso de mis pecados, me atrevo a comparecer ante tu presencia soberana. ¡No deseches Oh Madre de Dios! Mis humildes súplicas, antes bien inclina a ellas tus oídos y dígnate atenderlas favorablemente. Amén."*

Elliott Turner

# Chapter 1

Manny grimaced and trembled in pain on the hospital bed; he clenched his jaw to not shout in agony. The doctor had just delicately lifted the heel of Manny's left foot; that simple action shot lightning bolts of pain all up and down his shin. The doctor then slowly placed Manny's leg back on a pillow. The doctor's cold, brown eyes betrayed no optimism. Manny felt that the worst was likely the truth: he had broken his leg. The doctor suggested that they wait until tomorrow to do x-rays. In the meantime, hopefully a sling, ice, and Acetaminophen would leave Manny in better shape.

Only hours earlier, Manny had suffered a tremendous shock when, lying on the field of play, he had taken off his soccer cleat and felt his leg hanging by only muscles and skin. The freak accident occurred so suddenly and unexpectedly that his teammates at first only stood in a circle around him; they gawked in terror. Even the coach covered his mouth with his hand. Manny's teammate Bryce picked him up in his burly arms, carried him to Bryce's car, and drove him to the emergency room. Manny's left foot rested on the car floor with terrible consequences: every sharp turn and sudden stop shook his wobbly leg.

After the doctor left the room, Manny asked the nurse to turn off the light. She did so and also left. Alone, Manny checked his cell phone for messages. Bryce had found parking and would be up shortly. He had stayed with Manny for the first few hours, but left to find him toothpaste, a toothbrush, and deodorant at a nearby pharmacy. Manny marveled at the kindness of his teammate Bryce, whom he barely knew. Bryce had always been nice at practice, but this was above and beyond your typical good Samaritan.

Manny wondered about Hector. Three weeks had passed since they'd last spoken by phone. They'd exchanged a few Facebook messages, but that was it. Hector, who had been his best friend since childhood, seemed a complete stranger. They both lived in San Francisco, but never saw each other anymore. Manny also thought of his family back in Texas: his half-sister Maribel in Edinburg and the rest of his family back in Brownsville. They were in the same country, but it felt like the other side of the world.

Manny even thought of his dad. Manny hadn't known a thing about him for years, but wondered where he was, what he was doing, how he looked. Slowly, the Acetaminophen kicked in, the pain subsided, and fatigue forced Manny's eyes to shut. Dozens of memories raced circles in his head.

# Chapter 2

One fine spring day, a faded and black 1998 Toyota Corolla cruised up highway 281 in the deep South of Texas. Inside the automobile sat Emmanuel Hernandez, his best friend Hector Gutierrez, and Manny's half-sister Maribel. It was early morning and the April sun pounded the dash. The windows were open because the air conditioning did not work. Manny rode shotgun and gazed out at the mesquite trees, dead shrubs, and dying grass which constituted vegetation in the Rio Grande Valley. They zipped by familiar, small towns like Mercedes, Alamo, San Juan, and Edinburg. All led to one point: a date with destiny in Falfurrias, Texas.

Manny had just turned eighteen, the age of legal emancipation in Texas. He had also just fought with his mother for the seemingly thousandth time. She was a former schoolteacher and had insisted he get a high school diploma, then a college degree, and eventually some job behind a desk. Since he was a toddler, she had talked about him working in some office and wearing a black suit *con corbata* and pointed dress shoes.

Manny, a star soccer player for Lopez High School, harbored other plans. He threw away college recruiting letters in large part when he realized that all they offered were four more years of books and a miserable stipend. Maribel had just finished her third year at nearby University of Texas - Pan American, but had failed to convince him to follow her down the college path. She had infected Manny with a voracious appetite for reading, but the formalities of attending class and taking notes bored him.

To say Manny frustrated his high school teachers would be an understatement. In advanced placement Spanish, he would sit quietly in class most weeks, say nothing, and then suddenly unleash a perfectly worded diatribe in Spanish on a secondary character in *Cien Años de Soledad*. The next day, he would fail a pop quiz on properly placing accents.

When speaking, his tone suggested fluency, but his sentences fell apart grammatically near the end. He was a master of the subjunctive, but, when writing, found even the simple past-tense confounding. He was a textbook example of Chicano Spanish: insecurity impeded natural ability.

As for English, he devoured books on his own time, but clearly disdained the school's required reading list. He lived off Sparknotes and refused to crack open *Wuthering Heights* or any other Gothic literature. Yet, at the same time, he'd corner his teacher, Ms. Pribyl, during her planning period and wax passionately on a short story from *Drown*.

As Manny, Hector, and Maribel sped past the Buc-ee's gas station just north of Edinburg, Manny's stomach tightened and churned. Nervous sweat covered his wrists and palms. They were only an hour from Falfurrias. In that small town, the immigration checkpoint struck fear into the heart of any person without papers. Immigration officials stopped all motorists to look for drugs and *indocumentados*. In Spanish, the checkpoint was called a *"garrita,"* which means "claw." Manny thought of a giant claw and glanced nervously at Hector. Hector just smiled back and rolled his eyes. Maribel dozed off in the backseat.

It was easy for Maribel and Hector to relax. Both were US citizens. Manny's friends called them: *papelados* because they had papers. Manny, though, was another story. He had been brought to the US from Mexico as a child sans proper paperwork. His school social worker called him *indocumentado* or *migrante*, but his friends and family knew the right word: *mojado*. He was about to try and get past the *garrita* for the very first time. Manny was hopeful, but at the same time imagined the worst case scenario: a short stay in an immigration jail and then a one-way bus ticket to Matamoros.

Manny's dark fears contrasted with the pleasantly warm day outside. Manny felt the heat of the sun on his arm, which was sticking out of the window. Still, he could not relax. A sign said only ten miles to Falfurrias. He was terrified, but couldn't wait.

# Chapter 3

Hector and Manny sat in the front of the Corolla, dumbstruck. The car was parked in front of Stricklands, which was a mom-and-pop country restaurant in Falfurrias. Hector and Manny could look back at the *garrita* and chuckle. They'd done it. The officer stopped them, asked Hector if everybody was a citizen, Hector had nodded, and then they'd passed. No secondary. No further questions. *Pan comido.*

Manny could finally relax, but a new, equally powerful sensation gripped him. He looked outside the Corolla and saw the same South Texas shrub land, but the horizon now seemed endless. Ever since he found out about his legal status as an adolescent in the worst of ways - a school vaccination drive - he had felt fenced in. He viewed the Rio Grande Valley as a prison and his sentence was ad infinitum.

The fact his mother hid the secret from him for so long only made finding out ten times worse. In retrospect, a whole trail of clues from childhood pointed to only one explanation. His mother had insisted since high school that he never travel to Laredo or San Antonio for club soccer games. That's because of the checkpoints. He had never seen his birth certificate or Social Security card. His mom never got him a U.S. passport allegedly because it was too expensive. She had totally flipped out when, at fifteen, he talked about getting a learner's permit.

She herself never had her license on her when she got pulled over for traffic infractions. She always told the police that she had left it at home. This was technically true, but she was referring to her Mexican driver's license which was in a house in Southern Mexico. She had left it there decades ago. Officers just fined her and told her to go home.

Manny would never forget how he found out. As a freshman in high school, a well-meaning nurse had asked for his Social Security number to track down missing vaccination records in a database. His mom ignored the nurse's phone calls and letters. Then, the nurse sent a letter by certified mail. His mom ignored it. Finally, the Principal got involved, insisted on a meeting, and the truth came out. Manny had been born in Chiapas, Mexico.

Manny had felt angry, confused, and sad. Manny couldn't help but be a bit jealous of his younger brother and sister; both were born in Brownsville. They got Medicaid and could go to a Doctor's office to get shots. He had to go to the county health clinic, which was always *hasta la pata* and full of secretaries who filed their nails and looked down their nose at you.

Still, half of Manny's friends didn't have papers either, so life changed little at first. However, as high school games got more attention and soccer scouts appeared in the stands, inquiries came about Manny's age and his birth certificate. Scouts explained that they had been burned on high school prodigies that turned out to be baby-faced 24-year-olds. Nobody could commit to Manny without seeing his birth certificate. Manny had a sweet left-foot, but was also vertically challenged. At only 5'6 and 130 pounds, his stature did not help his case for recruitment either.

Manny grew even more resentful when, sophomore year, his friends with papers turned sixteen and could head over to Matamoros, Mexico and drink and go dancing. Things reached an apex junior year when kids started talking about applying to and attending colleges north of Falfurrias. They could pass the *garrita* without blinking. Manny resented them for this unseen privilege.

Today, though, Manny had passed Falfurrias, and he felt that America, the country he had always known and loved and called his own, was truly his. They went inside and the elderly Stricklands waitress took their orders. Manny requested a chicken-fried steak with gravy, Hector got a hamburger, and Maribel ordered chicken tenders with honey mustard. Nobody dared to ask about the tacos or enchiladas on the menu. In truth, each was eager to try anglo food prepared by anglos.

Halfway through the meal, two off-duty Border Patrol agents in lime-green uniforms entered and sat at a table near the entrance. Manny was sitting in the booth with his back to them and didn't notice, which was for the better; he would have trembled and fidgeted to his own detriment.

Maribel noticed that both officers were in their late twenties, had jet black hair, and were brown-skinned. They were presumably Hispanic. The one on the right was easily six-foot tall with broad shoulders and a muscular build. The one on the left had a goatee, buzz cut, and was *chaparro* and a bit *gordito*.

She also noticed that Hector watched keenly as the officers entered. He looked both up and down before settling his gaze on the tall one.

# Chapter 4

As San Antonio approached, the landscape changed slowly and then dramatically. In the Rio Grande Valley, the relentless sun and dried dirt choke life out of all but the fiercest plants. Manny had always thought that mesquite tree branches could easily pass for the roots of a normal tree. Mesquite trees looked to him as though God had grabbed and uprooted a regular tree, flipped it, and buried it head-first in the sand.

Now, from the backseat, Manny saw green bushes and even patches of native Buffalo grass. His cell phone hummed twice in his pocket. He ignored it.

Up front, Hector reached for the MP3 player which was plugged into the car radio. Maribel grabbed his hand. "Just wait until this song ends." Hector glared at her and withdrew his hand. He mumbled loudly: "*Basta de Bachata ya,*" and shook his head. Every song selection had been a battle for the past three hours, but Maribel had won by persistence. Hector's mumbling was a white flag.

They pulled over at a small gas station. Manny stepped out to pump gas and prepaid with a PayPal debit card. Manny was somewhat financially savvy for an eighteen-year-old and had helped his mother with her checkbook and accounts for years. He acquired the PayPal debit card by luck. When an uncle had been deported for the fifth time, said uncle had left the debit card and attached bank account with plenty of funds to Manny with one condition: a favor. Return said uncle's overdue Terminator 2 DVD to Blockbuster.

That infamous uncle, Jose, one of his dad's countless brothers, had crossed the border numerous times, often near Piedras Negras, but sometimes around Reynosa or Matamoros. Jose knew the lay of the land by memory. However, each day the *migra* and the *maña* made the crossing more dangerous. Before Jose was transferred to an immigration facility, Manny visited Jose in county jail and brought him his Mexican passport. Jose had a wife, kids, and unpaid debts to family members and Conn's, but only cared about Blockbuster. No matter how bad his credit or how many times he got deported, Blockbuster had always been there for him.

Manny had sworn to find the DVD in Jose's apartment and return it as expeditiously as possible. Thus, Jose rewarded Manny's kindness with the debit card. Months later, at the gas station, Manny recalled the promise he had made. The DVD was in his backpack, but, to his dismay, the last remaining Blockbuster in Edinburg had closed weeks prior to their passing through. Manny hoped there'd be another Blockbuster in San Antonio.

He finished pumping gas while Hector and his sister stood and talked by the side of the building. Hector puffed on a Virginia Slim, coughed, and ran his hands through his long, curly, and disheveled black hair. Since leaving the army months earlier, he'd really let himself go: he hadn't shaved in weeks, and had put on at least twenty pounds.

They all got back in the car. This time, Maribel drove. Manny's cell phone hummed twice. Then another time. At a red light, Maribel turned around and glared at Manny. "Is that *Catracha*? You did talk with her, right? *Right?*" Hector also looked at Manny in the dash mirror.

Manny remained silent. Hector rolled his eyes and Maribel cursed in Spanish under her breath. Manny pulled out his cell and read the first message: "*Dónde estás? LLámame.*"

# Chapter 5

A man's voice whispers into Manny's left ear: "*¡Marica! ¿A qué hora te levantas?*" A hand lightly shakes Manny's shoulder. Confused and only half-awake, Manny recognizes the man: his father. Manny opens his eyes and sees he is laying on the double-bed he shared with his younger brother during his childhood. Spiderman sheets are wrapped around his waist and legs.

Suddenly, a series of beeps fills Manny's ears and he wakes up a second time. The Spiderman sheets have disappeared and have been replaced by the sterile, white sheets of a hospital bed. He is groggy and wearing a green gown. His left leg is elevated and in a sling. He is alone in a small room in San Francisco General Hospital and it's two o'clock in the morning. His leg throbs. The Acetaminophen must have worn off. He also needs to pee, but can't stop thinking about his dad.

"*Marica,*" a pejorative similar to "fag," was what his dad called all boys and men with slight builds. His father had picked up the bad habit of saying "*marica*" while serving in Tampico, Mexico, with the *Fuerzas Marinas*. Other annoying habits of his dad's from the military were: rising before dawn, meticulously planning each day, and waking up people *to ask what time they would be getting up later*.

Manny smiled at the recollection, and then called for a nurse. She arrived shortly and started to help him get up and move his leg, but his screams threatened to wake up patients in other rooms. The nurse, a short and middle-aged white woman with green eyes, looked side-to-side with a knowing hint. Manny mumbled, but could not form words. Still, she nodded. "I know, I know. Wait here."

She scurried out of the room and left Manny to his thoughts. He texted Maribel to let her know that he was okay. She was probably in her dorm room in Edinburg, still awake, wired on coffee, and cramming for some exam. He sent an update to Bryce, who had gone home to sleep. Again, Manny looked at his contacts and stopped to look at one name: Hector. Almost a month had passed by since *the incident*.

The nurse returned with a bedpan in hand. She smiled. "Can you figure this out? Should I show you how to..." Manny's head throbbed, but he nodded no. He was embarrassed. She handed him the bedpan, turned off the light, and stepped out. Manny relieved himself, took some more Acetaminophen, and went back to sleep.

# Chapter 6

For the seemingly hundredth time, Hector reached for the MP3 player and Maribel protested with a low growl. She loved *música romántica* and *bachata*; he adored rap and reggaeton. Even the few genres they both enjoyed soon became points of contention. Hector swore that, in the Spanish language, Maná was the greatest rock band of all time. Maribel preferred the Argentine group Soda Stereo, or even Spanish rockers *Héroes del Silencio*.

Manny finally texted with *Catracha* and slowly worked up the nerve to maybe call her. In truth, he hated speaking with her when other ears could hear him. He preferred to isolate himself in a bedroom or bathroom in part due to intimacy. He would never admit it, but, equally important, he spoke to her in cutesy couple-speak and he never used that tone in front of other guys. He worried that Hector would have his balls if he heard Manny cooing like that.

He called her and tried not to coo, and the conversation lasted only five minutes. When she heard that he had gotten past the *garrita* in a car, she breathed a sigh of relief. A few years ago, she told Manny, one of her cousins had tried to pass the checkpoint by hiking in the dense woods. Nobody had heard from him since. Everybody in the Valley had a story about a friend or *primo* who had entered that labyrinth of mesquite trees only to get ditched by their *pollero*, the Mexican term for "guide" that literally means "chicken-handler." Not all the handlers were friendly, and not all the chicks survived the trip.

Hearing *Catracha*'s voice soothed Manny. He loved to hear her speak Spanish to him in her flowing Central American dialect. The cadence reminded him of an excited mockingbird; the tone flowed up and down as the sentences raced to reach the second-to-last syllable of the very last word. She also used proper Castilian terms he had to guess at, look up on Google, or ask his mom about.

Manny's dad was even around when *Catracha* first started coming by the house in high school. She initially won his father over with her use of the formal "*usted*" in Spanish and always called him

"*Don Hernandez*" this and "*Don Hernandez*" that. However, one day, his dad drove by her trailer lot and saw her mowing the lawn; she was wearing running shorts with a big white cotton shirt draped over a black bikini top. Seeing a woman doing physical labor disgusted him. His father still acknowledged her presence and was cordial, but disparagingly called her "*Marimacho*" and "*exhibicionista*" behind her back.

That actually made Manny love her more.

Unlike *Catracha*, Manny had made a mess of things when meeting her parents during that first dinner at her house. *Catracha's* mom pulled out all the stops and made a fine Honduran meal with several courses. Manny, though, after trying and loving *maduro frito* - fried plantain - had looked at the big, steaming plate of rice and beans and like any good Mexican asked: "*¿Dónde está el carne?*" The nervous silence taught him that Mexico is not Central America. One country's side dish is another's main plate.

Manny checked his Facebook and then napped. When he woke, the skyline of downtown San Antonio beckoned in the distance. He'd never seen with his own eyes a skyscraper taller than the twenty-story Chase building in downtown McAllen. The point of the Tower of the Americas loomed over all of San Antonio and threatened to cut a hole in the sky.

Hector checked his cell for directions and turned right off the interstate. He then took a couple farm-to-market roads before ending up at the gates of a mobile home park. The complex was about the size of a city block and had five rows of trailers. Each mini-street in the complex was named after a tropical fruit, like: "Pineapple Avenue." The sign on the gate said: "Welcome to Paradise Island." Below the text, a cartoon depicted the face of a blonde woman smiling under a palm tree. Below that, though, a piece of cardboard was taped to the fence and warned: "All visiters check in with gard."

Hector smiled, looked at Maribel, and then at Manny. "*Agárrense*," he warned. "Boros' trailer is supposed to be the nice one."

# Chapter 7

Since the fall of the Tower of Babel, languages have proliferated over the Earth. Often, who you can understand depends on the geographic proximity of your birth. Thousands of years ago, a raging river separating two human tribes could result in hundreds of years of little contact and the development of entirely distinct tongues. In the Rio Grande Valley, the *Rio Bravo* has long separated the US from Mexico and English from Spanish. Yet those inhabiting the border often speak both languages and have twisted the two tongues.

Hector spoke much more Spanish than Manny, but their close friendship and shared sense of humor led to a unique dialect of Spanglish intelligible only to them. For instance, they insisted on literally translating words and phrases from English-to-Spanish, resulting in nonsensical terms such as: *"Via del Sub"* for "Subway." In Spanish, a common Mexican phrase for hitting on a person is: *"echarle los perros."* On many occasions, Hector and Manny would see a beauty from afar, look at one another, and mumble: "Time to toss the dogs."

After a few honks, a skinny white teenager in a wifebeater appeared, unlocked a chain, pulled back the black gate, and ushered the Corolla into Paradise Island. Hector laughed, Maribel fretted, and Manny said in disbelief: *"El Toro* lives here? This place looks a little too *neighborhood."* "What?" Maribel asked. "You know, *barrio."*

As they rolled down the narrow gravel streets, they saw trailers that had withstood the test of time and more than a few windstorms. Cracked paint dotted the double-wides and wood decks sorely missed floorboards. Stray dogs roamed the area, just like in the Valley.

Finally, they arrived at the trailer on Mango Street. Nobody came out to greet them. In his head, Manny calculated the amount of money he had in his uncle's account and divided it by the $40 per night he'd have to pay at a motel. Finances dictated that he had no choice but to grin and accept Hector's plan to stay with *El Toro*. More importantly, Hector had assured Manny that *El Toro* still had useful connections with the professional soccer world.

They parked and slowly got out of the car. The double-wide before them had been painted baby blue in the 1990's and repainted light gray in certain sections, probably around the early 2000's. Broken blinds cluttered all the windows, but at least the wooden deck seemed relatively new and welcoming. Unlike the neighbors' decks, no boards were missing and it had been stained a dark brown. A small charcoal grill wore a gray tarp like a maternity dress.

Manny recalled the great moments of *El Toro*'s career in Liga MX, the Mexican professional soccer league, as recounted to him by his own dad before YouTube existed. *El Toro* won his first championship with his hometown club in Aguascalientes, then made a big money move to Mexico City, and then disastrously missed a penalty for *El Tri* in the World Cup. He was a hulking figure in his day with a fierce temper and a curly, black mullet. Part of Manny still refused to believe such a star could be living here.

Hector stood at the base of the deck stairs and called out. Nothing stirred. He took a few cautious steps up the stairs, and then the front door rattled and opened. Out came a red-headed white girl, probably mid-thirties, with a pudgy yet still hourglass figure, and nervous green eyes. She was clearly not *El Toro*.

# Chapter 8

Her name was Esme, and she was *El Toro's* wife. The fifth, by many estimates. Most had lost count, including *El Toro* himself. For two boys from the Rio Grande Valley, Esme's whiteness was exotically foreign and enveloped her every movement in mystery and allure. Manny hung on every word of her first utterance: "Who the fuck are y'all?"

The Southern intonation and third person plural sent shivers up his spine. He found adorable the way she ate the "g" at the end of gerunds and omitted the "s" entirely from certain contractions. When she turned to lead them into the trailer, her low-hung jean shorts and too short t-shirt offered a glimpse of a butterfly tattoo on her lower back; the ink had faded and the image had blurred quite a bit. Still, Manny failed this scribbly Rorschach test: he stared without shame.

Upon entering the trailer, Maribel's mind appraised this vixen in a two-note staccato of observation and judgment. The once white carpet in the main entry room had not been vacuumed in ages. *Floja.* Dirty dishes filled both sinks in the kitchen and a days-old bowl of macaroni loitered on the countertop. *Sucia.* Dust covered the TV stand and all the window sills. *Perezosa.* She also saw the pasty cellulitic legs that so enamored her brother, and, even worse, how Esme basked in the young boys' attention. *Sinvergüenza.*

If Manny and Hector shared a unique dialect of Spanglish, then Manny and his sister spoke an obscure language of literary references. Their love for reading sprung not from their mother, a burned out former teacher, but rather circumstance. One summer, when Manny's mom worked cleaning houses, she realized that the kids could spend all day at the library and she would save money on running the air conditioner at home. Thus, each morning, from May until August, Maribel and her younger half-siblings were dropped off at the James Sekula Memorial Library off Ruben Torres Boulevard. They learned to appreciate the written word *a huevo.*

The next summer, the pattern repeated itself. Maribel dived deeper into obscure literary fiction and dragged her brother down with her. As Manny and Maribel's young love of reading grew, their attention span for the audiovisual median shrunk drastically. Whenever they saw Manny's mom plunked on the couch and watching a *telenovela*, they sighed and complained about "The Entertainment." Only they got the D.F.W. reference, which was the way they liked it.

Thus, Manny pried his eyes off the tramp stamp and his ears perked up when he heard his sister utter: "this trip is about to jump the cruise ship." The *Corrections* reference was not lost on him, nor the ominous warning. "To jump the cruise ship" was, in their parlance, to lose the plot. Things could go downhill precipitously.

# Chapter 9

*El Toro* Boros still possessed a hulking physical presence, but moved with the speed of a disoriented turtle. Manny recoiled at seeing *El Toro* clunk along inside the trailer; the man's surgically-repaired knees struggled under his own weight. Still, *El Toro* was very tall and his hands were massive, even if they trembled. At times, *El Toro* looked on the verge of falling over, but still politely insisted that Hector stay seated in the recliner. One of the plastic patio chairs they used indoors would be good enough for him.

*El Toro* and Hector's father had been close friends in Michoacana, Mexico, he explained, where they grew up in the same *pueblo* of a few hundred souls. Their paths diverged when, at sixteen, Hector's dad and his family moved to Acapulco to open a t-shirt shop. By that time, *El Toro*, a legend in the state for a few *golazos*, trained with adults and it was only a question of when he would sign a pro contract. Still, *El Toro* never forgot the dark times of his youth, when, on the edge of starvation Hector's grandmother would *fiar tortillas* and invite him and his siblings over for rice with *sopa de frijoles*.

*El Toro* joked that Hector's dad had been the soccer star in their youth, and he had taught *El Toro* how to kick the ball off a defender's shin near the sideline to win a throw-in. He punched Hector on the shoulder and expectorated: "*¡Pura maña, tu papá!*" He then snapped in perfect English to Esme: "*Güerita*, bring these two young gentlemen some cold ones." He did not care about their ages, or that Maribel uttered a grunt of disapproval.

Despite *El Toro*'s sociability and rapport with Hector, Manny sensed something amiss. At times, *El Toro*'s tongue bumbled in search of the right word, like a flickering light bulb about to burn out.

The white roots on his trimmed mullet contrasted with his jet black bangs and eyebrows, and thus betrayed his age. *El Toro* had partied too hard during the good times, and the recent decade had aged him in dog years. Still, when *El Toro* thought nobody was looking, he glanced at Maribel like a *carne asada* and started to refer to her as *doncella*.

Esme noticed the nickname, was unsure what it literally meant, still was very annoyed, and the mutual enmity between her and Maribel was assured.

Maribel, often lost between books and daydreams, seemed to fail to notice the male attention. It was not the first time. Still, she had tagged along with Hector and Manny to keep an eye on her brother, but also to eventually head to Austin to see a boy. Once she was sure Manny could handle things, she'd be on her way. She had never once doubted in her brother's talent.

However, Maribel knew little of professional sports and had assumed Manny's early path would consist of only a tryout and then a contract. Like Manny and even Hector, she was basically clueless.

# Chapter 10

*El Toro* knew of a lower-division side in San Antonio and had the contacts to land Manny a trial session. However, the pride of the athlete swells eternally. Where once *El Toro* looked at players as rivals, he now viewed them as objects brimming with potential. Scouting greatness in others was his passion. Still, he dared not risk sending a player on trial to any club who he himself did not rank a nine out of ten. He had to watch Manny play with his own two eyes. And Manny's height worried him.

After everybody settled into somewhat awkward sleeping arrangements that first night, *El Toro* made a call and arranged for Manny to play an indoor game on the other side of town the next night. *El Toro*, Hector, Esme, and Manny rode out to the arena in *El Toro*'s old black van. Most of the players on the turf field were middle-aged Hispanic men, but they all had great first touches.

*El Toro* desired to see Manny's first-touch and speed of decision-making. Within minutes, Manny scored two goals and assisted another. One of his goals, a half-volley from thirty yards, was all the more impressive given the small size of the goal. *El Toro* recognized the familiar hissing sound as a ball sweetly struck with professional-caliber technique flew through the air. The kid was a natural.

About fifteen minutes into the game, *El Toro* shouted something in Spanish at the supposed coach on the bench. Then, the coach told Manny to play defense. Immediately, Manny's shoulders sagged and his energy level dropped. He was timid in the tackle, easily muscled off the ball, and failed to stay goal-side of his mark.

Hector saw his friend tanking it and heard the frequent sighs of *El Toro*. After five minutes, Hector rose to his feet and peppered a few insults at Manny. Manny's first response was an indignant glare, but then his eyes widened and he briefly stared into space. The rest of the half, he ran his socks off and even threw himself into a few late tackles.

At halftime, *El Toro* signaled for Manny to come over to them. *"Bien hecho, chavo, bien hecho"* he said, and then pointed for him to go to the showers. Confused, Manny walked toward the locker room. Esme handed him a duffle bag with shampoo, a towel, and a change of clothes. Manny thought he had played okay, but, based on his limited playing experience, he assumed that being taken off at the half was a bad thing. A very bad thing.

*El Toro* didn't say anything during the ride home and, when they got back to the trailer, he went straight to his room, shut the door, and fell asleep. Maribel, who had stayed behind to do some reading, greeted Manny with a warm smile and a hundred questions. Manny did not know how to answer.

# Chapter 11

Manny opened his eyes, glanced around, and saw a white curtain on all sides. He looked down and a bright blue cast covered his left leg from thigh-to-toe. The cast scared him at first, but slowly he began to relax. The support from the cast meant no more unexpected shakes. The surgery must have been a success, he thought. He took off his gown and put on his athletic shorts and long-sleeved soccer jersey.

Bryce had been nice enough to loan Manny a pair of crutches, and sat in the waiting room while Manny checked out. Bryce had even agreed to let Manny live with him at his sparsely-furnished row house in South San Francisco. The selling point, in addition to the camaraderie, was a first-floor bedroom and walk-in shower. Before, Manny had rented a cramped house with teammates in San Mateo, but his second-story bedroom was now a major hindrance. Thus, everybody agreed that Manny moving in with Bryce was for the best.

Manny sat in Bryce's car, but could barely speak. He had never been seriously injured before. Part of him had expected to walk out of surgery; the reality of rehabilitation slowly crept in. Upon arrival at Bryce's house, Manny saw a quaint living room with a reclining chair in front of a 40-inch HDTV. Next to the chair, there was a coffee table upon which sat the TV remote, Roku remote, a bottle of water, a bottle of orange juice, and a box of cereal bars. Unlike Manny, Bryce explained, he himself had been injured more than a handful of times.

At the far end of the living room, two sliding glass doors opened to a small patch of grass surrounded by six-foot fences. The curtains were drawn and Manny could see a few pots filled with cacti. Manny sat on the recliner and saw some puzzling things. For example, a shoelace had been fastened to the handle of the door that led to the first-floor bedroom. Bryce explained that the lace was for Manny to be able to pull and close doors behind him more easily while on crutches.

Manny thanked Bryce as best he could, but his head was a mess from painkillers and irregular sleep. He also had a problem with charity, even from friends. He just wanted to be alone and fall asleep. He could already sense that the enforced *ocio* - uneventful days of sitting - would make hours feel like days and days feel like weeks.

Bryce went into the bedroom and came back with two small plastic bottles. He placed one, labeled Acetaminophen, on the coffee table and then stared gravely at Manny. With a classic Southern drawl, Bryce asked: "you know what this shit does, right?" Manny glanced from side-to-side, and then furled his brow. "This stuff helps with the pain and you'll need it...but you're going to be *shitting bricks* man."

Bryce set the other plastic bottle on the table. The label said: "stool softener." "Take one of these every twelve hours. I'm going to head out and get you some yogurt. That'll also help. You like your yogurt blended or you want your fruit *in the bottom*?" Manny did not understand the question and missed Bryce's failed attempt at humor. He just stared. "Yeah you didn't seem *the type*. Okay, I'll just get you the blended stuff." Bryce chuckled as he exited.

Soon after Bryce left, Manny suddenly felt like ants were walking up and down his broken leg. He had never broken a limb before, and, in addition to the burning sensation, he felt the curiosity to move his leg. It felt great to lift his left leg up with the support of his cast, even if he could hear the crackle of still-forming-bones. He lifted his leg about four times, and, suddenly, he felt exhausted.

He leaned back, and, as he dozed off, he noticed an odd thing on the TV stand. In a framed, black-and-white picture, Bryce, smiling, donned a black tuxedo and had his arms wrapped around a short and skinny blonde woman. Manny knew the woman; Bryce had divorced her months ago, but there she was.

# Chapter 12

*El Toro* loved Manny's technical ability with the ball and silky first touch, but worried about the *chavo*'s size and athleticism. In his head, only two types of professional players existed: powerful bears and sprinting cheetahs. Thus, for those first few weeks in San Antonio, he drove Manny to a nearby high school football field to work on his fitness. *El Toro* ran the kid through short sprints and half-field sprints; no ball necessary. To his delight, Manny rose to each challenge and even pushed himself so hard he sometimes vomited.

*El Toro* only thought about one thing: the beep-test, that infinitely cruel measure of a soccer player's anaerobic fitness level. He knew his contact would likely ask for Manny's beep-test score before agreeing to see him. Still, *El Toro* liked what he saw: Manny pushed through stomach cramps, leg cramps, sore tendons, and even twisted ankles. Seeing him confront pain inspired *El Toro* and, in his head, dreams danced of Manny as a player for a *Primera* team like *Tigres* or even *Club América*. Of course, the frenzied journalists would want to ask *El Toro* about Manny and how *El Toro* had found and developed him.

Manny's extreme pain tolerance was not a product of chance. During his youth, his father had patrolled the sidelines of youth soccer games and watched Manny for signs of fatigue. His father constantly complained about the "*chiflazón*", a condition not formally recognized by medical practitioners, but that translates in English to "wussing out too easily." Manny's dad concocted all sorts of exercises to help his son's brain disregard physical fatigue. A few were dangerous.

Manny could not remember them all, but, his dad, proud of his son, would get drunk at barbecues and boast about the grueling workouts he put his son through. The cruelest of course was the *clavada*. On nights when there was a full moon, his dad would drive him and sometimes Pablo to the beach at South Padre Island for some swimming. In the distance, a green light glowed along the horizon and traced the ocean's edge. Manny's dad called that faint glow the *"Isla Esmeralda."*

Manny was to swim as far as possible and try to reach the *Isla Esmeralda*; he could use a kickboard which was tied to his leg. He also had a whistle attached to a wristband and was supposed to stop every twenty seconds and blow the whistle. If more than twenty seconds lapsed and he didn't blow the whistle, his dad, a former lifeguard, would dive into the water, swim up to Manny and pull him out. His dad boasted to others that, once, a wave had flipped Manny and filled his mouth and nose with water. Manny had turned upside-down, but he kept on kicking.

Every time Manny heard that particular story, he could feel his throat burn with seawater. He could even imagine his dad's arms grabbing him and tugging him to the surface.

After two weeks of sprint sessions, *El Toro* invited everybody in the trailer and a few neighbors to a barbecue. He had seen enough. He knew the kid was tough-as-nails and damn good at *futbol*. *El Toro* sung along to Vicénte Fernández and grilled *cabrito* and *pollo asado* while boasting that, come next Monday, Manny would be the newest signing for the San Antonio *Alacránes*. Manny and Hector again drank adult libations to the chagrin of Maribel, but even she downed a single Corona.

# Chapter 13

When Manny first arrived at the practice field for the trial, he saw a group of other guys already warming up, but also an older man standing on the sideline with a cigarette in one hand and a shiny cup in the other. He would learn that the man's name was Morelli De Charlus and he was the team's coach. The shiny cup was a "gourd," which was a container for *yerba mate*: a heavily-caffeinated South American tea ideal for neurotics and footballers alike.

Manny noticed that the gray hair on De Charlus' head had thinned and slowly migrated to the sides, and these remaining patches were unkempt and waved in the wind like a hand. Morelli's white dress shirt barely covered his gut and his green dress pants were four inches too long. The Argentine coach of the *Alacránes* was poorly dressed, but very confident. He intimidated Manny from the start.

During that first day of his trial, Manny beamed as he sat on the bench and first put on the yellow and black *Alacrán* training jersey. In his first week with the club, Manny scored goals in squad scrimmages, dribbled past defenders at will, and kept pace in both cone and sprint drills. His only problem was linguistic: Morelli's strongly Argentine Spanish sounded like Italian to Manny, and often the coach's rants were as unintelligible to him as an opera solo in Verdi's *Falstaff*.

The trial was to last two weeks and, on day ten, De Charlus took a break from sipping his yerba mate and finally grasped the gulf of misunderstanding between coach and player. Mexicans and Argentines both spoke Spanish, but a continent or two separated them and mutual understanding was not always assured. Thus, from that point onwards, he cussed out Manny in broken English with sprinkles of *porteño* Spanish, an even odder dialect of Spanish spoken only in Buenos Aires. "The *concha* of you mother!" "Think more rapider *pibe de mierda*!"

Manny understood based on volume: the louder the shout, the harder he ran.

However, this worsened matters; De Charlus belonged to a sect of soccer coaches who believed in pass-and-move soccer. He thought players should walk off the ball in certain areas and stick to certain zones. Running was often bad. This starkly contrasted with most Americans, many of whom viewed soccer as little more than a marathon.

Still, Manny's biggest problem was his blind spots. As a young player, he kept his eyes glued to the ball at all times and failed to survey the field around him before receiving a pass. The result was that he often feared defenders - *perhaps* behind him - who weren't actually there. The blind spots inevitably messed up his decision-making: he turned when he should pass and passed when he should turn.

In De Charlus' terminology, he was a *"regala-pelota."* On the last day of that second week, De Charlus took Manny out of his favored forward position and placed him out wide. He hoped the kid could run-and-cross like most Americans, and Manny did alright.

At the end of that very last practice, Manny sat on the end of the bench and couldn't stand up - his stomach turned knots and his legs felt wobbly. He had no clue if he would get a decision then and there. Eventually, De Charlus rambled over to Manny, lit a cigarette, and told him to plan on coming back for preseason. Manny resisted the urge to jump and punch the air. He just nodded and said: *"Sí, Señor."*

Back at the trailer, the elation smacked his head like a two-by-four. After weeks of being *incomunicado*, he texted and Facebook messaged everybody and anybody. He even called his mom. Ever since his dad had left, his mom had insisted on speaking English to prepare Manny and the others for university, but over the phone she broke into Spanish at the *emoción* of hearing her son's voice and the great news. Still, she sounded a note of caution.

She told him to focus on his soccer and stay away from *viejas*. The term meant "old woman" in Castilian, but "girlfriend" in Mexican. Manny couldn't help but joke: "Don't worry mom, I'll stay away from *viejas*. I'll only date *jovencitas*." His mother did not laugh.

# Chapter 14

*El Toro* made no plans for another barbecue, so Hector, Manny, and Maribel arranged to celebrate by finally tasting the nightlife of San Antonio. None of them had lived in a city with a population over 50,000, so they gleefully searched their phones and read reviews of bars, restaurants, and clubs. All concurred that, despite budgetary constraints, they needed to "Balbec it up," Manny and Maribel's literary parlance for *pachanguear*. However, a split soon emerged.

On the one hand, Manny and Hector let their hormones influence their restaurant preferences. They focused less on the food being served and more on the servers. They cared greatly about gender and the proportion of a waitress' skin covered by the uniform. Less uniform, greater interest. On the other hand, Maribel displayed zero interest in going to any breastauraunt or similarly-themed eatery. Hector had the car, but, ultimately, Manny refused to go anywhere sans Maribel.

They agreed on Titi's Taco Bar because of the patio and reputation for *tacos al pastor*. They arrived late-ish and the food was decent. Maribel even ordered a few beers, and then not-so-subtly passed them to her underage brother and Hector. The next stop was an allegedly over-eighteen club called "The *Licenciado*" on the River Walk, but disaster struck: Hector's Corolla would not start. His insurance did not include roadside assistance and *El Toro's* cell phone was disconnected. An attempted jump start from a passing motorist failed miserably.

A cab would be super expensive. They had to bum a ride, so Maribel stuck up her thumb and smiled at passing motorists. Eventually, a black Volkswagen Jetta pulled into Titi's parking lot. Out stepped two twenty-something Mexican females. One was *morenita* and wore a sleeveless black blouse with tight white pants and heels a mile high. The other girl wore hip-hugging faded blue jeans and a black dress shirt tied in a knot on the front and exposing her midriff. They both smiled, converged on Maribel, and unleashed a rapid fire torrent of Monterrey-accented Mexican Spanish.

Manny could barely understand them, but smiled and went along. The light-skinned girl insisted on Maribel sitting in the front passenger seat and the other girl sat in the back between the two boys. The girls were students and in their junior year at St. Mary's. Manny had heard about St. Mary's girls and now he knew what he had heard was true. They were gorgeous, but probably unattainable.

The dark one, named Maria, realized that Manny was having trouble *entendiendo*, so she spoke to him in her lightly-accented English. She shook a little in excitement when he told her that he was a soccer player for the *Alacránes*.

She was about the same height as Manny, which put him at ease. As they spoke, she eyed him *con hambre*. The girls decided to join them at The *Licenciado*. Maribel even seemed to give her blessing.

They stopped to get some Tecate, found the *Licenciado*, parked and pregamed. Before exiting the car, Maria leaned close to Manny and whispered sensually in his ear: "*¿Pero si eres un alacrán y me picas, voy a sentir una calentura en todo mi cuerpo, verdad?*"

Aside from "*alacrán*," he did not grasp another word. Still, he fully understood her fingers squeezing the inside of his thigh.

# Chapter 15

The music blared, hips gyrated, and laughs echoed all around. Only one thing interrupted the mirthful evening: Manny's cell phone. First, everybody chuckled at his now outdated Pitbull ringtone. However, the two *regias*, Maria and Gloria, exchanged suspicious glances when Manny merely checked the caller id and hung-up without answering. He eventually switched his phone to vibrate, but his pant pocket buzzed with life for a good half-hour.

Distance may upset the daily rhythm of a couple, but at certain moments they can still acutely feel the nearing precipice of a looming and even more profound absence. *Catracha* knew it was a Friday night, she had not seen Manny in weeks, and that San Antonio offered a diverse platter of nocturnal delights. She was naturally jealous and their relationship status was unclear, so his refusal to answer her phone and text messages at such an hour could only spell trouble. Each ignored call and text only enhanced her resolve: she had to hear Manny's voice before the night was over.

When Maria and Gloria went to the lady's room, Maribel grabbed Manny's arm to pull him closer and talk without Hector hearing. "What the hell is going on?" Manny tried to blow off her question, but she showed him her own cell phone. *Catracha* had sent her more than a few messages. "Fiendish," thought Manny. Maribel asked: "You did end things with her before leaving, right? Right?" Manny could only stare at the floor.

*Catracha* had dated Manny for almost three years, which was much longer than the average adolescent fling. Maribel thought of her as a sister and immediately set her sights on subtly sabotaging her brother's game.

Manny, on the other hand, could only think of one thing: sex. He desperately wanted to have it. Manny and *Catracha* had never gone all the way. He was a virgin and this bugged him greatly. In Maria's café eyes and olive-complexion, he saw an enchanting doorway to manhood.

That night, though, it did not appear meant to be. Upon returning from the bathroom, Maria suddenly took an interest almost exclusively in Hector. In fact, the two of them danced a few times, and then went to smoke in the patio area.

Manny, frustrated, tried to make small talk with Gloria, but they did not naturally click. The conversation stuttered like a car engine sans oil. She was about six inches taller than Manny, which always bugged him. Also, Gloria talked about McAllen and the RGV as if they were a magical land on par with Disney World. As a child, she explained that she had gone to Padre Island for *Semana Santa* and loved it. Manny pegged her as one of *"those regias"* who spent thousands of pesos at the designer outlet mall in Mercedes.

Gloria also didn't seem impressed by the *Alacránes* thing. She claimed she had friends who played soccer in Mexico and for schools in the US. She pointedly asked him why he didn't try to get a college scholarship. Manny politely feigned interest, but eventually ceased to ask questions and soon responded to her entreaties with three and four-word replies. Maribel and Gloria even hit a snag when they discussed school: Gloria couldn't see the value in any degree other than accounting. English? Worthless! Manny jealously watched the patio where Hector and Maria sat, smoked and laughed.

Soon, night turned to morning and the *Licenciado* closed. Maribel insisted that they scrape together funds and catch a cab back to *El Toro*'s trailer and not go visit a St. Mary's dorm room. Back at the trailer, Esme opened the door and greeted them with red eyes and a spacy smile. Maribel was furious at Manny and told him in Spanish that he owed it to *Catracha* to end things before "doing anything *pendejo*." She then pulled Hector outside and onto the deck to talk.

Manny stepped into the living room and sat by Esme on the couch. She was watching late night TV. After about twenty minutes, Hector and Maribel entered the trailer and walked straight to the second bedroom. Neither looked at Manny. It was Maribel's turn to sleep in the bedroom on the single bed while Hector dozed on the floor, so they left Manny to presumably crash on the couch after Esme retired for the night.

The very next morning, Manny, half-awake, sat up on the couch, picked up his cell phone and scrolled to the Facebook app. To his delight, both Maria and Gloria had sent him pokes and friend invites. First, though, he opened his profile and changed his status from "in a relationship" to "single." Then, he accepted the *regias'* invites, unfriended *Catracha*, turned off his phone, and went back to sleep.

# Chapter 16

Manny was so excited and so gullible that he signed the *Alacránes* contract the Monday morning before practice without even skimming it. Instead, he skipped to the last page, signed his name, and did not even ask for his own copy. He was in a rush because he had had to pay a cab to make practice, and was running ten minutes late. De Charlus hated tardiness.

During the customary two laps of jogging by the players, De Charlus laid a few tether ladders across the field. He then had the players perform a series of drills he called *"La Rayuela,"* where they either skipped, jumped, or high-stepped in a prescribed sequence. The goal was to improve the player's quick movement muscles, balance, and coordination. It also gave De Charlus a good look at the players' legs.

After a few *rayuelas*, a tall, lanky, black man in his early twenties appeared. He nonchalantly sat down on the bench at the halfway line and started to put on socks and a pair of cleats. Manny hadn't seen this guy once in the prior weeks of training. De Charlus waddled over to him, exchanged a few inaudible words, patted him on the back, and returned to the players. They played intense three versus three games with mini-goals while the black guy jogged two laps, stretched briefly, and then approached the group.

Everybody recognized him except Manny. As is common among Mexicans, chicanos, and Latin Americans, all the players referred to him as *"negro,"* meaning "black." After a few scrimmages, Manny got placed with him on the same team and, not knowing his name, screamed for a cutback pass after making a late run. With a head-fake and then a hip-fake, the man used his heel to roll a perfect pass to Manny in stride, and Manny then smashed the ball into the open net.

All smiles, Manny ran to the teammate, high-fived him, and said: "¡*Genial pase, negro!*" The man stared him down with an ice cold glare. In perfect Spanish, he declared: "*Sos nuevo, pero, para qué sepas, yo sí hablo Español y, de hecho, tengo un nombre: Junot.*" Manny was taken aback; he understood every word. The player, named Junot, spoke Honduran Spanish, similar to *Catracha*. Junot just wanted to be called "Junot" and not referred to by his skin color. Manny could understand that. He felt ashamed.

Manny stumbled out an apology in Spanish. "*Yo siento. ¿Me acepta mis disculpas?*" Junot smirked and answered: "Yeah, I also speak English bro. Just giving you shit. I grew up in Jersey. What's your name?" Manny was almost too nervous to answer.

# Chapter 17

Manny enjoyed modest success on the field of play, but struggled socially in San Antonio. Being born a Mexican and raised Mexican-American, this confounded him greatly. Everywhere he looked, he saw young, beautiful, and feisty *latinas* and *chicanas* as far as the eye could see. However, when approaching them, either in a bar, a cafe, or a bookstore, something failed to click. A wall existed between them and him. He could feel this wall, but not breach it. Thus, he hit his head against it over and over.

Eventually, he sought guidance. Maribel encouraged Manny to just be himself and try to ask sincere questions to girls. Back in high school, Hector, two years Manny's senior, had told Manny to be arrogant around women, aloof, and appear disinterested at all times. Manny struck a balance between the two extremes, but still struggled mightily. In his head, he made a list of ways to tell if a San Antonio *chicana* was too good for him. They were based on personal experience.

If she has jet black hair that is effortlessly wavy, she is too good for me.

If she is attending St. Mary's University, she is too good for me.

If she wears those outfits that reveal just a little midriff, she is too good for me.

If she is annoyed that I have to borrow an old car to get to a date, she is too good for me.

If she gives me her phone number, she is too good for me.

If she thought about attending St. Mary's University, she is too good for me.

If she looks stunning in tight, white dress pants, then she is too good for me.

If she is attending a community college part-time, she is too good for me.

If she has before and after pictures and gym pictures on social media, she is too good for me.

If she is a waitress who has recently served me a hamburger and french fries, she is too good for me.

If she smiled briefly at me on a street corner, she is too good for me.

If she can afford a knock-off designer purse, she is too good for me.

If she makes a funny face when I assume we are splitting the bill, she is too good for me.

If she wears clothes bought brand new at a store where the employees are well-dressed, she is too good for me.

If she does not give me her phone number, she is too good for me.

Eventually, Manny gave up hope and started to avoid making eye contact with unknown females. He did not realize that being from the RGV and Hispanic was not a point of solidarity for those cosmopolitan, San Antonio *latinas*: many perceived his old residence as a sign of poverty.

Maribel, who had spent a summer in Cambridge, Massachusetts, again tried to explain things to Manny. She had heard the East Coast term "JAP", which at first she mistook for a racial epithet targeted at Asians. Instead, the term was "J.A.P.", which stood for Jewish-American Princess. In the Hispanic world, she reasoned to Manny, you will find quite a few C.H.A.P.: Chicana/Hispanic-American Princesses. Basically, girls spoiled by a rich, doting daddy who are on the fast-track to trophy-wife status.

This knowledge entered Manny's right ear and exited the left. All the lessons of love for Manny would have to come the hard way, and he only added new lines to his list for the rest of his time in San Antonio.

# Chapter 18

Back on the soccer field, Manny's blind spots inhibited his game, but Junot played *futbol* with a bird's-eye view and the patience of an ocean eroding a mountain range. Junot was not muscular, but used every inch of his length to shield the ball from defenders. Junot was not fast, but moved with grace and anticipation. Basically, his intelligence allowed him to play the game one-step ahead of everyone else.

Manny had never played with anybody as good as Junot. Manny was used to being the star and felt a twinge of jealousy. He tried to hide his feelings, but they manifested themselves in multitudinous ways. For example, he was always the last to embrace Junot during a goal celebration. And one could easily mistake Manny's smile for a frown.

De Charlus noticed this, but still started Manny during scrimmages and practice games out wide. He needed Manny's pace on the flank more than maturity.

Still, the coach barked orders at Manny without pause. Manny felt suffocated at times: he was torn between focusing on a drill and trying to understand his coach. What most confused Manny was De Charlus' pronunciation of the "ll." Most Spanish-speakers pronounced "ll" as a "y". De Charlus, a *porteño*, said the "ll" as a "sh" as in "chachacha." De Charlus also conjugated verbs in the second-person by using *"vos"* instead of *"tú"*, but so had *Catracha*. Thus, Manny understood directions like: *"¡Reventálo, boludo, hijo de puta!"* And, as time passed, Manny learned more and more.

Most of the older players shrugged their shoulders at the animated coach's cursing, except for Junot. At one practice, De Charlus shouted: *"¡Corré negro! ¡Mováte o te saco!"* Junot ran halfway across the field, stood nose-to-nose with De Charlus, and shouted in his face: *"¡Oigame y oigame bien: tengo un nombre! Me llamo Junot. Y es la media que falla. ¡Déme un asistidor o cómase mil veces mierda!"* The scrimmage had stopped and everybody was watching. Manny stared in disbelief and only understood a few of the pejoratives.

Junot and De Charlus then stood silently and locked eyes for what seemed an eternity. Junot was red-faced and breathed heavily. De Charlus looked pensive. He puckered his lips and moved them from side-to-side. He scratched his ear. Suddenly, he burst out laughing. He slapped Junito on the shoulder, took a step closer, and said softly: "*Cálmese, querido boludo. Ya bajá de la punta y jugá de nueve falso, a pedir el balón. Y no se distraiga che.*"

Junot trotted back to the field, but stopped near Manny to smile and say: "*Uno se tiene que defender.*" A few minutes later, De Charlus walked up the sideline near Manny, offered him a water bottle, and pulled him aside for a chat. "*Es que Junot juega mejor cuando esté enojado. ¿No ves? Como coach, hago lo necesario para sacar lo mejor.*" Manny grinned. Both believed they were right and had just won the argument.

The rest of the scrimmage, Manny and Junot combined excellently and played give-and-gos at will in the opposing eighteen-yard box. As they left the field at the end of practice, Junot again approached the much smaller Manny, and put his arm around him. "Hey, Manuel, a word of advice: when we go to the university fields, bring a shirt and shorts to change into and *never* use the showers."

Manny asked Junot why. Junot paused and then explained in whispers that De Charlus had the unnerving habit of standing just outside the group shower area, looking at the players, and still talking to them about soccer. Even worse, he often made keen and usually lewd observations about a player's, ahem, *physical condition*.

"One time, I came back from Honduras a bit overweight. That fucker called me *nalgón caído* for a month!" Manny only half-smiled and did not quite get the joke. Junot translated as best he could: "Flabby ass." Manny laughed so hard his stomach hurt.

# Chapter 19

No matter how long Manny stared at his cell phone and sat on the recliner in Bryce's living room, he could not shake an odd feeling. He scrolled through old messages. He revised and edited his contacts. He deleted all the spam in his email. Still, seconds dragged on and stretched to infinities. Manny was a month into his recovery, and Hector hadn't called him once.

Bryce was nice, but Manny missed Hector and his sister Maribel immensely. Back in Texas, things were on the rocks between Maribel and her distance beau in Austin, so Maribel called or texted Manny daily. Manny knew things would change when he moved out of the apartment with Hector and started living with teammates in San Mateo.

Manny moved out largely because Hector's new friends were weird, slightly annoying, and always filled their shared room with obnoxious conversations and lame music. They always talked about fleet week, even though Hector was the only one who had served in the armed forces. Often, Manny felt like he entered the room and they spoke in code.

When a teammate mentioned that a room was available at his house, Manny had jumped at the chance.

Living with Bryce had been good and bad. On the one hand, Bryce was very thoughtful. He didn't play music from his room too loud, he kept the kitchen reasonably clean, and, at night, he tip-toed in the darkness to grab snacks from the fridge. Still, the music Bryce did play was "indie" and reminded Manny of a line from a sonnet: "Music to hear, why hear'st thou music sadly?" Even worse, Bryce was not super articulate and watched Fox News regularly.

Still, Bryce reminded Manny of that unique strain of Texan anglo who absolutely hated people of color in theory, but was nice face-to-face. Manny's biggest pet peeve was that Bryce talked about his divorce and ex-wife nonstop. When Bryce found out that Manny was still friends with her on Facebook - he himself had been blocked

- he insisted on logging in from Manny's username to stalk her online.

Manny still vividly recalled Bryce's wedding and reception. Bryce had invited everybody from the team, even the coaching staff and that aging drunk winger, from Holland, by the name of Petr Van Howten. Bryce had begged Manny to help him make sangria the night before the wedding. Even though Manny explained that the drink was native to Spain, not Mexico, he agreed to help. That night, they must have cut over two hundred green and red apples into tiny slices and used five bottles of Merlot.

Maribel had flown into San Francisco to be Manny's date, and remarked: *"mejor una boda de sangría qué de sangre."* At the reception, Manny and his sister could see that Bryce's wife was not ready to settle down. She gawked at the other Gales players with elevator eyes and was distracted by the large concentration of testosterone aka soccer players. To look her way was an invitation to flirtation.

Now, Manny listened to this story for the hundredth time from Bryce and between sobs; Manny's leg was broken, so he could not exactly leave.

Manny himself had finally ended things with *Catracha*. Still, he had misinterpreted the sagacious words of Maribel. She had told him that timing was everything and the timing of meeting and being with *Catracha* had just not worked out. Manny thus had seen *Catracha* as a puzzle-piece to his life that he found too early; he believed he could place that piece on the edge of the table and cycle back to use it later.

He attributed his lust for other ladies to simply: "Those pretty wrongs that liberty commits." If *Catracha* had loved him, she would always love him and forgive him.

Now, seeing Bryce, he witnessed the other side of the equation. Still, he did not connect the dots.

A decade later, Manny's heart would break in similar circumstances.

For now, though, his phone hummed. He had a message from Hector.

# Chapter 20

Manny felt uneasy. On the one hand, he had trained with the *Alacránes* for weeks and felt a part of the team. He had started in a few friendlies and the coach had just shared the development league season schedule with them. On the other hand, he had not been paid a dime. Each Friday after training, he had expected the players to crowd around the coach or some staff person and collect checks. It never happened.

Finally, he asked a short and chubby center back named Ernesto. Ernesto stared at him seriously for a few seconds and then grinned. "This is the third-tier, hoss. Nobody gets paid. That's why we only train once a day and in the morning. Everybody's got a real job." Manny told Hector and Maribel on the ride home from practice, and then the group confronted *El Toro*. He laughed it off. Manny could not have seriously thought he would jump to a pro contract so soon?

Hector's savings from his brief time in the army had dwindled considerably. Maribel still had some money left over from a Pell Grant, but the group now depended upon a pittance of an income source: banner ads from a website started by Hector and Manny years ago. The site's name was: www.anchorbabes.com.

It was not *that* kind of site. Rather, for years, Manny and Hector had endured the two-faced Texan embrace of Hispanic immigrants. On the one hand, work opportunities abounded and everybody had a Mexican live-in maid. On the other hand, radio talk filled the airwaves with demagogues and angry callers who detested the inconvenient Fourteenth Amendment. They pejoratively labeled the children of Hispanic immigrants as: "anchor babies."

In Iraq, Hector was often bored during his downtime at the army base. One day, he and Manny chatted about said term. Then, Manny had an idea for a site about "Anchor Babes," which would revolve around cheeky pictures - ideally selfies - of first-generation US citizens. The idea was a subtle *chinga tu madre* to immigration-haters. They used a basic WordPress template, posted a picture a day, started with family and friends, and invited folks to send a pic to a Gmail account. All the pics were PG:13 to prevent the site from becoming a revenge porn depository.

The site was a modest success and Hector managed most of the technical stuff. Still, they hit a few stumbling blocks. When Manny found out he was not in fact an "anchor babe," he considered deleting his pic and post. Also, they received some kinda scandalous pictures, which were almost always immediately deleted. Hector eventually took control of the associated email account and they perpetually revised the submission guidelines. Traffic swelled after a link on Facebook by an artist, and, after a year, they put up a few banner ads and started to earn about $200 a month.

That figure now seemed small in the real world. Maribel talked about returning to Brownsville for the rest of the summer. Her boyfriend in Austin had grown cold and always canceled his trips to see her last minute anyways. Hector and Manny convinced her to stay and promised to look for gainful employment. They got a replacement starter for the Corolla at a junkyard and scanned online job openings. They needed something that wouldn't be too physically demanding and would fit with the *Alacránes* practice schedule.

And that's how they eventually became the first part-time shelf stockers in Wal-Mart history to be fired *for cause*.

# Chapter 21

At first, Manny felt like a cheat. Guilt gripped his conscience. San Antonio was blistering hot that June, but Manny comfortably beat the heat. He used fake papers Hector got from the *pulga* to land a part-time job in an air-conditioned Wal-Mart. He kicked a ball in the morning and stocked shelves by night. Manny could not help but think of all his friends from the RGV who would love a similar life. Yet he and Hector would throw it away within a week.

The problem lied in a clash of personalities. The assistant store manager or "ASM", Judy, a middle-aged woman with long grey hair in a ponytail, glasses, and slightly overweight, insisted on rigid punctuality. By her estimate, if you were five minutes early, then you were five minutes late. Hector and Manny, conversely, believed that arriving and stocking items a half-hour or so later did no harm to anyone. In the RGV, as in ancient Rome, time and people moved slower. The saying was: *"Hora Latina."* Judy was a rude awakening to the concept of time as lived by most Americans.

Hector and Manny did not arrive on time a single night. After two tardies, Judy's policy was what she called "coaching." On Wednesday of that week, she pulled Hector into her office and yelled at him, and then did the same to Manny. However, they arrived fifteen minutes late Thursday, and a whole hour late on Friday. Judy didn't even bother letting them work that very last shift. She had them immediately sign termination papers and leave.

At practice next week, Manny mustered his courage and asked other players about their jobs. Some were in college and got support from mom and dad. Others worked as night security guards or parking lot attendants. Junot, though, sat Manny down and smiled. He asked him a question that totally caught Manny off guard: "You ever heard of Magic: The Gathering?"

Magic: The Gathering, known to many as "MTG", was a collectible trading card game. Basically, two players were armed with a deck of sixty cards and dueled one another. Different cards had different functions, but the goal was to reduce the other player's life. The cards had neat drawings, and Manny and Hector had dabbled in MTG during middle school. Still, the RGV lacked a decent comic scene so they lost interest fast.

In other parts of the country, though, MTG tournaments at comic shops for money soon turned into national events. A professional league even existed. Junot, the *aspiring* professional soccer player, was a *professional* MTG player. At first, he had started off trying to hustle individual players by feigning he was a dumb and black immigrant. He would go to a comic store on a tournament day, speak a purposely broken English, smile non-stop, play people in friendly duels, and lose early games on purpose. Then, though, he would play and wager money or a valuable card and out came the knives.

Manny briefly recalled his own MTG days, which were a maze of ghosts and specters. He remarked: "Yeah, back in the day I played with the black-themed cards and liked that one powerful card: Necropotence." Junot erupted in laughter. "Necropotence, you mean *negro*-potence. I was unstoppable with that necro-deck. They passed those new rules to restrict it because of me."

Manny did not believe Junot's boasting that Junot alone had caused a change in the game's rules, but soon learned from Junot about his reputation in the San Antonio comic community. It was rather low. You only have so many hustles in a single deck or town. Thus, Junot explained, he gave up the *tranza* and instead regularly played at regional and national tournaments. He'd missed the start of preseason because of an MTG tournament in San Marcos.

Manny's admiration grew immensely for Junot. This guy was a great footballer *and a helluva nerd*. Of course, the fact that Junot needed a part-time job made Manny's own dream of playing professional soccer – as in, getting paid - seem ever more distant.

# Chapter 22

The development league season started with a bang: the *Alacránes* won home games against Laredo, Austin, and El Paso. Still, the crowds were unimpressive: barely more than two hundred souls showed up to any given game. Among those people, Hector and Maribel appeared and shouted and sang. They also held their breath and waited for Manny to come on as a substitute, as was often the case.

Manny did not start a single game, but loved every minute. He adored the red-and-black *Alacrán* game day jersey, even if it was not even 50% cotton and did not have his last name on the back. He even enjoyed the pregame ritual: De Charlus drew dots and arrows on a dry-erase board and then barked orders during the warm up. The lack of pay and fans was a downer, but the quality of play exhilarated Manny. He had never had teammates this good, or played against opposition this talented.

The last weekend of June, the *Alacránes* had a doubleheader on Friday and Saturday away to Austin. The club had promised a nice hotel and to pay for meals, plus a ride in a chartered coach. Maribel planned on seeing her beau in Austin that weekend and promised to make the games. She and Manny viewed the respite from *El Toro*'s trailer with anticipation.

Hector said he was earning decent money as a night security guard at some *bodega* in North San Antonio, so everyone felt a bit better. Hector had stayed in touch with the *regias*, though, and this irked Manny. Rather than come home after his 7pm-to-2am shift, Hector also often disappeared into the eccentric nightlife of San Antonio and remained tight-lipped. Manny asked him point-blank if he was going out with Maria. Hector smirked and remarked: "What's it to you? Aren't you back with *Catracha*?" He then added: "Y'all need an automatic rotating Facebook relationship status or something."

This infuriated Manny. He and *Catracha* had long endured a rocky relationship of ups and downs. Despite years of being together, they were still adolescents who had not learned how to talk through problems. A jealous remark by *Catracha* could incite Manny. Conversely, back when they were in the RGV, a wandering eye by him towards a stranger would leave Manny in the doghouse for weeks. Manny actually liked that *Catracha* could not come to see him in San Antonio because she lacked papers: she was safely tucked down in the RGV and couldn't hover over him.

The weekend in Austin fast approached just as Manny started to notice how much Hector had changed. He'd shaved off his shaggy beard, buzzed the sides of his head, and now used gel to style the top of his hair. He wore contacts when possible, and he wore shirts and pants a size too small. Hector had traded in t-shirts for short-sleeve button ups and jeans for black dress pants.

Thus, Manny assumed Hector had gotten a girl. And Manny was livid that, instead of traveling to Austin for the *Alacrán* games, Hector was flying down to Monterrey for the weekend. He suspected the *regias* had invited Hector. He was not wrong on that account.

# Chapter 23

The *Alacránes* tied the Friday night game in Austin 1:1 despite arriving half an hour late after getting snagged in traffic on US 290. Afterwards, they immediately went to the hotel, which was a decrepit Day's Inn in South Austin where crack dealers loitered in the parking lot with an air of impunity. In the room Manny shared with Junot, they laughed and pointed out the broken chain lock, the torn curtains, and an odd stain on the carpet near the 1960's era A/C unit. Room 118 was basically a crime scene minus the chalk outline of a body.

Lights-out was 10:00 pm, but, the following morning, players could travel around Austin so long as they were back at the hotel by noon. Maribel had borrowed Hector's car and swung by the hotel to pick up Manny around 9:00 am. Manny noticed that she was hiding her eyes behind a pair of sunglasses. When she took off the glasses, he saw dark bags around them. She had been crying.

She soon confessed that things with the boyfriend had not gone well; they had gone terribly. He had broken up with her.

Manny and Maribel went to the Café Lorenzo, which was a quiet coffee shop located off Guadalupe street and bordering the University of Texas campus. While they sat on a couch near the entrance and his sister poured her heart out over espressos, Manny observed a trickle of white girls flow across the sidewalk just outside. All wore their hair in a ponytail and donned running shorts, athletic t-shirts, and flip-flops. "So this is what college girls look like," Manny thought to himself.

They returned to the hotel just before noon, Manny ate undercooked pasta for lunch with the guys, and then the team rode a charter bus over to the field. De Charlus stood near the bus door as each player got off and wore an icy glare. When Manny descended, De Charlus squeezed his bicep and pulled him aside. "*Tú sabes que* I know, *verdad*?" He asked. Manny shrugged his shoulders in confusion. De Charlus elaborated: "*Escucháme.* I no care if you girlfriend come to practice, come to games, but day of game, no *cojer, nada de eso.*"

Manny burst into laughter. He explained to De Charlus that Maribel was his sister, not his girlfriend. The Argentine grinned and asked: "But *dónde* is your *novia* then?" Manny explained his girl was back in Brownsville. Suddenly De Charlus' gaze went ice cold again. He shook his head. "She come visit?" "Not yet," Manny replied. De Charlus made an inappropriate gesture with his hands. "*Ahora yo sé por que* you always tense."

Manny had never had a coach butt into his personal life before. He remained silent. Suddenly, De Charlus slapped the boy's back and laughed. "*Relajáte, hombre. Te tomaba el pelo. Hoy serás titular.*" Manny's face lit up when he heard that word: "*titular.*" It meant: "starter," and was music to his ears.

# Chapter 24

Silence weighed heavily on the players for the entire bus ride home. They all sat motionless in their seats with shoulders slouched and disappointment painted across almost every face. One could only hear the slow slurping sound as De Charlus drank Yerba Mate in his metal gourd and he coughed from time-to-time. The *Alacránes* had just lost 4:1 to Austin. Even worse, they had been ahead at halftime, but conceded four goals in the second half.

Manny tried to imitate his teammates. He forced his shoulders to slouch. He bit his tongue to force a grimace. He stared at his feet to avoid eye contact. However, deep down, excitement brimmed and bounced and twisted and threatened to spill out. The team had laid an egg, but he had played the entire ninety-minutes and even assisted Junot's headed goal with a nice cross. For most of the first-half, he had stared at De Charlus and waited to be subbed off. Instead, the Argentine ushered him onwards with a wave of his hands and a "¡Corré, loco! ¡Concha de su madre, corré!"

They arrived in San Antonio and Junot even dropped off Manny at the trailer. Manny had barely stepped out of the car when he heard *El Toro*'s shouts. The front door swung open and out stormed Esme; she was crying and shaking. She went straight to her Buick, sat in the driver's seat, and buried her face in the steering wheel. Manny glanced around and was unsure how to proceed. Junot just drove off.

Maribel arrived shortly thereafter, and, after seeing Esme and hearing from Manny, the two of them slowly entered the trailer. A faint squeaking, like an ungreased wheel on a rolling chair, came from the back bedroom. "*Toro*, everything cool?" Manny asked with trepidation. The giant emerged a minute later; hot tears streamed down his cheeks. He held up three empty condom wrappers. Manny's eyes opened wide as saucers.

*El Toro* confessed to both of them that he had long suspected Esme of cheating on him; they had not had relations for months. However, he never expected her to do so in *his* own trailer. He had found the condom wrappers in the bathroom while looking for toilet paper under the sink.

What most angered *El Toro*, though, was this: he suspected that the man who used those condoms with her had to have been a serious sneak... *or recently moved in*. He clenched his jaw as he stared at Manny and inquired as to Hector's whereabouts.

# Chapter 25

After Manny had lived with Bryce for a few weeks, he started to pick up the same living rhythm as Bryce, but also detected differences in their personalities. Both accepted Jesus Christ as their savior, but Bryce was a Baptist who did not care for images of the Cross, Jesus, the Virgin Mary, or even Manny's Rosary. Catholicism and Catholics were a foreign and thus dangerous species to him. Still, Bryce openly expressed his frustrations to Manny about being the Southern, religious outcast in the bay area: there was no Baptist church within a reasonable drive.

Thus, Bryce did what any God-loving American would do: he hopped to different Protestant services each sabbath like a child choosing scoops at an ice cream parlor. One Sunday, he would be Lutheran. The next Sunday, he would try Unitarians. Another Sunday, he would give Presbyterians a shot at saving his soul. And, if he woke up with a hangover or sore from training, the Methodists had a decent band at their teen life early evening services. The drummer was especially skilled, but leaving soon for college, so it was a packed house and sometimes standing room only.

Manny felt that his broken leg was taking too long to heal, so he found himself praying and even reading The Bible. When Bryce nonchalantly asked him if he wanted to attend church, Manny could only think: why not. He resolved to not take communion and not register with the protestant parish to cover his Catholic behind, but was really looking forward to getting out of the apartment.

The warmth and exuberance of each Protestant church blew Manny away. He had never seen so many happy and welcoming white people in the same place at once, and was overwhelmed. He was so nervous at the first church service, he couldn't even speak. He just smiled and nodded his head, and the gracious Lutherans presumed he was not fluent in English. They informed him as best they could - speaking really loudly and slowly - that they offered free E.S.L. classes on Wednesday nights and even had *Servicios En Espanol* on Saturday evenings.

Bryce intervened before Manny could finish politely registering for E.S.L. classes, but Manny really appreciated the love of his Protestant brothers and sisters in Christ and began to make mental notes on the few sects he encountered:

**Lutherans--** Lots of blondes and redheads. Definitely need to spend more time around here. Very Nordic vibe. However, the Ocean Spray cranberry juice does not taste like blood, and has not been properly refrigerated.

**Methodists--** Gritty as fuck. Bryce fears them and claims they won the Civil War for the North. He was nervous the whole service. I kinda sorta believe him.

**Unitarians--** Preacher smiles almost *too much*; ditto for his wife and children. I am not a doctor and cannot diagnose an opiate addiction based on the facts available. However, suspicion lingers.

**Presbyterians--** A little too pushy with possible new recruits, but who doesn't want to feel needed even if you are backed into a corner? Suffocating hugs are sometimes the best. The coming hiking trip to Lake Tahoe is of great interest, but before my leg will be healed.

**Episcopalian** - Just Catholic enough to make Bryce squirm. Nice. Cool to see a woman priest. If reform-minded Catholics just keep pushing, hopefully this can happen in 300 years.

**Church of Christ--** No drinking. No dancing. No deal. Preacher has lots of adolescent daughters who eye-fucked me all service; it reached a point where I believe Sin was involved. Why are these always so close to army bases, along with pawn shops, payday lenders, and tattoo parlors?

Finally, Manny convinced Bryce to attend a Catholic Mass. Bryce was incredibly nervous, even if the faithful were polite in a somewhat cold, distant, Catholic sorta way. Bryce had inquired beforehand if he could take the Blood and Body of Christ. Manny laughingly told him that if he tried to do so, the Catholic super police would arrive and toss him in a Vatican jail.

Bryce did not smile and did not take Communion. Manny felt bad that his Protestant brothers and sisters had opened their doors to him and so gleefully shared the Body and Blood, yet felt unwelcome in his own House of worship.

# Chapter 26

The trailer in paradise had suddenly become a cauldron of suspicion. Manny and Maribel had become ensnared, and neither could vouch for Hector. They realized they had to start looking for other lodgings. Maribel calmed down *El Toro* and got him talking like a sane human being. What he revealed, though, struck a nerve with Manny.

Like many great athletes, *El Toro* possessed confidence and dedication, but lacked a middle-class background. Thus, when he reached the *Primera* and started to make serious money, he spent cash quicker than he could earn it. Friends and family came out of the woodwork to ask for loans and money for half-assed business ideas. *El Toro* operated on the assumption that he would earn more money each year and play for at least a decade. He was wrong on both counts.

By the time his knees gave out and nobody would sign him, he faced bankruptcy squarely in the eye. Of course, the numerous divorces had not helped. Still, *El Toro* remained a hopeless romantic. Every first kiss and early morning pillow talk inevitably pushed him to the altar. He said "I do" when he had no business exchanging vows in a chapel.

Immediately after his playing career ended, he hustled up money by selling life insurance to active and retired pro players. However, things went south when one of his clients passed away unexpectedly from a stroke and the life insurance company made the poor guy's widow jump through hoops for two years before paying out. Word spread like wildfire and his brief career peddling life insurance was finished.

He squeaked by off his player union pension, which was paid to his cousin in Querétaro in pesos, who then sent it to him via Western Union in dollars. *El Toro* was embarrassed to be a Mexican in the US who *received* money from family, instead of sending it, and he drove all the way to the white people HEB on the other side of town to get his money.

Hector returned from Monterrey a few days after the domestic incident. Esme and *El Toro* seemed fine. Manny filled in Hector and they resolved to never be alone with Esme, lest they arouse the suspicions of *El Toro*.

Maribel, who spent a decent amount of time in the trailer, was the most perplexed: she couldn't recall a single thirty-minute span when Esme could have sneaked a man inside.

The whole incident had made Manny recall the tumultuous marriage of his own parents. One day stuck out in his mind: when his mom found his dad's second cell phone while cleaning the truck. The ensuing symphony of slammed doors, punched walls, and heated voices had caused his younger self to feel as if the world was crashing down around him.

After all the trailer drama in Paradise Island, Manny's *picazón* over the *regias* passed. He even asked Hector how Monterrey went. "You have fun down there? I hear that city is wild." Hector looked Manny in the eye and replied without blinking: "It was cool. F.Y.I., nothing is going on with Maria, but, yeah, you could say I had some fun."

Manny didn't believe him, but could maybe forgive him.

# Chapter 27

The *Alacrán* season hummed along with wins and ties and losses. July weekends filled with road trips to Odessa and other small Texas towns forlorn by civilization, but full of humidity and dust. Manny did not start any more games, but regularly came off the bench at halftime. Junot, though, caught fire and scored in five consecutive games.

De Charlus arranged a friendly with a professional team from Oklahoma. All the *Alacrán* players trained extra hard in the week of practice leading up to the game. Scrimmages suddenly filled with sliding tackles, body checks from behind, and elbows to the throat. Everybody wanted a piece of everybody else and a starting spot in that friendly.

When Manny returned to *El Toro*'s trailer on Wednesday with a black eye, Esme lavished him with attention. She said "poor baby" and got bags of ice and a wet towel for his face. Once Maribel got back from the library, though, Esme vanished like smoke.

Since the fight with *El Toro*, Maribel shadowed Esme most of the day because she hoped to catch Esme's lover and clear the good names of Hector and Manny. She had even spoken with a neighbor named Milton, who, donning a wife beater and with oddly stained teeth that looked melted, confirmed that Esme cheated often and Boros had to know.

Esme detected Maribel's surveillance efforts, and detested them. She sought vengeance in petty ways, like locking Maribel out of the trailer "by accident" or making passing remarks about Maribel's weight.

Far away from the trouble in paradise, Manny's soccer career got a kickstart. Right before the start of the friendly, De Charlus announced his lineup, and unexpectedly started Manny at striker alongside Junot. However, Manny played poorly. His first touch was off, he shot when he should pass, and his movement lacked crispness. Various times, he opted to run and dribble at a double-team instead of passing to Junot. The Honduran grew frustrated, held up his hands and shouted: "¡No sos pinche Messi!"

At the half, everybody circled around Manny and gave him a piece of their mind. He felt frustrated at himself for sucking, but being berated by so many folks at once only left him defensive. After about five minutes, De Charlus parted the circle, approached Manny, and asked: "Tell me, Mr. *Crack*, why I no cut you *ahora mismo*? What *hiciste vos* for the team?" Manny lowered his head and tears formed in the corner of his eyes. This only infuriated De Charlus more. He grabbed Manny's chin, lifted it, and shouted face-to-face: "¡Decíme ahora mismo!"

Junot stepped in and pulled back De Charlus. He shouted and reminded everybody that Manny was young, and a few other guys also were playing nervous. The offense had sucked, but the defense had held firm. After 45 minutes, they were tied 0:0 with a pro team. That was not so bad. Everybody nodded. He then looked at Manny and said four words: "¡Más bolas! ¡Más bolas!"

Junot's words worked wonders. Manny played the second half like a man possessed: he hustled for loose balls, ran himself ragged, and always tried to play the ball as quickly as possible to Junot. In the dying embers of the game, Junot scored two headers at the far post: Manny assisted both with crosses. The *Alacranes* lost 3:2, but De Charlus pumped his fist at the whistle and even pinched a few players' heinies as they left the field.

The following Monday, Manny arrived early for training and wanted to thank Junot. The rest of the guys trickled onto the field, changed shorts, put on cleats, stretched appendages, and softly kicked the ball about. De Charlus ran them through the *rayuelas*, some intense two-a-side games, and ended things with a full field scrimmage. Manny thought it odd Junot had failed to show up.

After practice ended and all the players had just finished a cool down lap around the field, De Charlus gathered them in a circle. He grinned and announced that Junot had made the leap: he had signed a professional contract with the Oklahoma club. Everybody applauded and a few guys pumped their fists.

Manny felt sad. He hadn't even gotten Junot's cell number to stay in touch. Within weeks, though, he too would be leaving San Antonio.

# Chapter 28

The relentless Southwestern sun pummeled the black Corolla's hood as Hector and Manny zoomed down Interstate 10. Cities and towns and desert flew by until the boys at last reached Tucson and switched highways. The barren desert outside reminded Manny of the Valley and home, even though he headed in a different direction. He thought of Maribel; she was probably already on that *Conejito* bus which stops in Edinburg. A part of him envied her.

Still, he looked ahead to California with that same excitement he had once felt about San Antonio. With August coming to an end and cash reserves depleted, Manny had worked up the gumption to ask De Charlus about any professional contacts. The Argentine fought back tears, squeezed Manny in an uncomfortably long hug and promised to make some calls. Manny had suspected it was a hollow promise, but, sure enough, the next day, Manny received a weird phone call from an unknown number with a (415) area code.

Manny thought it was a bill collector. However, the voicemail was a man who spoke in accented English and asked for an "Emmanuel." Manny prepared to delete it when the man mentioned a possible trial with the San Francisco Gales. The *professional soccer-playing* San Francisco Gales. At practice the next day, De Charlus approached Manny and asked about any "*llamadas*." Manny grinned and didn't know what to say. De Charlus then pointedly asked when Manny would be leaving. The Argentine's face grew red and covered with sweat when he learned Manny had not returned the call.

He made Manny take a break from practice to immediately call back a certain Coach Van Ongeval. Manny found the Dutchman to be very excitable over the phone; apparently, De Charlus had sent him promising prospects in the past. Van Ongeval just kept asking over and over Manny's age, position, and contract status. The Dutchman confused past tenses and demanded Manny's assurances that: "he is not contracted since age eighteen."

Van Ongeval invited him to come to San Francisco and train with the Gales the last month of the season. If Manny played as well as De Charlus said, he could train with their amateur team in the offseason until March, coach at Gales camps to make ends meet, and, of course, attend the next preseason. If that went well, he'd be a Gales player. Manny said "yes" without thinking. Only later did he even recall that he had an uncle in the Bay Area where he could maybe stay.

Still, Manny had forgotten about a promise he had made; only on the open road did he recall his uncle's DVD. A date with Tijuana beckoned.

# Chapter 29

To Manny's dismay, Blockbuster had closed throughout the US. However, Hector saw on his phone that the chain still thrived in Mexico and two stores operated in Tijuana: one on Boulevard Salinas and the other on Boulevard Industrial. He graciously volunteered to personally deliver the DVD.

They drove through San Diego and headed south. Manny felt pangs of jealousy as they parked in a lot near the San Ysidro pedestrian crossing to Tijuana. As Hector walked up the sidewalk and towards the metal gates underneath the *"Bienvenidos a México"* sign, a handful of US immigration officers in blue uniforms with bulletproof vests stood around and joked. Not one paid attention to Hector as he crossed that imaginary division between the two countries.

Manny wondered what the air felt and tasted like over there. When he had realized in high school that any trip to Mexico would be a one-way visit and thus should be avoided, he had grown obsessed with the country of his parents' roots. He had always begged friends to bring him a souvenir from their day-trips to Matamoros and Reynosa. Once, an aunt brought him *queso de Oaxaca* that spoiled in the fridge after a month because Manny dared not eat it. Instead, he smelled the cheese each day before and after school.

Manny left the bridge and walked back to the parked car. He recalled Hector's sarcastic words before departing: "If I'm not back by the end of the day, I'm dead and just head on to Cali without me." Manny stared at a Google Map on his phone and saw both Blockbusters were near the border. "What could take so Hector long?" He mused. Hector had simply explained that things down south move at a different pace than in the US.

Manny sat in the car with the windows down and used his phone to read up on Saint Anthony and Saint Francis, the Saints responsible for the names of his past and future residence. Saint Anthony of Padua was Portuguese, Franciscan, born rich, and canonized lickedy split. He was the Patron Saint for lost people.

Conversely, Saint Francis of Assisi was Italian, also born rich, founded quite a few religious orders, and had actually fought as a soldier before becoming a priest. He was the Patron Saint for animals. A tough choice, but Manny preferred animals to lost people.

When the lunch hour approached, Manny walked to a taco stand and got some *tacos de fajita*. The handmade flour tortilla was thicker than he liked, but the vender diced the raw onions into miniscule squares just like Manny's mother back in Tejas. Manny wondered about Hector and the mysteries of Mexico, but also what awaited them in San Francisco. Could he make the Gales team? What was the coach like? Would his uncle let them stay with him?

Manny could not fathom Hector's errand taking more than three hours, but, around seven at night, Hector had not returned and Manny walked to the taco stand. This time, he ordered *tacos al pastor*, and, to his delight, Maria, the regia from San Antonio, replied to his WhatsApp messages. Manny and *Catracha* were in fight-mode, and, of course, that entitled him to chat up all the attractive girls in his contact list. He even posted on a few girls' Facebook walls; he knew *Catracha* would see it, and delighted in jabbing his finger into the festering wound of her jealousy.

Finally, around nine at night, Hector appeared. Manny didn't even notice the red mark on his friend's neck or his now tousled hair. Instead, he hugged his friend as a wife embraces a soldier returning from war. When Hector showed Manny the selfie of him returning the DVD to a Blockbuster clerk, Manny shook in delight. *¡Misión cumplida!*

They got in the Corolla, headed north past San Diego, and soon started looking for a place to stay. They decided on a decrepit two-story motel named The Spouter Inn. The place looked old, but the price was right and they were officially down to their last hundred dollars. On a queen-sized mattress hard as plywood, neither slept very well that night.

For Manny, though, physical discomfort had little to do with it. He tossed and turned because he believed that he was only six hours of highway from his dream.

# Chapter 30

Left foot forward. Stop. Breathe. Right foot forward. Stop. Breathe. Bend at the ankle. Stop. Breathe. Manny was in water up to his chest at the YMCA pool and carefully took baby steps. For over an hour, he had walked from one side of the pool to the other. Bryce watched from a nearby chair and was stretched out like an iguana on a rock. The San Francisco sun barely produced a freckle, though.

Manny's ankle and knee were stiff from a month in a hard cast that had covered his leg from thigh-to-toe. When he had gotten the cast off, his shriveled and pasty leg looked like a cross between a prune and cottage cheese. Still, he had delighted in feeling the air on his calf. With each step in the pool, Manny could feel his tendons creak and strain.

For the past two weeks, Bryce had accompanied him to the YMCA to do "aquatic therapy." Manny lacked the money to pay for proper physical therapy, so he watched some videos online. He decided on "aquatic therapy" for a simple reason: there was no risk of falling and re-injuring yourself when you walk in water. Plus, YMCA monthly membership was only fifty dollars.

Manny was also elated to leave Bryce's apartment. He had devoured novel after novel, but yearned for the spontaneity of the real world. He had grown sick of his lethargic daily routine: wake up - eat - read - eat - TV - eat - sleep. Even Yahoo Chess had grown tiresome. He yearned to resume normal activity. He also wanted to be walking before Hector's big party in a few weeks. Hector had never seen Manny injured before, and Manny didn't want to appear weak.

The Gales coach, so affable at practice, had not returned any of Manny's phone calls or text messages for months. When the medical bills began to arrive, Manny used the last of his money to talk with an attorney. The guy wrote a letter to the club on Manny's behalf, and, within a week, his overdue paychecks appeared via mail and the club told him to forward all medical bills to them. The club had even agreed to pay Manny for a few extra months.

Manny was relieved, but still felt uncertain about the Gales. He also could sense the precarious position of Bryce, who still played for the club and relied on the cash he earned working as a coach at their youth camps. A part of Manny wanted to go to some Gales practices and maybe even games. He missed his teammates. However, he mused: had his lawyer letter tanked his career? A few of the guys still texted him and they were friends on Facebook, but Manny felt alone and increasingly isolated. He knew he couldn't rely on Bryce's charity forever.

He wanted to move out, but felt he had no place to go.

# Chapter 31

If God wiped Sodom and Gomorrah off the Earth with fire and brimstone, then He will wash San Francisco away in one magnificent wave. Situated on a tiny, sloped peninsula and sandwiched between the Pacific Ocean and a bay, residents feel in their bones the inevitable day they and the city will go crashing down into the sea.

For a person raised under the Texas sun like Manny, it was depressing to witness the stillborn days die one after another. The never-ending gray clouds always mask the sunlight, overcast afternoons stretch into evenings, and then the day abruptly ends before it could begin.

When Manny and Hector first arrived in San Francisco, they had different expectations. Manny had heard from his Uncle Julio Luis, aka *Tio Julio*, that the weather was cold by Texas standards. The city was also expensive. Thus, Manny entered the foreign city with a head full of doubt.

Hector, meanwhile, had secretly daydreamed about the city's seedy nightlife. In the small towns of the Rio Grande Valley, everybody knew everybody and their grandma. Thus, rumors swirled like cyclones and news traveled fast. Hector viewed San Francisco as a clean slate and a place to experiment. He looked forward to some anonymity.

Manny's *Tio Julio* lived in Oakland and had a modest two-bedroom loft in a renovated warehouse. In his late forties, *Tio Julio* had dyed his hair jet black, grown a bit pudgy in the middle, and always wore tight, baby-blue polo shirts. He was a professor of literature at a local state college.

Manny vividly recalled his uncle's handful of visits to Texas for the holidays; he would bring Manny and Maribel paperback books as gifts like: *Twenty-Thousand Leagues Under the Sea* and *The Wizard of Oz*. Manny had once read a short story published online by Julio about a roller coaster that didn't work because the engine's oil had mixed with water, but had failed to grasp most of the jokes.

*Tio Julio* agreed to let Hector and Manny stay and share the second bedroom, which had been used as a study. While Hector reorganized the stacks of papers and magazines, Manny couldn't help but peruse his uncle's bookshelves. His hands shook as he held a second edition of *Roughing It* by Mark Twain. He started to read the Moncrieff translation of *A Remembrance of Things Passed*. The pages were yellow, the hardcover binding was in tatters, and his uncle had made corrections in blue ink of typographical errors.

For the first few weeks, Manny noticed that his *Tio Julio* was rarely in the apartment. Manny's mom had always referred to Julio as a classic *solterón* - a swinging bachelor. Manny chuckled because he believed that his uncle's lifestyle had not dimmed with age. "*Estos gallos tan gallos!*" His mother would have said.

# Chapter 32

Johann Van Ongeval had the mannerisms of a well-traveled salesman. Like many other Dutchmen over the centuries, he had covered the four corners of the Earth to proselytize and pander to the unfortunate savages uneducated in his own enlightened ways. However, he was not a missionary of Christ. Rather, he taught the nuances of Dutch soccer's philosophy of *"Totaal Voetbal,"* or "total football." As the coach of the San Francisco Gales, he had enjoyed years of personal stability and modest professional success. At this later stage of his life, he valued the former more than the latter.

He calmly shook Manny's hand on the first day of training and explained that the team practiced twice a day. He informed Manny that, while the season ended soon, Manny could still train for a two-week probationary period. Of course, Manny would be paid for those two weeks, regardless of if he made the team or not. Van Ongeval spoke to him with unflinching directness and did not ask Manny if he had any questions after the brief chat. Instead, he told Manny to go to the office to sign a probationary contract and then get dressed for training.

Unlike De Charlus, Van Ongeval preferred pull aside chats to public shouting. During the first few practices, he would slowly walk towards Manny, wait for a break in action, and make a "sh" sound to get Manny's attention. In his lightly-accented English, where the "th" sounded like a "t", he would tell Manny with a grave tone that: "I think we have a problem to discuss." He would then pause, not for dramatic effect, but to assess the grammatical precision of his next sentence. "You did not use your left foot there. What is your reasons?"

The question at the end of these mini-lectures was always a trap. Any player who tried to justify a bad decision or a poor touch received a verbal barrage, often in Dutch. Thus, players learned to remain silent and nod.

Manny naturally bowed to authority and Van Ongeval prized Manny's demeanor as much as his youthful pace. Unlike De

Charlus, Van Ongeval wanted Manny to dribble at defenders, cut inside, and shoot on goal. He cursed in Dutch to himself and shook his head every time Manny crossed the ball into the box. "That is not *Totaal Voetbal!*"

Johann always smelled of smoke and suffered from a chronic cough, yet the players never saw him smoke a cigarette. Not even a single time. He detested sprint drills and practicing setpieces. During one scrimmage game, he apologized to the team for briefly fielding a 4-4-2. It was the only time anybody could recall him saying he was sorry for anything.

From the onset, Manny felt he was playing well and could handle the level of competition. A player named Bryce, one of the few white guys on the team, immediately took Manny under his wing. He was a Southerner and Manny was brown but a Texan, which was close enough. Bryce explained Van Ongeval's 4-3-3 formation to Manny as best he could.

He also revealed a trick: the Dutch harbored very different views on pain threshold from your average American. Basically, if you told the coach you felt sharp pain in your ankles, he would immediately make you stop training. No questions asked. This was a particularly good stratagem for the morning session if you woke up with a hangover.

Manny thanked Bryce for the tips. He had not yet tasted the San Francisco nightlife, but would remember that advice for a later date.

# Chapter 33

For the last month of the season, Manny was a Gales player, but he *wasn't* a Gales player. He signed a thirty-day contract and trained with the team, but did not dress for home matches or travel to away games. He was paid, but did not play. Coach Van Ongeval explained that the team had limited roster spots, and all but assured Manny a spot on the team and actual games come next March. Still, Manny felt trapped in purgatory. Even a night out on the town with Hector to celebrate Halloween couldn't lift his spirits.

When the season came to an end, the Gales put him to work at youth camps all around the Bay area. One week, he would coach twelve-year-old boys in Alameda County; the next week, he would train eight-year-old girls in Palo Alto. Hector had gotten a job as a bellhop at one of those fashionable hotels off Market Street.

Hector worked nights and Manny worked days, so the two saw each other less and less. They started to help *Tio Julio* out with rent, but both Manny and Hector secretly itched for their own place. Just not with each other.

As the months dragged on, Hector and Manny grew more and more distant. Many nights, Hector wouldn't even return to the apartment to sleep. Manny suspected a significant other in his life, but Hector kept his lips sealed. He said folks at work always stayed in vacant rooms if they worked too late.

Manny thought little about it because Hector had always kept his cards close to his chest in matters of actual feelings and emotions. Still, with a tinge of jealousy, Manny saw comments on Hector's Facebook wall from new coworkers and friends he had never met. Hector even got a mattress for himself in their shared room: no more sleeping on the floor.

Sometimes, Manny would text his mom and Maribel forty times a day, other times he would disappear into a blackhole. He tried to see his younger brother and sister on Skype at least once a week. If he had any extra cash at month's end, he would send money his mom's way to help out with groceries.

Manny's daily mood could be determined by if he had blocked or unblocked *Catracha* on his social media profiles. He had treated his pet hamster Sisyphus in the RGV better than his on again, off again girlfriend: Sisyphus had been clearly given to a responsible cousin. *Catracha*, meanwhile, felt both the ire and passion of Manny. Neither friendzone nor *amigos con derecho*, the two were *something*, but not quite a couple; it was painful, but neither could cleanly end it. At least not yet.

On Christmas Eve, Hector, Manny and *Tio Julio* went out together to get Chinese food, but they might as well have been strangers. Julio ordered some vegetarian plate and complained about how his students only cared about grades and viewed the acquisition of knowledge as superficial competition. Manny and Hector just listened, but their minds drifted elsewhere. Back at the apartment, they did not exchange cards or gifts or anything. The three of them slept under the same roof, but lived in separate spheres.

Later that night, Manny felt his heart jump up into his throat as he watched his younger siblings on Skype during the *Noche Buena*. He had forgotten how his little brother Paolo would bite his thumb when he got nervous with excitement. Manny almost cried when his little sister Phoebe shouted with delight at getting a new white dress.

Eventually, Manny decided to move into a house in San Mateo with other Gales players. He was resolute in his decision, but still dreaded the conversation with Hector. If he moved out, Manny reasoned, Hector would undoubtedly have to move out too. Of course, the thought of Hector also moving into the house in San Mateo with him had never even entered his mind. Gales teammates were a separate realm from Hector, unlike the *Alacrán* days when Manny's social circles formed concentric rings. Hector had also breached roommate etiquette a few times; he did some little things and one big thing that pissed off Manny.

To Manny's surprise, Hector took the relocation news well. Hector confessed that he was also itching to move out. They agreed to shut down the "Anchor Babes" Tumblr, sell the domain name, and split any profits. They also promised to stay in touch and grab lunch sometime, but neither believed the other. Or himself.

# Chapter 34

For six months, the banality of being a not-playing soccer player on a lower-division club ate away at Manny. He could go out with his roommates to bars and say he was a Gales player, but no pictures of him in a Gales uniform appeared on TV or the newspaper. The local press simply didn't care. Nobody was a fan. Every two weeks, he collected a check printed on neat, watermarked paper and signed by the team's office manager and CFO: Willem deGroot. The checks cleared, but Manny still felt cheated.

Once February arrived, things changed. He and two roommates joined a gym and jogged in the mornings before coaching at Gales youth soccer camps. Manny entered preseason in the best shape of his life and easily won every sprint drill that Coach Van Ongeval tossed his way. The coach played Manny as a wide striker; this meant he now normally faced defenders before receiving a pass. He had more time on the ball and his blind spots were no longer an issue.

As March neared, Manny grew excited about the season's start. Two weeks before the opening game, he scored in a friendly. Manny had been offside and scored a tap-in when the other team's keeper dropped the ball, but the goal blew wind into his sails. In that friendly, Manny wore the purple-and-navy blue Gales jersey for the first time. On the back of the shirt, his last name was above the number thirteen.

Manny impulsively bought ten Gales jerseys with his name and number. One paycheck flushed down the drain. Still, the hair on his arms and neck stood on end every time he thought about the fast approaching season and his first official game. He knew he was no lock to start, but his head spun circles at the possibility. He often wore his jersey and marveled at himself in the bathroom mirror. He even Skyped with his mom and siblings to show it off.

A week before the opening game, the team started practice with three versus three games on a small field but with big goals. Players on the sideline joked and stretched as the six players tussled for the ball. When Manny's team entered the field, he never for a second considered pulling up his socks or putting on his shin guards. A few minutes into the game, he dribbled past one defender and the ball bounced unexpectedly after rolling over a clump of grass. Manny seized the chance to hit a hard shot on the half-volley; he slowed down, balanced himself and then whipped his leg with all his might. He was so focused on striking the ball cleanly that he never saw a defender sliding into his path from the side.

His shin snapped like a twig over the defender's knee. The sound of the breaking of bone echoed like a gunshot.

# Chapter 35

Manny had never believed in dreams. He had them, but they never lingered. Like dew on a bed of grass, they evaporated from his mind without a trace at each day's start. When friends talked about dreams, he mentally checked out. For him, dreams simply lacked any basis in reality. They were brain farts; a way for the mind to exercise while the body rested.

One of his last nights in San Francisco, Manny vividly dreamed of waking up at his mom's apartment in Brownsville. Before he even opened his eyes, he smelled and heard wondrous things. Handmade flour tortillas warmed on the *comal*, diced potatoes fried in a pan, and *huevo revuelto* sizzled in another. He heard a knock at the bedroom door and then it opened a crack. His little brother asked in a low voice: "*¿Ya te despiertas?*"

When Manny awoke on Bryce's sofa, there was no food being prepared on a stove. Just silence. He looked down and saw his left foot in a plastic boot. He burst into tears. In fact, he had cried every day since the injury, always by himself, but today was the worst. He couldn't stop.

He cursed himself for not wearing shinpads that day of practice. He cursed his coach for starting off practice with a scrimmage. He cursed his teammate for sliding into his leg. He cursed his tibia for being so weak. He almost cursed God for placing his dream in his hands and then taking it away so suddenly, but refrained from doing so out of fear. Things were bad, but things could always get worse.

He stood up and wobbled around the apartment in his large plastic boot. He neared the fridge when his cell phone burst to life. Five messages from Maribel entered in succession. Apparently, a brutal tropical storm, not uncommon in July, had just hit South Texas and Northern Mexico. UT-Pan Am had canceled classes, folks had evacuated Padre Island, and the City of Monterrey, Mexico was an absolute mess.

The thought arrived like a gust of wind: home. He needed to go home. His mind jumped to the next query: how? Riding Greyhound buses would be an invitation to getting picked up by *la migra*. Manny also could not fly: his bogus driver's license had zero chance of fooling an airline. Another gust arrived: Hector's car. He needed Hector's car.

Manny had harbored doubts about going to Hector's party before, but now he had to. Would Hector give it to him? Sell it to him? They had barely texted in months and Hector had even blocked Manny from seeing his Facebook wall. Hector, though, knew the Valley and Manny's family. He would understand. Despite the silent treatment, he had invited Manny to the party after all. Manny only had to attend, and, once there, find the right time to speak with Hector alone.

The night of the actual *fiesta*, though, the right time never seemed to materialize. Manny was nervous and out of his element. Limping in front of Hector was awkward. Manny did not know most of Hector's crew and they struck him as odd. Also, Hector frequently got lost in thought and could barely keep a conversation with anyone, let alone Manny. This guy Matt kept butting into Manny and Hector's conversations. Something else about Matt threw Manny off: he felt him making faces at him behind his back.

It wasn't until the early morning, after most people had left the *fiesta*, that Hector and Manny got a chance to speak. Hector agreed to sell Manny the Corolla at a bargain and they started to have a real conversation, but Manny felt rushed and left abruptly.

The next morning, Manny awoke groggy and felt torn. Part of him smiled at the thought of going home and seeing his family and maybe even *Catracha*. Had she waited for him like Penelope? The other half believed that his soccer dreams had died forever that day and the taste was bitter.

He packed his scant possessions in a single bag, thanked Bryce, met with Hector to pick up the car, and drove off. No going away party. Only a few goodbyes. He did not want anyone else to see the tears swelling in his eyes. In his heart, he had failed and that was that. Family won. Soccer lost. He had lost. His brittle tibia and fibula had lost. And not just lost today, but forever. He loved soccer with a passion, but the love was not reciprocal.

He promised himself he would never kick a ball again for the rest of his life.

He also promised himself that he would someday walk without a limp.

He had no clue how many more chances life would throw his way.

# PART TWO

*Oración a la Santísima Muerte:*

"White Child, Holy Death, bless my day, bless my luck, bring happiness to me and my loved ones, do not abandon me, care for me always, keep distant evil, that it not come near, and that my enemies flee from me, that today success will arrive, and prosperity accompanies me always, hear me as I beg, Holy Death, and each day I will do so again.  Amen."

Elliott Turner

# Chapter 1

The burning incense made Manny's nose run, but he vigilantly made sure each and every candle flickered with life. The Lee & Simon funeral home was a modest, one-story brick building located off Jefferson Street in the Southeastern corner of Brownsville. Manny stepped outside the dark visiting room, into the entryway, and stared at his reflection in the glass door. The crow's feet near his eyes, the stray white hairs, the lines on his forehead, where had they come from?

Over twenty years had passed since that first time he left the Valley and he was now over forty years old. He checked the messages on his phone: his younger brother Paolo and younger sister Phoebe would arrive at Harlingen International Airport about 10:30 am after a connecting flight in Austin. Even Maribel was driving down from San Marcos, despite the fact she was not a blood relative of the deceased.

He turned around and wandered around the funeral home. It was only ten o'clock in the morning, but he felt like he had been there for hours already and the day would never properly start. A tactful reef with scattered white flowers hung on a stand near the entrance. Slowly, staff started to trickle in, including Michael Lee Jr., the son of the owner. He wore a tactful black suit, black tie, and even a black dress shirt.

Manny entered the men's restroom. He saw a familiar pair of white sneakers underneath the wall of the first stall. The shoes belonged to his son: Fher Antonio. Manny hated his son's first name, which his *then* wife had picked without his consent. Manny asked with a hint of urgency: "*M'ijo*, you fine? The *tios* arrive soon in Harlingen, so you gotta leave now to pick them up on time."

He heard a grunt from inside the stall. Then, pants shuffled and a belt buckled. The door opened and out stepped Fher, who was the spitting image of Manny at seventeen-years-old. Fher washed his hands while Manny gave him directions to the airport. They exited, and, in the funeral home's entryway, Manny asked Fher if he wanted to see grandma before leaving. The mortician had done a great job on her face; he'd borrowed a photo to do her makeup just right. Fher coldly replied: "No. I'm pretty sure she'll still be here when I get back."

Manny's jaw clenched and his eyes shook with anger. Here he was, about to bury his own mother, and his teenage son was giving him shit.

# Chapter 2

Years before the funeral, Manny had lived with Fher in Houston for only a short time before they headed to Brownsville. He had visited his elderly mom and the border town on long weekends from Houston, but, after relocating to the Valley, he noticed and marveled at the minor changes. For example, Highway 77 was now five lanes, not four. There was a new federal courthouse on Harrison Street. Major restaurant chains had slowly sprung up like weeds, strangling the local mom-and-pop Mexican places. Nearby Harlingen had even renamed a street after a massive three-story fishing and hunting store.

Manny sat among family and friends at his mom's viewing, but his mind traveled elsewhere. He vividly recalled that muggy August afternoon when he packed up his house in Northeast Houston. He had only been back in the United States about seven years and had only lived with Fher for about ten months. The two sorted through their things and bickered like a couple. They simply could not agree about necessary items versus trash. Despite being in middle school, Fher clung to his childhood stuffed animals like an overboard sailor to a life preserver.

By mistake, Manny had already sold Fher's desk at a yard sale and thrown away half of his comic book collection. Manny was not the most organized person, and pinched a nerve by discarding one of Fher's neurotic childhood obsessions.

Manny tried to explain away the mistake, but his casualness made things worse. For him, he had confused one box with another, and it was an accident, so that was that. Fher's entire body trembled with rage. He wanted to talk to his mother. He hated his dad. He hated the world.

Manny briefly pondered the irony of his son's claims: if he hated the universe, would that not include the mother to whom he now wished to see? The mother who had dropped him off without a word at the house and all but disappeared? Manny's long pauses before answering only made Fher angrier.

Manny only had one option: he promised to buy Fher comics. As in, a ton of comics. Thus, when they left the house the following day in a moving truck, they had barely driven an hour towards Brownsville when, in some small town, Fher demanded that they pull over the car and check out a comic shop.

Once inside, Fher flipped through the quarter comics boxes with the meticulousness of a faberge egg collector. Two hours later, they exited and Manny was $50 poorer and Fher was twenty comics richer. Fher had barely buckled his seatbelt when he insisted on borrowing his dad's smartphone and then Googled all the comic shops near the highway.

They stopped at Corpus Christi, Kingsville, and Harlingen. They had left Houston at nine in the morning, but arrived in Brownsville around midnight. The drive was normally five hours. Manny spent more on comics for Fher than on gas and the Uhaul rental combined.

They even stopped at the white rose memorial for Selena in Corpus, but that was Manny's doing. He struggled to place into words and explain to Fher just what she had meant to so many people. Fher, borrowing his dad's cellphone, pretended to listen at least. Manny could only sigh and smile. With four decades under his belt, he could smell that the year was going to be especially challenging.

# Chapter 3

Fher stuck out like a sore thumb in Brownsville. His white skin freckled under the blistering sun and he struggled to speak even basic Spanish. The other kids wouldn't even call him *"güero."* He was a *gringo*, plain and simple.

However, Fher's curiosity in learning the language inspired and even tickled Manny. His son's approach to learning was verbal and ad hoc: when dad spoke Spanish, Fher often made a mental note of the context and phrase. Later, he would write it all down in a pocket notebook.

This methodology produced odd results. For example, one day, the two drove to McAllen because Manny had a meeting with his financial advisor at the Chase Tower building. Upon leaving McAllen, they got stuck in a traffic jam on Highway 83. When they finally arrived back home, Fher ran inside the house to grab a notebook and pen. He then started writing feverishly. After about five minutes, he smiled and approached his dad with his notebook in hand.

"Daddy," he asked, "when driving and somebody is driving behind you too closely, you say: *'bríncame ya pendejo'*, right?" Manny bit his lip to suppress the smile. "And when you are driving behind somebody, but they go too slowly, you should say *'písale idiota,'* correct?" Manny gave up repressing his smile and let out a full belly laugh. "But, *papy*, I still don't get exactly when to say *cabrón*."

The seriousness returned to Manny's face. He resolved to clean up his potty-mouth.

While Fher slowly adjusted to Brownsville by learning Spanish, Manny tepidly tested the local job market and struggled living under his mom's roof. Her condition had deteriorated drastically. The morning after their arrival, he spoke with the neighbor woman who had regularly checked in on his mom the past few years. She warned him that she had twice caught *Doña Rosa* trying to eat raw meat. Just days earlier, Manny's mom had prepared *tacos de fajita* in the strangest way: she put pieces of beef in a skillet, sprinkled on salt and seasoning, and forgot to turn on the burner.

His mom could not even remember Manny's name half the time. Sometimes, she would confuse him with her half-brother "Hernandes," who had died decades earlier. Other times, they would sit on the couch, watch a movie, and she would suddenly stand up. She'd grab her walker and go to the door, and then struggle to open it. Manny would inquire what was going on, and she'd claim that: "Hernandes he coming to get me now."

When these things happened in front of Fher, Manny forced out a smile. He would joke and say: "But *abuela*, I'm Hernandes. Sit back down."

Privately, it killed him. The mother who gave him life now couldn't recognize his face. As an adolescent, he had hated her rules, but over time he'd grown to appreciate her authoritative attitude. He came to see her as a rock; she was the foundation upon which he had built his own life. Dementia had blown that foundation to pieces, like a pillar of salt in the wind.

One day, he asked her who she was. She answered in Spanish: "*No estoy yo aqui que soy tu madre?*" He could only answer yes.

Each night, she could still remember her *oraciónes* in Spanish, and, before putting her to bed, they would pray the Rosary, *Padre Nuestro*, and *Angel de mi guarda*. Silently, Manny would ask for the Lord to deliver her to Heaven as quickly and painlessly as possible.

# Chapter 4

Manny enjoyed at least one thing about Brownsville: his lingering reputation as a soccer prodigy. From Laredo to McAllen to Harlingen, folks from a certain generation still recalled Manny's name and face. Thus, he was elated to find out that his old youth club, the RGV Rayos, was still in existence and holding tryouts for middle-schoolers. Would Fher follow in his dad's footsteps?

There was one problem: motivation. Fher naturally took to the soccer field like a bird to flight, but lacked a competitive spirit. At recess, he disdained the playground and sports and preferred to sit in a circle of friends and talk. He also hated running, especially in the heat. During the first few Rayos scrimmages, Fher never went to ground to make a tackle. In fact, he never tackled. Or blocked shots. Or tried to.

Instead, Fher viewed the field as a geometry puzzle to solve, especially near the opposing goal. The ball had to be at "spot x" and struck with "curvature y" to beat the goaltender and enter the netted box. He was lazy and moody, but the kid scored goals by the handful.

Manny could only think of one sensible solution for his unfocused son: bribe him. First, Manny offered Fher a new game system if he made the RGV Rayos team. To Manny's delight, Fher roasted the other tryout players and scored a hat-trick.

It made matters easier that Manny's old youth team coach was now the team's director. The two chatted and stood side-by-side for most of the tryout; both saw Fher score one minute and then lose all focus the next. He was either bored or lazy. After Fher's third goal, the director smiled at Manny and said: *"Tal palo, tal astilla, no?"*

The problem with bribes, of course, is you have to keep paying them. At first, Manny promised Fher ice cream after every practice. Fher, though, demanded high-end ice cream. None of those *paletas* from Wal-mart. He wanted a proper *salidita* to an ice creamery in an affluent part of town and numerous scoops of Rocky Road. Manny, though, stuck to his guns and took him to a small wooden shack in an HEB parking lot: they got *nieves*, the Mexican equivalent of Italian shaved ice.

Fher kinda liked the cherry flavor, but still felt betrayed.

As the season progressed, Fher's demands grew more onerous and impractical. His threats grew disproportionately as well. He once even scored an own goal while defending a corner kick and glared at Manny afterwards.

Rather than realize that, perchance, Fher did not like soccer much and this was a bit of awful parenting, Manny sweetened the pot to a video game per goal. Of course, Fher scored and demanded a new release, while Manny insisted on a used game.

Manny had once foolishly signed an amateur contract with the *Alacránes* decades earlier; he was now getting worked over by his agent-less son. And things were not about to get easier.

# Chapter 5

Manny could not remember which President or political party had passed amnesty laws that legalized immigrants like him. All he recalled from that time, over a decade ago, was paying some sleazy attorney three grand, getting papers within six months, and almost immediately moving to Houston. Those four years he had spent in Brownsville after returning from San Francisco had been a dark time for him.

His lack of papers had seriously hampered his goal to work and help his family out. Instead, he had to look for under-the-table jobs at *pulgas*, Home Depot parking lots, and even in the fields. He recalled his dad's old rule-of-thumb: only take a job where you get paid in cash at the end of each day. If you don't get paid that first day, then you probably never will. Manny seldom worked without getting paid, but also spent lots of time between jobs.

In his rush to return from San Francisco, he had foolishly left behind his fake Social Security Number and lacked the connections and gumption of Hector to track one down. He often helped his mom clean houses. The hours were long. The pay was unstable. Still, he grew closer with his two younger siblings. His mom also got to take Sundays off for the first time in her life.

When Manny finally got his papers and decided to move to Houston, he had a plan. First, he completed an online G.E.D. program. Second, he took out a loan and enrolled in a Certificated Nurse's Assistant school. By his calculations, he could get his CNA certificate in less than a year and start earning decent money. The plan was to send money back to Brownsville whenever he could.

Manny became a CNA and worked primarily in old folks' homes and saw firsthand how dementia crippled the elderly mind. When talking with family members of his patients, he explained the process as follows: first, short-term memory became fuzzy. A patient would have trouble remembering which grandchild just came to visit or what they had for dinner. Second, mid-term memories became jumbled into one another. A patient would confuse the names of two sons or even what school that particular son had graduated from decades earlier. Lastly, and finally, the line between past, present, and future disappeared. People re-lived events from decades earlier, but with names and roles switched. The dead soon came to visit, and often.

Despite having worked for years in Houston and taken care of patients afflicted by dementia, Manny still held out hope for his mother when he returned to Brownsville. He had some ideas on how to jog her memory. For example, he found and downloaded old Mexican TV programs that she had watched in her youth. He also always started sentences by stating his name and her name.

He opened a can of Miller Light to see if a light of recognition sparked in her eyes. As a child, the sound of his dad opening a beer would normally have provoked a groan, and, eventually, a fight. Now, she only blinked and looked confused. She even forgot the lyrics to 'Chente songs.

Still, Manny was not easily dissuaded. He had cared for hundreds of patients and slowly watched their minds melt, but this was *his mom dammit* and he considered himself an expert on the matter. He printed and framed countless family pictures and labeled them. He showed her old videos of weddings, graduations, and even a funeral or two.

Despite all this effort, his mom had clearly been in stage two of dementia for some time and was dangerously close to stage three. There was nothing he could do to stop that. Deep down, he knew his mom's decline was a 99% probability, but he clung to that 1% chance of recovery.

That first year back in Brownsville, the hardest day for Manny was his own birthday. She forgot it, and even Manny's light prodding couldn't help. Delusional, he spent the whole day expecting her to remember. He even recalled how, as a child, she had always been the first to wake him up in bed and sing him *Las Mañanitas.* No matter how poor they were, she always had a cake with candles ready by dinner time. She had even sent him a card with twenty dollars after he had ran off to San Francisco.

But that morning he awoke without a song. He just got up and started to cook breakfast. Eventually, his mom got up and pushed her walker slowly to the breakfast table. Then she sat down and stared at him with the affection of an irate Inn guest.

He had enjoyed his mother's love for decades, but never appreciated it. Now, he had to reciprocate it with no prospect of thanks or recognition. Still, he knew that he was all she had; the other siblings had left Dodge a little over a decade ago. So he gave her every ounce of his love and compassion.

# Chapter 6

A return to Houston? The question lingered in the air, like that famous Texas humidity which makes August days unbearable. Manny, Fher, Maribel, Phoebe and Paolo sat around the long wooden table in his mom's house and ate tamales. His sister Phoebe, now living in Raleigh with her boyfriend, had asked him the question. "After all," she reasoned, "who would want to live in *the Valley*?"

Manny looked at Fher, but neither had an answer. Both missed the diversity and activity of Houston. The Mexican food was amazing in the Valley, but if you wanted Indian or Chinese food, or even decent Italian, you were out of luck. Still, after over a decade of travels, Manny felt comfortable. Fher was doing well at school. The house was paid for. In the RGV, taxes, gas, and food were cheap. Fher had even started to make friends.

Manny had even grown to like the "bump-ins," as he called them. From time-to-time, he'd see an old classmate in HEB or at the gas station. What struck him was how fickle memory was and unevenly distributed among people, and sometimes even within a single person. One older woman recognized Manny's face and talked about the time he started a petition to allow comic books in the school library in fourth grade. Another guy he saw in line at the bank recalled a goal Manny had scored in a high school playoff game.

These moments helped Manny remember that his childhood was more than an empty stomach and parents yelling. Still, sometimes an old wound opened. For example, at his mother's funeral, Fher had wandered around the family plots and a statue caught his attention: a concrete angel stood and held a single flower while watching over a young girl seated at the angel's feet. Etched on the gravestone read the name: "Gemma del Socorro Hernandez" and the dates "1988-2002." Fher asked Manny who Gemma was, and Manny ignored him.

Fher correctly read his dad's silence and stopped inquiring. Still, Fher was curious. Who was this little girl who passed away so long ago? Fher tried to catch one of his *tios* alone to ask, but the right opportunity never arose. He dared not ask in front of his dad: that would be an affront to paternal authority. Instead, Fher played detective by taking a renewed interest in the labeled family photos hanging on the walls in grandma's house. He scanned the older pictures and asked: "Who was who?" "That was your aunt Paola." "That was a family friend." Finally, he hit the jackpot. "That was your aunt Gemma."

He stared at the young girl's long black hair, dark brown eyes, cinnamon skin, and radiant smile. "Aunt Maribel, what happened to her?" he asked. Maribel answered in Spanish: "*Se nos adelantó, mi hijito.*" In Mexican Spanish, the phrase "*adelantarse*" can mean both "cut in line" and "predecease." One guesses the meaning from context.

Fher heard it for the first time, but got the drift. Still, Fher wanted to know "how" and "why?" He was in high school, and the concept of death had started to both fascinate and terrify him. Gemma was younger than him when she passed, and that didn't seem fair.

Maribel, who lived in San Marcos with her husband and kids, expertly changed the subject and prodded Manny again about returning to Houston. "But *hermano,* there are no white girls to hit on around here!" Manny blushed.

Paolo couldn't resist, and jumped in. "We all know you got a type, bro. *G-ü-e-r-a.*" Manny rolled his eyes and got up to grab a beer. He made a remark about Pablo's girlfriend back in Boston being whiter than milk.

When Manny sat back down at the table, the conversation turned serious. His younger siblings asked if mom had a will and what would happen to the house. Manny had to clarify: he had never actually *given* the house to mom. Rather, he had bought the house and let her live there rent-free. The blood drained from Paolo's face, but he said nothing.

Still, tension lingered. In the eyes of his younger siblings, Manny had always been his mother's special one. He had gone, in their childish eyes, on a "trip" to San Antonio and San Francisco while they had wallowed in poverty. He had been the golden child with good grades. He had been the local celebrity.

They also assumed he was a millionaire because he had played several years in the Mexican first division of soccer.

# Chapter 7

Ironically, Manny's path to Mexico was made possible by his northern move to Houston. Fresh after getting papers, Manny relocated to North Houston and quickly settled into a quiet and monotonous existence akin to a carpenter ant. He worked the midnight shift at an old folks' home, and, like all fine medical businesses, the home turned a profit by both milking government benefits and understaffing services.

For his ten-hour shift at night, Manny was the only Spanish-speaker in the entire building. He was also the sole CNA in charge of an entire hall, which meant six rooms filled with twelve elderly persons. He worked so hard that after leaving work he slept all day and had no social life.

His boss, a taskmaster African-American woman named Allison, was near the end of middle age yet retained the vigor of a teenager. She was strict, but fair. Most importantly, she overlooked Manny's problems with punctuality after seeing how deeply he cared for the residents. He learned their names the first day, and usually learned their food preferences and daily rhythms within a week. Most other employees could not name a single patient.

Manny's nightly tasks revolved around two common occurrences: nightmares and poop. Residents regularly screamed in their sleep and emptied their bowels all over the sheets, often at the same time. Thus, all night, Manny skipped from room-to-room, and calmed down one elderly patient while changing the diaper of another. The worst was when a female resident would empty her bowels and there was no female CNA on staff. Manny would have to ask a female resident nurse (RN) to do the dirty work, which upset the typical balance of power.

After two months of wipes and screams and paychecks, Manny befriended a co-worker named Mark Washington. Mark was black like the rest of the staff at the old folks' home, but he went out of his way to make Manny, the only Hispanic who was not a patient, feel welcome. Manny soon learned that Mark had a fetish for Latina women, and Mark hoped Manny could pass along some romantic tips and key Spanish phrases.

The two often worked the same four days of the week on purpose so they could go out together on their days off. Manny would take Mark to Latin clubs, bars, and restaurants. In time, Mark learned the basics of dancing bachata, merengue, and even salsa. Sometimes a latina with a thing for black guys would fall into his lap, but, more often than not, he would struggle to connect with latinas.

Manny explained that talking about family, food, and music was fundamental. For Mark, the Hispanic version of these topics might as well have been a foreign language. Still, Mark was nice, smart, reliable, and counseled Manny on an amorous topic of mutual interest: white girls.

And thanks to Mark, Manny met his wife.

# Chapter 8

Manny's shyness around the opposite sex sabotaged most of his attempted conquests. Once, as a teenager, he rode shotgun with his friend Santiago, and, at a stoplight, a car of cute girls pulled up alongside them. Santiago rolled down his window and began to serenade the ladies with *piropos.* Nothing offensive, but not exactly charming. The girls ignored him, so he began to furiously honk the car horn. They still ignored him. He turned to look incredulously at Manny and ask: "Are these girls deaf or what?" There was one problem: Manny was not visible. He had ducked down and hid his head in his lap.

Mark's advice to Manny for hitting on white girls was simple: don't act like a white dude. In Mark's estimation, most white dudes were either too passive or of the "drunk and aggressive frat boy" variety. This was not objective truth, but Manny needed a prod more than concrete knowledge. Mark encouraged Manny to approach a girl, open with a tactful compliment, and then ask lots of open-ended questions. Even if the girl was not that into you, they all liked compliments and talking about themselves. Worst case scenario: they would let you down gently after a few minutes.

One night, Mark and Manny prowled a country-themed bar in North Houston from door-to-door. The place was packed, a few televisions showed a local sports game, and rock music blared in the background. Manny had never really listened to *Journey* or *Aerosmith*, and struggled to fathom how two people could dance to electric guitar riffs. Manny and Mark eventually sat at a table in the back corner.

They had barely ordered a drink when, across the way, Mark saw a young lady in a short and sleeveless green dress approach the bar. Her dirty blonde hair barely reached her shoulders, and Mark noticed that her green-blue eyes never left Manny.

Mark could not stand to see Manny pass up the invitation. Every time they went out, he had to push Manny to make an initial approach. Manny's fear of rejection was both risible and annoying.

This time, Mark threatened to leave the bar immediately if Manny didn't get up and talk to that blonde girl.

Manny pedaled the same old excuses: maybe later, maybe the girl was looking at somebody else, etc. Mark shook his head and had heard enough. He stood up abruptly and began to put on his coat. "Weak ass shit," he growled.

Manny, worried they might be seen, gestured for Mark to sit back down. Once he did, Manny took a deep breath, repeated a word of encouragement to himself, and stood up.

As per usual, Manny relied on liquid courage to fuel that first approach. He downed his beer in one gulp and then took a step towards the girl standing at the bar. She was at last five inches taller than him, but her eyes enchanted him. They were neither green nor blue, and he lost himself staring into them.

She stared back without blinking.

# Chapter 9

Manny awoke with a throbbing headache and found a foreign body in his bed. He had little recollection of the prior evening, but delighted at seeing this person sound asleep beside him. The blonde, female creature made adorable sounds as she slept. Manny counted the seconds between her mini-coughs. His memory was blank, but he could deduce what had happened. After about ten minutes, he got up and decided to make breakfast.

At first, Manny didn't hear her enter the kitchen. Out of the corner of his eye, though, he caught a movement. He turned and saw her wearing one of his football jerseys. She must have grabbed it out of his dirty laundry hamper. *"Buenos días,"* he said, grinning from ear-to-ear. She giggled and replied with a terrible accent: *"Buenos días."*

Manny spoke to her and openly admitted to not recalling most of the prior night, but omitted a key fact: he could not recall her name. Instead, he asked her how she liked her coffee, her toast, and other food-related queries. By focusing on minutiae, he tried to get a sense of her. He also stalled for time. He hoped the name would come to him or maybe she could get a phone call and answer by stating her name.

She devoured the *huevos rancheros*, but took her time sipping the dark coffee. She quizzed Manny on the neighborhood, his job, and his preferences in "the scene."

By "the scene," Manny presumed she referred to bars, restaurants, and nightclubs. He claimed that he did not go out that much, but she gave him a defiant glare of incredulity. His ears raised a fraction of an inch, as they always did when he was nervous. He finally blushed, shrugged, and admitted to hitting up a few Latin clubs every now and then with his friend Mark.

Her eyes flickered to life. She put down her coffee, leaned over the table and stuck her tongue down his throat.

The kiss was interrupted by her cell phone buzzing on the table. She withdrew to answer it, and, to Manny's dismay, then she said she had to leave. However, she asked Manny for his phone number. She entered in his digits, but then paused and asked: "I'm sorry, but I didn't catch your full name, just your nickname"

He smirked. So, she had forgotten his name as well. "My actual name is Emmanuel Hernandez, but 'Manny' is fine." She typed in his name and immediately called him. He saved the number and asked her: "And, *muchachilla*, what is your full and proper name?"

She replied without pause: "Albertine. Albertine Blume."

# Chapter 10

Every fiber of his essence urged Manny to text Albertine. His body yearned to touch her again, and a vibrating cellphone with a screen full of sentences was the closest surrogate. She had even sexted him only a few hours after leaving his apartment.

The texts contained numerous grammatical errors such as a lack of punctuation and capitalization, yet still sexually aroused Manny. His heart beat a bit faster and the hairs on his body stood on end every time his phone buzzed with a new message.

At work, though, Mark urged caution. He looked down upon Manny's "condition." In Mark's opinion, Manny had become too clingy, too soon. He urged Manny to try and go days between messages and calls.

Manny thought of the song *La Habanera*: "If you love me not, if you love me not, then I love you." He tried to not text, but failed. He was enamored and in the worst way.

Albertine told Manny that she worked as a paralegal, and she claimed to work really long hours and six-days-a-week. Thus, most of their encounters were nocturnal affairs, often at Manny's apartment. Still, sometimes their schedules aligned and they went on proper dates. Once, they fed the overweight squirrels at Hermann Park near downtown Houston. Another time, they toured the Bicycle Museum. They even went to Galveston for a weekend and took the ferry to the lighthouse.

In addition to conflicting schedules, punctuality posed a problem for the budding couple. Albertine lived her life with her eyes glued to the clock. She planned her days well in advance.

Manny, of course, had never worn a watch. He had always believed in the Spanish maxim: *"Hay más tiempo que vida."* When he arrived a half-hour late to a date, he always blamed traffic.

Albertine rolled her eyes. She always started drinking by herself if she had to wait more than ten minutes.

The two eventually reached a compromise: Manny would pick her up at her apartment before dates, and she would not start to get ready until after he had arrived.

Manny's lack of punctuality frustrated Albertine, but, at the same time, she adored his patience and good nature. She often had to cancel plans at the last minute due to work, and he rarely questioned her or showed frustration. She was also taken aback by how openly he expressed his feelings and how early on in their courtship he had told her: "I love you." In those three simple words, she detected a sincerity that frightened her. After only a few weeks, she reluctantly agreed to date exclusively.

After only five months, she agreed to move in with him. She told herself it was just a test, and the practical side of her liked paying less rent. Still, things started ominously. The first night together in *their* apartment, things were heating up in the bedroom when suddenly audible flatulence slipped between her thighs. Even worse, Manny's face occupied a nearby region.

She immediately tensed up and covered her mouth. She felt embarrassed and could not continue.

Manny, though, merely laughed. He couldn't help but be inspired and thought of an alternative title for his favorite Gabriel García Márquez novel: *Amor en los Tiempos de Cólicos*.

# Chapter 11

To Manny, Albertine represented the polar opposite of his last serious girlfriend: *Catracha*. If *Catracha* had been a bit jealous and demanded constant attention, Albertine placidly co-existed sans attention like a cactus without water. Instead of co-dependence, Albertine insisted on time away from Manny. A week could not pass without her wanting a girl's night out and she often worked late. This arrangement suited Manny, but only for a time.

As the months passed, Manny began to view Albertine in an even more serious light. However, the more he tried to get closer with her, the more distant she remained. She hardly talked about her family; her dad called her once a month, but she had not spoken with her mom in years. Manny sewed together facts to form a quilt of her life, but holes stubbornly remained. Her parents had divorced when she was young, *but why?* She had chosen to live with her dad, *but how did she feel about that at the time?* Her mom had remarried and had a few more kids, *but where were they now?*

To Manny, the most striking thing about Albertine was her lack of emotion. Or, in a negative light, her inability to express and understand her own feelings. She closed her eyes and her teeth rattled when she was angry, but she would insist she just "needed a minute." She avoided all films from the following genres: romantic comedies, family dramas, and "downer" documentaries. She only cried when she chopped onions.

Still, after they moved in together, things hummed along well enough. She was a wizard with bills and finances. Manny soon got a grasp on his credit card debt and even opened a savings account. However, the coasting came to an abrupt halt the first time Manny brought her to Brownsville for his little sister's high school graduation. Albertine did not care much for Brownsville or Manny's family, and they cared little for her.

She filled the entire 48-hour period in South Texas with countless complaints. It was too humid. Everybody spoke Spanish and she didn't. During one barbecue at a neighbor's, she insisted on staying in the car and playing with her cell phone. The second day, Manny's mom spent the entire morning preparing a special chile sauce for enchiladas. Albertine torpedoed any hopes with her future *suegra* by declaring herself "sick of Mexican food" and insisting on going to a burger joint for lunch.

Things started poorly, and only got worse. At dinner that last night, Manny could feel his mother's heated glare as Albertine ate with less than pristine manners.

His mom watched the *gringa* out of the corner of her eyes and she imagined her future grandchildren slurping their fingers, resting their elbows on the table, and even belching without covering their mouth. After only ten minutes, Manny's *madre* lost her appetite and asked to be excused early from the table.

On the return drive to Houston, Albertine smiled from ear-to-ear at the approaching Houston skyline. Earlier, an uncomfortable silence had filled the ride between them.

When Manny tried to broach the subject of his family and that failure of a first meeting, she dismissed all complaints as "nobody gets along with their boyfriend's family."

Yet, as the relationship started to stutter, he foolishly responded by trying to tighten his grip on her. He furiously exerted efforts to improve things and viewed all problems as his personal failings. He sent her flowers at work. He bought her moderately expensive dresses and jewelry. He took her to nice restaurants. Still, a stubborn gap loomed large between Albertine his girlfriend and Albertine the woman he wanted to know and love.

Finally, a drastic solution presented itself: he had to marry her. Matrimony could open her heart. Or so he hoped.

# Chapter 12

Manny knew for sure two facts about Albertine: she loved Las Vegas and adored weekend trips. Based on this knowledge, he crafted the perfect marriage proposal. First, he meticulously planned a trip to Vegas well in advance. He spent hours scouring hotel websites to find the most romantic yet still affordable option. He also tracked down chapels for shotgun weddings and rates. Then, he cooked up an excuse for the trip: discount airfare.

Albertine bit at the bait. However, Manny nervously walked on eggshells that first day of the trip. While Albertine rested her head on Manny's shoulder during their late night flight out of Hobby Airport, Manny again resorted to liquid courage. He reclined his chair and drank by himself an entire bottle of Merlot. After arriving in Vegas and catching a cab to the hotel, Manny, still tipsy, popped the question on the wrong knee just after she had opened the hotel room door to a trail of roses and a live mariachi band.

Albertine grabbed her chest and said: "Yes," but she did not cry or scream or cover her mouth or tremble with joy. Rather, she said: "Yes" as one might say: "Yes" after a cashier at a fast food restaurant repeats an order out of a drive-thru window.

However, that single, glorious word "Yes" blinded Manny to his bride's reticence. He could already see a house full of children and a picket fence. Marriage to Albertine was a first step towards a closer and happier future together, he thought. They did the Vegas chapel thing; both were drunk on adrenaline and vodka.

Manny's mom flipped out after hearing of the marriage. She had already disapproved of Albertine as a girlfriend, and the *güera's* willingness to marry in a chapel far from family forever sealed her place in the outhouse. Of course, Manny was arguably even guiltier, but, in his mother's eyes, he had fallen under a spell. The *suegra* started to reconsider her long-held Catholic beliefs on the sinfulness of divorce. She would not become a renegade Jesuit overnight, but she would reexamine her objections to Vatican II.

Months passed and the marriage solved none of the problems in the pre-existing relationship. Albertine remained a frigid workaholic with family issues. Manny, though, viewed her flaws as mere bumps in the road. He used his status as a "husband" in his quest for information and also to try and warm her frigid heart. However, she still refused to share email passwords and carefully guarded her own cell phone.

Manny, still somewhat idealistic, attributed her fierce privacy to childhood issues.

A much darker truth, though, would soon come to light.

# Chapter 13

Despite the weight of his mother's recent funeral, Manny was happy to be sleeping under the same roof as his siblings again, even if only for a short time. He woke up early the day after the burial to make breakfast. No donuts. No cereal. No, Manny decided, this would be a warm Mexican breakfast and he knew just the plate: *chilaquiles.*

While living abroad, Manny had learned how to make a dish he labeled "*Chilaquiles*-express." The premise was simple: the same savory taste of the Mexican plate, but a quicker and more efficient method of preparation. First, and essentially, you need quality tortillas. Ideally, one would get a bag of still warm, freshly-made corn tortillas. However, not everybody lives near a tortilleria. Also, sometimes you don't want to wake up, drive to the store and back, and then still have to cook for thirty minutes. Manny developed a taste for Guerrero brand corn tortillas, but they could never be more than a week old. And they should never be stored in a fridge.

Some folks prefer flour tortillas, including his younger brother, but Manny dismissed those types as *raros*. When making Manny's *Chilaquiles*-express, the tortillas must be medium-sized or small; no burrito-sized behemoths. Ideal diameter? Five-to-seven inches. Size matters because, for step two, the cook tears the tortillas into smaller pieces, preferably triangular and of the isosceles variety. Next, one must dice lots of onions. Yellow or white onions will work.

After dicing onions and tearing up tortillas, the heavy guns come out. One absolutely must utilize a heavy-duty skillet. This skillet should be at least four-to-five inches deep and have a diameter of ten inches. A good rule of thumb is: it must be light enough to hold with one hand, but solid enough where one could use it to bludgeon a home intruder. Place the skillet over the stove and turn up the heat.

At this stage of *chilaquiles* preparation, a robust debate exists. On the one hand, many prefer to toss the tortilla strips and diced onion into the skillet and pour in cooking oil. Manny, though, preferred to preheat the cooking oil in the skillet before adding the onion and tortilla bits. He also used corn oil, but vegetable oil also works. Manny believed that preheating the oil would prevent said oil from skipping into the air and possibly taking out an eye. He always wore long-sleeved shirts when cooking.

Forget timers; no clock can tell a person when the tortilla bits and onion are ready. Speaking in minutes and seconds would be futile. Instead, one must rely on a nose and a pair of eyes. Black is a bad sign. A burning smell is another. When the tortilla bits become a golden brown and the diced onion caramelizes, turn off the stove immediately. Manny preferred his tortilla bits extra crunchy, and was willing to burn a tortilla bit or two if that left the rest well done.

Next, one drains the oil from the skillet, but leaves the fried tortilla bits and onion inside. Some folks remove the bits and onion and place them on paper towels to dry. Manny viewed this step as unnecessary because, a minute later, one places the bits and onion in the skillet again and cooks eggs over them. Manny preferred his eggs very well done, but others disagreed. At Fher's request, Manny also removed the yellow from the eggs before performing this step.

In the second-to-last phase, another debate exists. On the one hand, purists preferred to buy a hard block of white cheese at a grocery store and then use a *raspa-queso* to grate the cheese over the still hot egg and tortilla bits. Manny's Americanness, though, triumphed over conventional Mexican cooking. He just bought grated cheese in a bag.

Lastly, Manny again showed his Americanness by heating and pouring red Pace picante sauce on top. For many older Mexicans, the use of pre-made sauce bought in a container from a store was a Cardinal Sin. Red salsa sauce holds a special place in the heart of the Aztec descendants, and many cooks spend hours dicing peppers and mixing spices to create the just right blend. However, the preparation of a proper *salsa roja* by itself can take more than half-a-day. Hence, Manny preferred Pace.

As Manny finished cooking, the aroma drew his family members to the dining room. His siblings had not eaten a warm breakfast for years and scarfed down their *chilaquiles*. On the other hand, Fher had eaten *chilaquiles*-express probably every day for breakfast since arriving in Brownsville. He still cleared his plate in minutes and asked for seconds. Only one thing ruined the morning: Manny's ex-wife called and insisted on speaking with Fher. Fher grew visibly upset after the brief conversation. He didn't even finish his second plate of *Chilaquiles*-express.

After she hung up and Fher was almost in tears, Manny grabbed his phone and threw it against the wall. He hugged his son and wondered aloud how he ever could have married *that woman*.

# Chapter 14

Mark was the first person to openly cast doubt on Albertine's character. Manny could not answer a basic question: why would a law firm pay for a paralegal like Albertine to travel so often for cases in other parts of the state? This simple question, posed to him by Mark during a break at work, loomed over Manny like storm clouds. During one lunch break at the nursing home, Mark stopped eating a ham sandwich, looked around to be sure nobody else was present, and said to Manny: "She is porking other dudes. You have to know that. Are you okay with that?"

Manny lacked concrete evidence, but adultery just made sense. In his heart, he knew it to be true, but preferred to turn his head away rather than contemplate it. Instead of assigning blame to Albertine, his rationalizations stretched beyond the realms of logic and morality. "So what if she cheated," he thought to himself. "Lots of people cheat when they're young."

Their outings as a couple became dull and rote; the coldness between them papered over simmering tensions. Manny watched Albertine's subtle glances at other men and asked himself: "what does she see in them that I don't have?"

Like a skilled poker player, Manny began to pick up on Albertine's "tells": the subconscious signs the body emits when one is dishonest. She would stumble over words. Her palms sweated. She had trouble maintaining eye contact. At first, her explanations for her "work travels" were elaborate tales that would have made Scheherazade blush.

Like all talented liars, though, she changed tactics. Applying the principle of Occam's razor, she now explained her "work trips" in single words like "deposition" or "trial." When pressed for further details, she would roll her eyes and sigh.

Manny felt a fool. Years earlier, Maribel had looked at one picture of Albertine on social media and warned him. He had dismissed her claims as tainted by prejudice: "You never like *güeras*." Now, despite all the circumstantial proof, he retained one sliver of hope: would Albertine settle down *after kids*? However, this stupid idea met with ice cold reality. Albertine had no interest in having kids yet and refused to stop taking birth control.

Manny accepted his role as the cuckolded husband by distracting himself with a hobby: he returned to the soccer field for the first time in years. And the hobby turned into an obsession. On Saturday mornings, he played in a park with Nigerian immigrants. On Wednesday afternoons, he played futsal with Russians at a Jewish community center. On Friday evenings, he sipped Tecate after playing indoor soccer with fellow Hispanics.

However, one incident jarred him. For his wife's birthday, he went to her office with flowers to surprise her. The secretary told him that Albertine had called in sick.

Manny took a full five minutes to compose himself and then left the office. He tossed the flowers in the trashcan near the exit. The rest of the day, he didn't call Albertine or even text.

Around two o'clock, she texted him that she would be working a bit late.

Manny did not reply. Instead, home alone, he turned off his cell phone and drank himself to sleep.

# Chapter 15

Silence swirled throughout the house like a frigid draft. Manny could hardly muster the energy to say: "Hello" to Albertine when she got back, and he made no attempt at conversation. She barely noticed his change in attitude; her mind was always busy with other matters.

The relationship was probably never well, but that was the night it died. Manny started to hate their couple routine. She got up early, ate toast, left for "work," and then came home late, usually well after dinner. They shared a bed, but little else. She even started to "work" on Sundays.

They were on the same cell plan, so Manny checked her text and call records online. He anticipated finding a smoking gun: a single number she called often. Instead, Manny found about *five* regular numbers. When he called them anonymously, the voicemail greetings were always men whose voices sounded similar in age to himself. Nobody answered.

Manny finally realized his marriage wasn't dead; it had never been born. A part of him had internalized his own parents' split and viewed all relationship failures as devastating, world-ending events. He had seldom thought about his parents' separation, but part of him had foolishly believed that any relationship could work with enough effort. With the blinders now off, he could finally see his own stupidity and naiveté. A relationship takes two.

Even his place of solace, soccer, had grown weird. One of the co-owners of the indoor arena, a pudgy and bald Mexican man with a huge moustache, had started to obsessively watch Manny's games on Friday nights. After one game, the man, nicknamed *"Piojo,"* came over to Manny and asked him: *"¿Por qué chingados te estás pudriendo acá?"* Manny struggled to understand the man's *chilango* accent, but got the jist of it: "why are you wasting your time *here*?"

It turned out that *Piojo* was a former professional player named Virgil Cantu; he had retired to Houston to live with his *gringa* wife. Virgil still scouted talents in Texas for his old club in Ciudad

Victoria, the capital of Tamaulipas. His demeanor was friendly, but he refused to believe that Manny could be older than 25-years-old. He also insisted that, despite a noticeable limp, Manny had played *futbol* professionally at some point. When Manny admitted to his time with the *Alacránes* and the Gales, Virgil smiled.

After one indoor game, Virgil invited Manny out for a drink. Over margaritas at a local bar, Virgil suddenly turned angry, grew red in the face, and pushed Manny's chest with two fingers. He said that Manny should be playing professionally in Mexico; Manny's first-touch was too good to be wasted on some indoor league in *gringolandia*.

Manny smiled and said: "*¿Y qué?*"

Virgil leaned close and said in a low voice: "I can get you the two-week trial with pro team. Paid. Would you go? *¿O eres un chiflado?*"

Manny, skeptical, said: "But my wife. She has a good job here." Virgil rolled his eyes. "*¡Búscate otra entonces!*"

# Chapter 16

Inside the bus station, Manny sat on a bench with his backpack at his feet and his cell phone in his hand. He stared at the email confirmation, but could not quite believe it. He had just bought a one-way ticket to Ciudad Victoria. He had also called to take two weeks off from work, just in case things didn't work out. However, the bigger question loomed: what about Albertine?

On the one hand, Manny wanted to disappear completely. He delighted in imagining Albertine as distressed by his sudden and unexplained departure. Still, he thought things through. Would she track him down online or contact his relatives? Would she file a missing person report? Would she think to call his work? What would they say? These questions obscured the more likely truth: she may simply not give a damn.

For the past three months, soccer had become Manny's salvation and an escape from his reality. The mess of his personal life faded after he put on a pair of boots and kicked a ball for a few hours. After games, he'd beg teammates to go out for drinks just to delay the inevitable return home. On Friday nights, he'd even come home long after Albertine had gotten back and gone to sleep.

The ticket on his cell phone screen offered him a clean break from his life and his wife. He called his half-sister Maribel and opened up about Albertine.

Maribel bit her tongue and listened. Instead of rushing to pass judgment, she asked Manny open questions about his thoughts, his feelings, and his dreams. She asked him if he needed money or a place to stay; she assumed he was filing for divorce.

He laughed. He told her he was going to travel around Mexico for a break and to collect his thoughts. He was also changing phone numbers and email addresses, but had written down her number and email. He would contact her shortly after arriving in Ciudad Victoria. He also told her not to tell anybody, even his mother, about where he was. He didn't tell Maribel about the soccer trial because he feared it was either a scam or, worse, he might not make the team.

The loudspeaker announced his bus's departure, so he hung up. On the drive from Houston to McAllen, he wrote on his cell phone a message to Albertine which was long, nasty and accusatory. He called her out on the telephone numbers and the affairs. He called her every offensive term that came to his head. Most importantly, he accused her of dishonesty and giving up on their marriage before it even had a chance. He did not tell her where he was going or why. She could burn his things for all he cared. He had left his car with Mark.

He clicked "send" and then immediately closed that email account, his other social media accounts, and turned off his cell phone.

The bus stopped briefly in McAllen, then crossed over into Reynosa, Mexico and headed South on Highway 97. Manny looked out the window and felt a weight lift off his shoulders.

He never received Albertine's reply ten minutes later, in which she confessed to everything and begged for forgiveness. She even admitted to lying about going to work on her birthday. The day of her birthday, though, she had not gone to see another man. Rather, she had gone to visit an OBGYN. She was scared because she didn't know how to tell Manny *he was going to be a father*.

She was sure it was his.

It would be several years before Manny and she would speak again.

# Chapter 17

For three decades, Mexico had existed in Manny's psyche as the Borgesian Library of Babel: it was a seductive world of ever-expanding possibilities. Manny arrived at the bus station in downtown Ciudad Victoria at eleven o'clock at night and with only a few hundred dollars to his name, and reality vanquished fiction. Only one thing stood out: the heat. The sun had set hours earlier, but it was still hot as hell. Manny sweated profusely. It was even worse than Brownsville.

Eventually, an assistant from the club showed up and drove Manny to a reasonably nice hotel near the city center. He explained to Manny in a mixture of broken English and rapid-fire Spanish that the hotel and all meals were paid by the club. Tomorrow morning, a taxi would come to drive Manny to training, also paid for by the club. For a second-division outfit, Manny thought, they had already spent more on him than the Gales and *Alacránes* combined. He slept with his curtains open and admired the view of the surrounding mountains.

The next morning, he arrived at the club's training ground and tried to correctly say the club's name, *Tzompantlis*, but failed miserably. He recalled a friend from Houston who had mistakenly thought the first syllable of the word "Oaxaca" was pronounced like "oaks." He felt ashamed and resolved to learn how to say the team's name.

Manny did a quick medical with the club's doctor and then got escorted by a young female intern to the locker room. A training uniform, shorts, socks, shin pads, and cleats rested in a pile on a wooden bench. A few other players had arrived early and greeted him.

As he changed, Manny heard a strange sound from outside the room: English. The voice came in scattershot bursts, and Manny made out unfamiliar terms such as: "bloody hell," "wanker," and "rubbish." He deduced that the speaker was from England, not

America. He stepped out of the locker room and into a hallway. The smell of cigarette smoke and body odor assaulted his nose.

Before him stood Terry Hodgson, the English manager of the *Tzompantlis*. Skinny as a pole, Terry donned a blue and white jumpsuit and wore Nike running shoes. Alongside him stood a male intern, who ostensibly was translating Terry's various grievances to other members of the club's staff. Manny tapped Terry on the shoulder and said: "Hey, I'm Manny, the trialist from Texas."

Terry turned around quickly and looked startled. He eyed Manny up-and-down, then smiled and warmly embraced him. "Finally, another English-speaker! I thought you'd never arrive!"

# Chapter 18

The first two weeks of training flew by. Terry asked Manny to play every position on the field but goalie. The pale Englishman complained constantly about the heat and what he perceived as a lack of support from the club. Terry professed himself to be a "training ground coach" and was flustered when the club would not pay to erect him a mini-tower from which he could watch practice.

However, the training pitch was the nicest Manny had ever played on in real life: two groundskeepers kept the Bermuda grass immaculately green and trim.

Coach Terry doubted the ability of his translator, and started to rely on Manny to communicate ideas and concepts to the team. Through practice and immersion, Manny's *mocho* border Spanish improved considerably. Divorced and desperately lonely, Terry also invited Manny out to dinner a few times at some of the better restaurants in Ciudad Victoria. Over *ceviche*, Terry drowned himself in cheap beer and blasted everybody involved with the club. He even talked bad about the players and his sentences started with "he's a good lad, but…" before ending in a vicious attack.

Manny made a mental note: the term "good lad" served as a warning shot before Terry's diatribes.

At the end of two weeks, the *Tzompantlis'* General Manager, a tall and overweight bearded man named Jose Vergara, invited Manny to his office after training. He closed the door and Manny sat on a black, leather chair. From his desk, Jose grabbed an envelope and a stack of papers. He handed both to Manny. The envelope contained Manny's first paycheck, and the stack of papers was a first contract offer. Jose explained that the club had recently lost a major sponsor, so they could only offer Manny one million pesos per year.

Manny blinked and felt the urge to pinch himself. One million pesos converted to about sixty thousand dollars per year, double what he earned as a CNA. He signed the contract without even thinking of talking to an agent and walked briskly out of the office.

He cashed the check at the nearest bank, it cleared, and then went to Plaza las Adelitas where he bought a Mexican cell phone at Wal-Mart. Suddenly, for the first time in his life, money was no longer an issue for him.

He did not impulsively purchase a car because he wanted to avoid the hassle of getting a driver's license. At his hotel that night, though, he fantasized about big purchases. He perused local real estate listings online.

He attended the *Tzompantli*'s home game that Saturday and sat in the club's executive box. He wore a dapper black suit and red tie provided by the club; he felt handsome. During the game, the *Tzompantli*'s center back elbowed another player in the face and was shown a red card and they lost 1:0. Afterwards, Manny headed to the locker room, where Coach Terry was ripping into the center back, but the translator was clearly softening the verbal blows. When Terry shouted and called the player a "bloody idiot" and "disgrace", the translator softly said a single "*estúpido.*"

Terry was less than impressed. Less than fifteen minutes later, though, Coach Terry gave a press conference and called the referee's decision too harsh. He publicly defended the player and refused to budge.

Afterwards, Coach Terry saw Manny and invited him for a bit of whiskey at his office in the stadium. After a few drinks, Terry explained his "philosophy." Basically, a coach must view players as a sculptor sees a boulder: inside lurks a beautiful essence, but he or she must chip carefully to find it. A coach cannot change what lurks inside; he can only discover it.

Manny talked a bit about himself, and Coach Terry flipped out when he realized that Manny had been coached by De Charlus.

Terry prodded Manny for details on the training methods, fitness regime, and dietary regiment of De Charlus. Apparently, De Charlus had coached quite successfully in Argentina and even Europe before moving to San Antonio and leading the *Alacránes*. Terry revered De Charlus and spoke of him as a philosophy student would of Aristotle. He asked Manny point blank: what most stood out from his time with De Charlus?

Manny immediately recalled the single time he had disregarded Junot's advice and showered at the training ground after practice. As Junot had warned him, De Charlus lurked near the showers and blatantly peeped inside. He spoke openly with the bathing players. After one glance at Manny, De Charlus gave him the nickname: "*poronguilla chueca*," which an Uruguayan teammate later translated for him. It either meant "little prick," or, even less flattering, "little curved dick."

Manny replied: "It would have to be...the *physical* aspect. He was big on the player's *physical* aspect." Terry's eyes widened and he smiled and nodded.

# Chapter 19

Manny couldn't shake this odd feeling: was he worse at futbol than when he was younger? He was often last in sprint drills. He was not the best in finishing drills. He did reasonably well in passing drills, but he even got muscled off the ball by smaller guys at times. He looked at himself in the mirror during one weight room session, and noticed a tiny, little gut starting to form. How had he got to where he was? Why him?

The weird part was, younger guys always came up to him to ask for advice and admired him. He spent most practices talking to his teammates, putting his arm around a kid who was having a bad day. He was probably the slowest on the team, but Coach Terry always appointed him to stand in the center of the field when the team won a corner kick: Terry didn't trust anybody else to snuff out a counterattack.

In his head, Manny made a list of the things he did for his team:

Stick my thumb up an opposing forward's butthole when defending him on a set piece or corner kick.

Always fall to the ground and shout and moan when fouled, even if fouled lightly.

Stand in front of the ball after a free-kick is called against us.

Stand in the wall when we defend free kicks and blow kisses at the opposing forward while insulting his mother's chastity.

Not allow young players to get too happy or too sad.

Say really bland things at press conferences to bore journalists.

Flick the tip of the penis of an opposing forward when defending him on a set piece or corner kick.

Not allow coach to get too happy or too sad.

Show up on time for practice and always sober.

When doing really poorly on a distance run, pretend to cramp up or force myself to vomit so coach thinks he is helping me push myself to my limit.

Grab the jersey(s) of opposing player(s) until I get a second verbal warning from the ref or am shown a yellow card.

Show up on time and sober for the Friday night lock-down in a local hotel before home games on Saturday.

Say really stupid things are press conferences to confuse journalists.

Self-doubt gnawed away at Manny; he hated to watch game video because he cringed at seeing his old man limp. He remembered himself as young and graceful, yet thousands of fans in person and on TV watched him hobble around a field for 90 minutes. He thanked the Lord and vowed to enjoy the view from the summit while it lasted, but also prepare for the inevitable descent.

# Chapter 20

Coach Terry praised Manny on the training pitch and Manny soon started most *Tzompantli* games. However, Coach Terry puzzled Manny by constantly shifting his position. One game, Manny would play as a sole striker. The next game, he'd play as a holding midfielder. In one game, he even played left back for the first time in his life. In his heart, Manny felt that he was a striker. However, he recalled what De Charlus had told him: "Every single soccer player believes he's a striker. Most are wrong."

Manny bit his lip and came to marvel at the two faces of Terry. During one game, Manny failed to defend his man on a corner kick and that player headed in a goal. At halftime, Coach Terry gave Manny the hair-dryer treatment: while Manny sat on a wooden bench, Terry stooped down and yelled into his face from a foot away for a good ten minutes. After the game, though, Terry refused to single out any player at fault in the press conference. Rather, he rambled on to journalists about marking systems and zones and man-to-man. The reporters eventually grew bored and changed the subject.

Manny's role as de facto translator grew. He did his best to translate word-for-word Terry's British English pejoratives to the Mexican Spanish equivalent. The adjective "bloody" turned into "pinche" and could be heard most weekday mornings throughout the training ground. A few of the younger players saw Manny as a suck-up, but the veterans appreciated his efforts. Eventually, Manny became assistant captain of the team.

The *Tzompantli*'s results were erratic, even if Terry imposed a clear and coherent style of play. The team fielded a deep, defend-first, four-four-two that counterattacked down the flanks. The press called this the *Estilo Ingles* and were enthralled by the speed of the *Tzompantli*'s attacks. Manny knew the system well from his time in America, where he disparagingly called it "Gringo ball." Despite his doubts, he trained hard and tried to make the system work. Once he had raised his fitness levels, he solidified his place as a holding midfielder.

The paychecks kept coming, and Manny started to send money back to his mom. An idea dawned on him: he could buy a house in Brownsville and let her live there. During the day and in-between practices, he would scour online real estate websites for listings while eating at the club's cafeteria. One day, though, at the cafeteria, another player sat by Manny. He had heard that Manny still didn't have an agent. He handed Manny a card.

Manny's first instinct was not to call the agent, but rather to speak to Coach Terry. In Terry's office, Manny had barely mentioned the word "agent" when Coach Terry stood up, slowly walked over to his open office door, closed it, and walked back to Manny. He leaned in closely and said softly: "Get as much money from these muppets as you can, *as quickly as you can*." Terry's wording took Manny aback. Terry smiled mischievously: "Mate, there's a saying: today's best friend will toss you under a bus tomorrow. This business is brutal."

Manny paused and reflected. He would get an agent. He knew he needed somebody else to fight those battles for him.

# Chapter 21

Manny arrived at practice on Monday morning but had no clue what to expect. The prior night, a stream of text messages had violently shaken his cell phone to life around midnight. Messages arrived from several players and even his agent. Then came the group messages. Apparently, Terry was no longer coach. Manny and the other players, though, were in the dark on whether he had resigned or been fired.

Manny went to training and could smell bad blood in the air. He had barely sat down at his locker when an executive in a gray suit entered. The older man read from a sheet of paper and explained that Terry and the club had experienced a mutual disagreement and decided to part ways. He offered no details. He also said that Terry would not be allowed near the club's stadium and his old office. Terry's assistant, Phil, the physical conditioning coach, would be the interim manager.

The man left and the players chatted among themselves in low voices. The older guys had seen quite a few firings and resignations, so they barely bat an eyelash.

Still, not letting Terry say goodbye rubbed the younger players the wrong way. A few of them asked Manny for Terry's number and then they texted him thanks.

Manny had resisted the urge to call Terry, but finally caved and "rang" the Englishman. Terry answered and sounded perfectly normal. However, he explained that confidentiality was part of the severance package, so he couldn't reveal many details.

Before, the *Tzompantlis* had coasted along to mid-table security, but the new interim coach made a royal mess of things. He arbitrarily benched veterans in favor of younger, but untested, players. Squad harmony turned into constant bickering and discord. Phil experimented with odd formations, at one point playing four forwards. However, he overlooked a serious problem: the *Tzompantlis* didn't even have one decent forward, let alone four.

Players, confused by their tasks and new assignments, made basic mistakes and blamed one another.

Manny benefitted from being named captain, but the team nosedived in the standings. Manny held numerous player-only meetings and met with Coach Phil one-on-one, but Phil stubbornly refused to admit any mistakes or change anything. Manny missed Terry and even yearned for the inappropriate glances and nicknames of De Charlus. Phil, from South America, frustratingly combined the assurance of a champion with the intelligence of a grade-schooler. In press conferences, he ascribed all losses to the players' lack of dedication and fitness.

The players prayed for a new manager and hoped the "interim" tag meant something. However, as with many small clubs in Mexico, once the team starts losing, things soon go to hell in a handbasket. Suddenly, sorely needed sponsorship money dried up and cash disappeared. The club started to pay the players once a month, as opposed to every fifteen days. A few guys complained that their paychecks bounced, but the club President paid them cash after a few tense meetings behind closed-doors.

Inconsistently paid and poorly managed, the *Tzompantlis* hemorrhaged points and dropped in the standings like a diving falcon. On the last game of the season, they needed a draw to stay in the second-division. They played at home and hosted the second-worst team in the league. Coach Phil finally relented and fielded a basic 4-4-2. The *Tzompantlis* scored in the fifth minute off a corner kick, but conceded a penalty kick and goal in the 80th minute. Then, in injury time, disaster struck. One of the players scored an own goal while defending a corner kick. The game ended to boos and hisses. They were getting relegated, and, even worse, the few fans who had shown up tossed rocks and little plastic bags of urine at the players as they left the field.

Manny sat on the wooden bench in the locker room and could not stop crying. They delayed the press conference by a half-hour to allow him to get himself together. Before the vicious media, he bit his tongue as Coach Phil again ascribed the loss to fitness problems. Manny's face turned bright red when Phil talked optimistically about the team fighting for promotion next year and Phil's own hopes to stay on as manager. When finally allowed to speak, Manny vomited the recycled "we lose as a team" mantra over and over. He was sad and mad, but too mature to get baited by journalists.

That night, he drank Tequila alone in his apartment until passing out on his black leather couch. In only ten months, his personal dream had turned into a nightmare.

# Chapter 22

The *Tzompantlis* were no more. A few days after the very last game, players showed up for end-of-season meetings and found the office doors locked. Manny and a few other players sat in their cars and waited in the parking lot for over two hours. They feverishly texted their agents and were furious. The club had not given them their last paycheck. Manny was even owed a bonus for having made a certain number of starts and appearances.

Unlike other players, Manny had not bought a sports car or too many designer clothes. He had even avoided the *pachangas,* the groupies, and only gone on a few dates. For the most part, he hoarded cash and entertained himself by watching American TV shows on iTunes. He also reignited his torrid love affair with literature. When he came into training with dark lines around his eyes, the players and manager assumed a wild night on the town. In reality, he had been unable to put down *La Fiesta del Chivo.*

Manny and a few other players left the parking lot and went to a local mall. They ate at a sushi restaurant inside, loitered for a bit, got heckled by some fans and hugged by others, and then went to their respective homes. The next day, Manny's agent broke the bad news: the *Tzompantlis* were bankrupt. Even worse, the owners had not paid fees to the Federation and probably owed taxes. The former was the kiss of death in Mexican soccer. Even if a new owner tried to buy and reorganize the club and win promotion, the interest and fines on the missed fees would be astronomical.

Only two positives emerged. First, the players' union and Federation had a wage fund for such cases. Manny should not expect his bonus anytime soon, but he would still get his wages for a few months and via direct deposit. Secondly, and most importantly, Manny was now an undisputed free agent. Any club from any division of Mexican soccer had the chance to buy his contract.

"Great," the cynic in Manny thought. "The captain of a team relegated from the second division is now a free agent." That same day, he packed up his apartment. He invited his landlord, an elderly woman, to lunch and explained the situation. He said he was low on funds and needed to move out. She agreed that he could pay one month's rent and leave early if needed. She only asked one favor: he give her a signed jersey before leaving town. He agreed.

That night, he sat in his bed while reading a short story by Juan Pablo Villalobos, sipped a rum and coke, and went to sleep around ten. At midnight, he cellphone buzzed and awakened him. He saw the Mexican area code "744", didn't recognize it, and didn't answer. The person didn't leave a voicemail, but called another ten times. Manny's head raced in circles: did he owe somebody money? Was this one of those robo-kidnapping scams that happened in bigger cities? Finally, a text message arrived.

"Manny u bloody idjit pick up its Terry. U wanna come to Acapulco? :) :) :)"

# Chapter 23

Fher rolled down the car window, stuck his face out, and inhaled the salty sea air. Manny did likewise. The sun had barely risen and they had already crossed the bridge connecting Port Isabel with Padre Island. Manny's siblings sat half-asleep in the back of the mini-van. Manny drove north along the beach past the hotels and stripmalls and tourist shops of *La Isla*. When they finally reached the dunes, sand covered one side of the narrow, two-lane road. He stopped at the very last parking area before the road ended. He smiled. When his siblings woke up, he thought, they would recognize the spot instantly.

Manny and Fher jogged a few miles up and down the beach, and then played soccer with a volleyball. When they returned to the van, Maribel and Phoebe had already changed into swimsuits and had even unloaded the beach umbrellas and cooler. Paolo still dozed in the backseat, so Manny lowered the van windows and left him inside.

They set up the umbrellas, opened the lawn chairs, and spread two blankets over the now hot sand. Fher jumped in the ocean with Phoebe, while Maribel and Manny sat and spoke. He told her about the difficult last few months with mom. He had had to sleep on the floor next to mom's bed so she would not wake up and fall during the night. In fact, "sleep" was not the right word. He had laid down, but had to remain awake and vigilant.

At night, while she tossed and turned, mom constantly spoke to dead relatives. A few nights, she would wake up and insist that her brother Hernandes had brought her tacos as a snack and they were in the fridge.

Maribel just listened and let Manny release his grief as a balloon slowly deflates. When Paolo woke up, he meandered over and joined them. Maribel left the two boys to go for a swim.

Paolo ribbed Manny for giving Fher a cell phone so young. Manny admitted that he had resisted, but the phone would be useful in case of emergency.

This was a half-truth. In reality, Manny decided to let Fher keep the phone after Manny received his very first sweet message from Fher. The smiley face and *"Papi te kiero"* had melted his heart.

Inevitably, the conversation turned to their own father. Manny looked out at the azure ocean and asked Paolo if he remembered the *Isla Esmeralda*? Pablo scoffed. He remembered their dad always drove them to the beach at night and let them run around, but he also recalled a key detail unseen by Manny: dad would always go swimming with a lady while the two boys were playing. Dad would get in the water, some lady would walk towards them, dive into the water, and swim out to him.

Manny suddenly recalled that, once, he had found a dress and women's sandals on the beach. Another time, he remembered hearing a lady's laughter carry over the ocean.

The two boys, now men, then talked about mom's last few days before the stroke. Manny explained to Paolo how dementia had slowly killed the person inside their mother's body. On some days, mom would wake up and believe she was still a teenage girl and be mad that her parents were not home. Other days, she would confuse Manny and Fher for distant relatives. She would swear she was a prisoner in her own home.

Manny said the stroke was a blessing; it was a peaceful exit for his suffering mother. Paolo, however, was speechless but clearly upset. Manny gazed into Paolo's eyes, and Manny saw his brother futilely searching for lost time. Manny told him that Mom's last lucid comments had been worries for her sons, neither of whom were married.

Paolo had a live-in girlfriend, but couldn't help asking Manny about his brother's own romantic life. Many viewed Manny's asexual lifestyle with curiosity and skepticism, including Paolo. Was Manny a player or had he switched teams?

Manny deflected his little brother's questions with vague answers. Paolo, though, turned the screw and asked more pointed and specific questions. Exasperated after a few minutes, Paolo asked Manny: "when was the last time you *slept* with a woman?"

# Chapter 24

Yet again, Manny signed a contract without reading it first. However, Acapulco FC was coached by Terry and safely mid-table in the first division. Manny felt secure and also got handsomely compensated. Still used to dollars, his eye balls jumped out of their sockets when he saw how many zeroes were on the first few paychecks. In fact, they weren't even paychecks. He got paid direct deposit. He struggled to believe that only a few years ago he had been toiling away in a nursing home for ten dollars per hour. He thanked the Lord and promised to go to Mass sometime in the near future.

Manny's relatively advanced age and the fitness levels of first division soccer did not jibe. Terry pushed him hard in training, but Manny could only give a good 70 minutes before becoming a liability on the field. However, his maturity and professionalism quickly won over his new teammates. As a youth, he would grow angry when he didn't start games, when he didn't play entire games, and when he wasn't fielded as a striker. Now, as a middle-aged man, he contented himself with playing holding midfielder.

Manny's tenure at Acapulco FC was marked by one major scandal: the "*patadon*." In a cup game versus one of the big clubs from Mexico City, Manny slid into a tackle to win the ball and the opposing forward turned unexpectedly. Manny's cleats connected with the player's ankle and tore various ligaments of said ankle. Even worse, the player was a budding star for the Mexican national team.

The newspapers tore into Manny as the "*Gringo patadon*" and opposing fans invented songs to insult him. Manny got worried and grew a bit paranoid, but Terry laughed it off. "If they're talking about you, it's a good thing. No exceptions. And I love a full-blooded tackle."

As a first-division player in a rich resort town, Manny received no shortage of invitations to VIP parties with alcohol, designer drugs, and ladies of ill repute. Despite pressure from his

Colombian agent Sergio to do a few promotions, he still preferred to stay at home and read a good book. He explained to teammates and others that he was still *technically* married and his wife was in the US, so things would look bad if he constantly went out *de pachanga*. He omitted the fact he and his wife had not spoken in several years.

He had also grown strangely religious as he had aged, but hid this fact for one simple and stubborn reason: older people had warned him that this would happen, and his younger self had mocked them.

A social invitation arrived, though, that Manny could not refuse. Jay Guzman, the CEO of a multinational conglomerate, was considering an investment in Acapulco FC. He invited Manny to a private party at his castle-inspired mansion in the exclusive *Lomas de Chapultepec* neighborhood of Mexico City. Manny and his agent were the only persons from the club invited, and they would attend after the next away game in the capital. The Acapulco FC President had personally met with Manny and explained the importance of the meeting. Manny would be an ambassador for the club and expected to "do his part."

The night of the game in the *Distrito Federal*, Manny did not start and only played ten minutes as a sub. When he asked Terry why, the Englishman merely winked and said he would need his energy for later. As the rest of the team showered and got onto the team bus, a chauffeur led Manny and Sergio to a black Rolls Royce and then drove them across town. They arrived at a neighborhood more akin to a fort. They passed two security checkpoints and the car was searched each time. When they finally rolled down the long driveway that lead up to Guzman's mansion, Manny realized why it was nicknamed the *Castillo de Torres*. The elaborate three-story house featured several spiraling towers.

After handing their coats to the butler, Manny and Sergio had to leave their cell phones with another person. They were then escorted to the backyard. Various sofas were scattered around the edges of a shallow pool which was the shape of a figure eight. Dance music hummed softly in the background; the only light emanated from the in ground pool lighting and a few candles on small square tables. The host, and other guests, clearly wanted things dark.

This struck Manny as odd because in the rest of the house he had counted over two dozen mirrors. Outside, men with gray hair wore black designer suits, sipped on *mojitos*, and enjoyed the company of female dates half their age. Manny counted more bodyguards than guests.

Manny asked Sergio to introduce him to Jay Guzman, but his agent laughed. Mr. Guzman, Sergio explained, rarely attended these functions. Before Manny could ask another question, a thirty-something woman with a strapless black dress, shoulder-length dark black hair, and café eyes approached and interrupted them.

Her eyes absorbed every inch of Manny. She smiled, extended her hand, and said in perfect English: "You must be that rough American we've all seen on the TV. Manny, right? Nice to meet you. I'm Flor Buchanan, Jay's wife."

# Chapter 25

Flor Buchanan was beautiful, but not in a way that intrigued Manny. In South Texas, he had grown up with and grown bored of curvaceous *morenitas*. He also smelled a hint of desperation about her. She donned a white diamond necklace that, he deduced, served two purposes. First, the necklace provided a pretext for any male to stare at her surgically-enhanced bust. Secondly, and more importantly, the necklace allowed Flor to assume that men and even women were staring at her surgically-enhanced bust.

Flor promised to take Manny on a private tour later, and then disappeared. A half hour passed and Manny was bored as hell. "Why was he there?" He thought.

Sergio had called some contacts beforehand, and explained to him that the small guest list had been carefully curated by Flor. She referred to them as *"los fieles,"* the "faithful," and were people who were wealthy enough to belong to the same country club, but discrete enough to keep their mouths shut. This tight-lipped loyalty, though, made for dull conversation.

The insularity also bred contempt for newcomers. Manny tried to talk to a few people, but they spoke as if writing a telegram; their brief and Hemingwayesque replies gave the impression they had to pay per word uttered. He retreated to a sofa with Sergio and they talked soccer for a spell. Manny knocked back a few Coronas, but grew restless. If Jay Guzman was not there, what was he doing there? How could he be the club's "ambassador" if the foreign dignitary was not present?

Flor reappeared and socialized among a few nearby tables. She was a master of the art of standing too close to old men and laughing at unfunny jokes.

Sergio spoke to Manny in hushed tones, and Manny could barely hear him. "For the Mexican, you know who is the *sancho?*" In the few years that Manny had lived in Mexico, his Spanish had improved immensely. He confidently rolled his "r's" and he even pronounced the hidden "y" in most diphthongs. He mastered the difference between *ándale* vs. *órale*. He also learned to pronounce English words with a Mexican accent, adding a superfluous "e" to words that started with consonants. For example, he said "e-sport" instead of "sport." Still, Manny heard the word "*sancho*" and assumed it was a proper name and referred to a particular person.

Flor came to their table and Sergio immediately shut up. She sat beside Manny on the couch, uncomfortably close, and squeezed his right bicep. "You're pretty tan for a gringo. I bet you have a lot of girlfriends down there in Acapulco, no?" He clarified that he didn't have any girlfriends in Acapulco. Flor grinned as wide as the Cheshire Cat.

She reminded Manny about their private tour later and promised to show him her husband's yellow sportscar, a Zenvo St1. She then got up suddenly and skipped to another table.

When she was out of earshot, Sergio clarified what Manny had started to suspect. Jay Guzman, like many other people present, probably operated in Mexico's illicit economy. He was likely out of the country due to an arrest warrant. However, the legitimate arm of his business was considering a deal with Acapulco FC and Jay wanted his wife "to approve." Manny's job was to stay until at least midnight and be sure Flor Buchanan "approved."

Manny felt affronted, but also a bit flattered. That's it, he thought, he just had to be charming and flirt with a CEO's wife a bit. It sounded easy, but why was she avoiding him?

He soon stopped drinking. Every twenty minutes or so, some *mesero* would try to get him to take shots, but he steadfastly refused.

At the stroke of midnight and bored out of his mind, he stood up to leave with Sergio. Maybe there would be no private tour with Flor. Most of the guests had cleared out by that time, and he had not seen Flor for over an hour. Manny and Sergio were escorted to the entryway and got their coats when a short, pudgy bodyguard in a black polo shirt and jeans approached Manny. *"La dama de la casa pide su presencia."*

Sergio gathered his belongings and left. Manny followed the bodyguard back to the pool. He didn't dare to look at himself in any of the hallway mirrors.

# Chapter 26

A few days had passed since that night at the Buchanan's, but Manny still felt sick to his stomach. Everything had been so surreal and upsetting. He had been *played* despite having anticipated it; he racked his mind trying to piece together how. First, Flor Buchanan had insisted they go swimming, and he only acquiesced partially; he put on a pair of borrowed shorts and only stuck his legs in the water. Second, she had suggested they relax in the hot tub, which he flat-out rejected.

However, when they sat side-by-side in lawn chairs, she suddenly grew emotional and seemed to pour out her soul to him. She talked about her impoverished childhood, her verbally-abusive dad, her rise to fame as an actress-model, and, of course, her unhappy marriage to an emotionally-distant husband. She cried and asked for him to just hold her, which he allowed. By the time he realized what was up, she had already undone the bottom half of his dress shirt. His resistance melted at the touch of her palms.

Manny's complicity and naiveté bothered him in equal part. The morning after the *polvo*, he watched reruns from an old *telenovela* featuring Flor Buchanan. To his disgust, he saw on the small screen the exact same character - an "emotionally distressed Flor" - as the night of their encounter. Manny marveled at how, ten years later, she could still transform herself into *that* persona. He shuddered at the thought of Flor at her next party, where she would brag to her friends about having tagged the "rough American."

At least Manny's club was happy. Jay Guzman's business signed the sponsorship deal with Acapulco FC. Manny even got a renovated contract with a pay raise months later. Still, Manny's career had entered a decline. He enjoyed Terry's confidence, but physically could only play and contribute for an hour as a starter or make thirty-minute cameos as a sub. He spent most post-game Monday morning practices in an ice bath or getting a massage. Almost every day, he woke up in pain; his ankles swelled, his back ached. More and more, he consulted the club doctor about which painkillers were permitted and which would trigger a positive on a doping test.

Manny handled the reduced minutes with tact, in large part because his internal flame of competition had extinguished. He no longer lived and died with each game. He had accomplished his childhood dream, but felt alone; he was a stranger in a foreign land. He was paid handsomely to kick a ball, and that was that.

He retreated into the life of the mind. He read long and trippy novels by an author who was either Chilean or Mexican. He even fell in love with an unpublished collection of avant-garde poetry by a long-deceased Uruguayan-French writer named Rocamour Galeano. He thanked his lucky stars he had downloaded Galeano's complete works as a PDF just days before the piracy site hosting said work was shut down by the Swedish authorities.

Already in a state of physical decline and spiritual malaise, Manny received a long-delayed sucker punch from his past: one day, after a practice, a strange man was loitering around the club's parking lot. Manny tried to avoid eye contact with the man and walked directly to his car, but the man recognized Manny and approached him. The man asked if he was Emmanuel Hernandez, and Manny said "Yes."

Manny figured the man was a journalist or a fan. He was wrong. The man was a process-server and handed Manny an envelope with a formal stamp and seal. Manny opened it, and pulled out a letter. He read at the top of the first page in black and bold letters: *"aplazamiento jurídico,"* or "legal notice." Manny read on and learned that his biological father had passed away recently in Mexico.

Manny had been named one of the heirs in the will.

# Chapter 27

"Juan Joaquin Hernandez." Manny had not even recognized the name at first. Then, he recalled that relatives called his dad "J.J." and white people called him "John." The legal letter had Manny's full name and date of birth and even his place of birth. It looked legit.

He called his agent, who then called a lawyer in San Cristóbal de las Casas, Chiapas. A few days later, his agent confirmed that a will had been filed in the local court, and a man named Juan Joaquin Hernandez had passed away from a heart attack about a month ago. Juan left behind a widow and two daughters, both of whom were older than Manny. More importantly, Juan Joaquin's family spoke to the local attorney and wanted to meet Manny; they gave the attorney their phone numbers, email addresses, and physical address.

Manny's head spun. His first instinct was to call his mom, but then he restrained himself. As a camera lens slowly comes into focus, he could suddenly see his own past a lot clearer. His parents had fought over money because his dad worked a ton and earned little; it did not add up. This was probably because dad sent money back to Mexico for this other family. If these half-sisters were older than him, then his mom had put up with his dad's infidelity because she herself had once been *the other woman*. His dad had not disappeared after getting deported for the fifth time: he'd just returned to his first wife and family.

Manny thought he had gotten over his adolescent rage and his violent hatred of his father. He was wrong. Time had started to mend the wound of his dad's departure and disappearance precisely because Manny had filled the void of knowledge with a fictional play, one in which his dad was just another tragically unfaithful and unreliable human being. Manny had given up hope that his dad was still alive, so instead he had imagined that his dad had died trying to cross the *Rio Bravo* and return to his mother and him. This was not true. Reality bit, and bit hard.

Curiosity, though, defeated anger. He accepted the invitation and went to San Cristóbal. Part of him wanted to meet his half-sisters and see the family his dad had once left and then returned to. He had heard a few stories about San Cristóbal, a small town in a valley surrounded by mountains. *Tio Julio* and his mother had always referred to the place in hushed tones, as if it was a magical land, but full of evil; Manny only knew that his family had left the city in a hurry shortly after fighting broke out between the Mexican military and Marxist rebels.

When Manny stepped off the bus in San Cristóbal after a two-hour journey from Tuxtla Gutierrez, the state capital and closest city with an airport, his legs wobbled as if returning to land after an eternity at sea. He was not fatigued, just nervous. A short and stout woman with cropped black hair and dark brown skin held a piece of cardboard with "Manny" on it. To her right and left stood two women, both middle-aged, who looked uncannily like his sister Phoebe and half-sister Maribel. All three were dressed to impress in designer blue jeans, heels, and colorful blouses.

The younger one, Xoco, recognized Manny, shouted, and tried to run towards him in heels; she staggered like a newborn deer, almost fell, and he caught her. She was a foot shorter than him and couldn't weigh more than one hundred pounds. Before he could blink, the older woman, Grimilda, and older sister, Anselma, had joined the embrace. Grimilda shook with delight as she smiled and tears ran down her face.

This was not the reception Manny had expected.

# Chapter 28

Manny awoke in the guest bedroom of his dad's two-story house to the smell of *chile*, eggs, corn tortillas, and tomato sauce. The unmistakable odor sneaked in under the crack between the floor and door. He heard a woman singing, the sizzling of pans, and the constant hum of a plugged-in fan. He felt the soft comforter and queen-sized mattress under his back. He looked at the white wooden desk in the corner, finely painted blue walls, and carefully hung black-and-white pictures of long-deceased relatives. Despite being much wealthier at this point in his life, he recalled his childhood and felt envy stir inside him.

Yesterday, after visiting his dad's grave and leaving flowers, Xoco and Anselma had taken him on a tour of San Cristóbal in their yellow BMW. They showed him the ancient chapel where they were baptised, took first communion, and were confirmed. They drove by the Catholic *prepa* where both had studied from preschool to *colegio*. Then, they showed him the small campus of a private university where Anselma had recently finished her Pharmacy Doctorate.

Manny rode around, but his mind drifted elsewhere and he thought of his dad's red truck and his mom's faded gray Camry without working A/C. He remembered having to bum rides to school from Hector his freshmen year. After returning to Brownsville from San Francisco, he had also had to bum rides from co-workers. As a small child, his family's cramped apartment had meant that he often slept on a twin mattress, no box spring or bed frame, with Pablo. His sister had slept on another mattress on the other side of the room.

Both his half-sisters lived with boyfriends in nearby Tuxtla Gutierrez, but came home most weekends. During the two days Manny was there, a constant stream of visitors came to the house; the guests sipped *café con leche* out front in nice wooden lawn chairs and chatted about the weather, *la política*, and neighborhood *chisme*. They introduced Manny as their brother from the US, and a few guests recognized him as a *futbolista*.

The smell was too much, so Manny sat up and got out of bed. He tossed on some clothes and his mouth watered. Every time he smelled that combination of *huevo revuelto*, corn tortillas, and *chile*, he recalled Saturday mornings in grade school when his mom made the stuff by the truckload. He thought of that famous line: "Nothing but a moment of the past? Much more perhaps…"

His cell phone rang. His agent had news about the legal case regarding his dad's Last Will and Testament. Apparently, Manny enjoyed a right to one-third of the house and a ranch just outside San Cristóbal, but there was one problem: they were heavily mortgaged to the tune of at least six-figures. The family's attorney had subtly intimated to Manny's agent that the family would like for Manny, the millionaire footballer, to pay off those debts. Manny hung up the phone and suddenly lost his hunger. He laid back on the bed.

An hour later, Xoco knocked. She had brought Manny a plate of food. She called him *dormilón* and claimed he was just like *papy*. Later, after eating, she showed him a box in the attic; Manny was surprised to find a few of his old soccer jerseys. There were also a few old Polaroids of him, Pablo, and his dad. One of them was taken at a barbecue; it was from one of the very last times Manny could recall seeing and being with his father. The memory still burned like a red hot pointer.

Manny grabbed the jerseys and a small St. Christopher medallion he vaguely remembered. Still, he consciously left the photos in the box. He had no use for them. He packed his things, thanked his half-sisters for hosting him, and invented an excuse to leave. He said their attorneys would be in touch. They begged him to stay and asked what was wrong, but Manny flagged a cab and left.

In the taxi, Manny realized that his mother might not have been *the other woman* because he had forgotten a key fact: his older sister Gemma, who had passed away. Gemma probably had been born before Xoco and Anselma. That would mean his father had betrayed his mother not once, not twice, but *three times*. The fact Manny had forgotten about Gemma tore his heart to pieces. He promised to light a candle and say a prayer to the Virgin for Gemma's soul that very night.

A few weeks later, Manny's attorney filed a notice to the San Cristóbal Court that Manny was giving up his share in the estate. He never heard from Gimilda, Xoco, or Anselma again.

# Chapter 29

The house felt empty and foreign. Fher had gone to school and Maribel, Pablo, and Phoebe had all left early to travel home. Manny sat in his recliner in the living room, sipped on a coffee and jotted Thank You notes. Various relatives from both the US and Mexico had sent cards and flowers for his mom's funeral. He feverishly scribbled notes in his chicken scratch handwriting; he knew that if he delayed the task more than a week, then he would never do it.

A name caught his eye: Julio. His *Tio Julio* had been battling cancer for years, still lived in the Bay area, and had become a recluse. A few nights ago, though, Julio had called Manny to express his grief and even sent a gorgeous flower arrangement to both the funeral home and the gravesite. Julio explained that his health did not permit him to travel, and Manny appreciated the calls and flowers.

Instead of a note, Manny picked up the phone to personally call and thank him. Despite his serious health issues, *Tio Julio* could still make Manny laugh. His uncle had stoically undergone two rounds of chemotherapy with nary a complaint, but still cried at the little inconveniences and injustices of daily life. He was neurotic to the max.

For example, during one talk with Manny, *Tio Julio* had suddenly unleashed a vicious diatribe against the manufacturers of a particular shoe polish company. Their crime? Not filling their plastic bottles adequately. The background? Earlier that day, just before leaving for a date with chemo, *Tio Julio* had only been able to polish satisfactorily one of his dress shoes before the bottle ran out.

For Julio, chemo was bad, but leaving the house with a single shoe polished was apocalypse. Just like Manny's mom said: "*Antes muerto que sencillo.*"

The phone rang a few times, then went to voicemail, so Manny just hung up. However, a few minutes later, *Tio Julio* called. Soon, the receiver and Manny's ear were filled by his uncle's heavy, labored breathing and a high-pitched "*¡Aloooooo sobrinillo!*"

The two talked about the funeral and Manny painted as vivid a picture as he could. *Tio Julio* felt bad for not attending, but was a bubbly and superficial optimist beyond remorse. He would sound as if he was fighting back tears one moment, then, a minute later, he'd gasp upon hearing about a suit worn by someone and say: "*¡Ayyy que chuloooo!*"

"The pictures you put on social media were nice. Back when I lived down there, the funeral homes never did showings - they just prepared bodies for burial. They used all that space at the actual home to store bricks of *mota* and run clandestine bingo parlors. It's...it's...nice to see change can happen and be good. But..." Julio's pauses always warned of dissatisfaction. "Your off-blue tie with that baby blue shirt...your mother...she....it's for the better she didn't live to see that."

Manny rolled his eyes.

*Tio Julio* had lost his job as a professor shortly after Manny left San Francisco due to allegations of inappropriate alcohol use and conduct around students. Julio, though, had grown sick of teaching, especially bickering with students about grades, and gleefully accepted a hefty buyout package. He had invested very prudently all his life and spent his golden years watching his money grow while writing simply for the pleasure of writing. Saying *Adios* to the publish-or-perish rat race had also been liberating.

Now that Manny's mom had passed, though, he had a few questions for Julio; things his uncle would never have revealed while Manny's mom was alive. For instance, Manny had never understood how exactly he himself had come to the US at such a young age. He also now knew about his dad's life and earlier family. He asked *Tio Julio* to elucidate those years as best he could. Julio had no firsthand knowledge of the crossing, but had heard the story. Manny was stunned at hearing how a young Manny, his mom, and his older sister Gemma had crossed. Manny had assumed his mom had bought fake birth certificates and crossed at a bridge. Instead, she'd waded across the *Rio Bravo* at night with two kids. They could easily have died.

Then came the next question: why? *Tio Julio* explained to Manny about the crushing poverty he and Manny's mother had all faced as youths: their dad died in a mining accident and their mom was a street vendor, so they didn't have the money to even rent their own place. Instead, they had lived the *posadas*: they stayed at the house of any relative or friend of mom who would let them. They lived on the whims of charity and patience of others; it was awful. Manny's mom had gotten close to Manny's then-married dad because he offered her stability. He had also promised to get divorced and marry her and take her to America, where he had lived once.

Before any of that could happen, though, the war between the Zapatista revolutionaries and the Mexican military broke out. The heavily-armed Communists entered into towns at night, forced the locals to participate in faux-trials and lynchings of the landed elite, and then retreated back into the mountains and forest. If you didn't attend a trial or lynching, they marked your house. Then, when the military came later, often during the day, if you had attended a trial or lynching, you were considered a collaborator. Your house was marked. Manny's dad fled first, succeeded in crossing into the US, and sent money for his pregnant wife and Gemma to come.

Julio paused and asked Manny if he was writing this down. Manny laughed and asked: *"para qué?"* Julio asked Manny if he still kept a handwritten diary, like back when he lived in San Francisco.

This blew Manny away; he had thought his diary a secret. He asked how did Julio know? His Uncle laughed. Before Manny arrived in San Francisco, he said, Maribel had read it and called *Tio Julio* to warn him in advance about skanky lady friends that may want to loiter about.

Manny's face grew red with embarrassment, then pink with a touch of anger. *Tio Julio* then asked Manny a strange question: "Do you still talk to any of your friends from then? Like that Bryce fellow?" Manny had forgotten all about his old teammate, and even that *Tio Julio* had met the guy. *Tio Julio* found it odd the two had not remained in touch; after all, Bryce had helped Manny so much in his moment of need.

That night, Manny had a strange dream. He woke up alone on the mattress on the floor in his old childhood room, but was an adult. He left the room and wandered around his family's old apartment. The TV was on and Mexican soccer team Club America was beating Pumas 2-0. A 'Chente song played in the background. Nobody else was there. Empty Miller Lite cans rested on the floor by the side of the couch. As Manny approached the small, black folding table in the dining room, he saw a large black book of photo albums in the center. He picked up the book and flipped through it, but all the pictures were fuzzy.

Manny awoke the next morning and made *chilaquiles* for him and Fher. All the house was packed up in boxes except for the dining room table, a few chairs, the couch, the TV, and the TV stand. Manny rummaged through one particular box and found what he was looking for: his old diary, which was a collection of spiral notebooks. His mom had kept them and he had absentmindedly packed them without recognizing them. He resolved to read them later, probably over a drink. For now, he placed them in the same old backpack he'd once used to transport Unce Jose's Terminator 2 DVD.

Fher wandered into the dining room and sat at the table. He was wearing athletic shorts and a white shirt instead of pajamas because that's what his dad wore. Suddenly, Fher stood up, walked towards his dad and embraced him. He said nothing; it was all hug. Fher may have been older and bigger and moodier, but these sudden hugs were still a frequent occurrence. Manny loved them.

"Whoa Fher, *buenos días.*" "*Buenos días Papy.*" Fher stepped back and looked down at his feet. "*¿Qué pasa, m'ijo?*" Fher asked Manny if he was sure about moving. Wouldn't he miss the Valley? Manny answered honestly: "*Puede ser.*" Then, Fher smiled and hugged Manny again. "I know why you moved back from Mexico, Papy. You don't have to move again if you don't want to." Startled, Manny inquired. "And tell me, why did I move back from Mexico?"

"Mommy says you came back to be with me." Manny's mouth dropped. "Damn," he thought to himself. "Sometimes ex-wives do the darndest things." He made a mental note to send her a birthday card this year.

He also hugged Fher again, just because.

# Chapter 30

Manny left Mexico for a variety of reasons. However, one thing truly pushed him to leave: he felt alienated. Despite Mexico being the country of his birth and heritage, he never stopped feeling like an American living abroad. He viewed his time in Mexico as an adventure, not a homecoming. Beyond the postcard facade, he found genuinely warm and caring people, but certain things just really bugged him.

From the decadence of the uber rich in *Las Lomas* to the depravity of his middle class half-sisters, Manny associated Mexico with a caste system. In his head, he saw an inverted graph for wealth and morality. The richer you were, the more you could do, and the more immoral you became. In Manny's mind, his half-sisters had idly enjoyed the fruits of wealth in Mexico while he and his siblings put up with a drunken and negligent father. Manny and Pablo and Phoebe had eaten quesadillas made of stale tortillas and moldy cheese in a cramped apartment in Brownsville while Xoco and Anselma feasted on *tacos de fajita* in their palace in San Cristóbal.

The exact event that precipitated Manny's departure occurred in Carcosa, a mid-sized town in Southern Mexico. Acapulco FC traveled there to play the local side, and, because an international break followed the game, the players were given a few days off afterwards. Manny stuck around town for two reasons: first, a girl he had met long ago in San Francisco had contacted him via social media. Second, Carcosa had a neat, colonial-era theater. A university acting troupe was performing the classic Spanish play: *El Rey de Amarillo*. He got tickets to see it.

Manny had a driver in Acapulco, but rented and drove his own car in Carcosa. He figured the short ten-block drive from his hotel to the downtown theatre in the late afternoon would be safe. However, he'd barely driven two blocks when a rusted piece of metal in the street popped one of his tires. Still, he didn't panic and was more annoyed than anything. He used his cell phone to call the car rental company, who then called the insurance company's roadside assistance.

He stood and waited by the car, but then the wind changed directions and suddenly a putrid stench burned his nostrils. He saw an open dumpster in an alleyway across the street, but no rotten food could smell that bad. He looked around: *nada*. He crossed the street and approached the dumpster. Once he got within five feet, he saw a human hand sandwiched between two trash bags. He fell to his knees and vomited.

Eventually, Manny composed himself and went to a nearby restaurant to seek help. He told the cashier that he had seen a body in the dumpster. The cashier, a short and plump man, clearly did not care. The cashier simply said that, when he got a minute, he would tell a manager. "Manager?" Manny thought. He was confused. "What about the police?" The man scratched his moustache and asked Manny where he was from. Manny remained silent. The cashier leaned forwards and whispered to Manny a bit of advice. "If you report a crime, how could you be sure the police would not implicate *you*?" Who had been with Manny most of the day? How had he found out about the crime?

Manny left the restaurant and returned to his car. Despite the heat, he sat inside and rolled up the windows. He texted the woman to cancel the date and waited a half-hour for the tow truck to arrive.

That night, he resolved to return to Brownsville as soon as possible. He called his agent and told him he wanted to retire at season's end.

Since that day in Carcosa, every sore knee and ankle confirmed his decision. Fortune also smiled upon him. The club noticed that Manny had lost his motivation and starting place, so they offered to buy out his contract. His agent had not told them about the retirement, so Manny gladly accepted

Manny was only in the US for a handful of days when he got a big surprise. After waiting in line for two hours at the Brownsville DPS office and paying a fifteen-dollar fee, his application for a Texas driver's license was denied. The clerk looked at Manny strangely, printed out a form, and handed him an official-looking letter. Manny read it, and was dumbstruck.

Allegedly, Manny owed the State of Texas over $20,000 in child support. "Child?" Manny thought. He closely read the paper, and then asked out loud: "Who the hell is *Fher Hernandez*?"

# Chapter 31

Manny sat alone on a recliner, held his phone up to his face, and read his mom's obituary. Still, the words did not register. The small, plastic screen said that his mom had passed away one week ago, yet he could still smell her in the house. Near the sink, a dish rack was full of glasses immaculately washed and dried by her hands. In the refrigerator, on the top shelf sat little plastic cups of her favorite yogurt. In the master bedroom, her blouses and underwear filled two boxes. Framed pictures of her still dotted the walls. Manny had been unable to take them down just yet.

Manny called his mom's cell phone number. The phone rang a few times before beeping and going to voicemail. His mom's voice, with her slight accent, filled his ear: "Hello, I am not available to answer the phone right now. Please leave me message and I call you back." A tear rolled down Manny's cheek. He got up, went outside, and meandered around the backyard. His mom's two lemon trees stood erect in the back right corner. To the left, *yerba buena* covered the ground all along the fence.

He returned inside and read the obituary another time. One life. Six decades. Three paragraphs. Twelve lines. This painful thought led to another: Manny recalled reading Hector's obituary online almost ten years earlier. In his last season at Acapulco FC, his mom had called him on his cell just before a game. The line was scrambled and fuzzy, but he still could make out: "*Hectorín está muerto.*"

The two had ceased talking many years earlier, but it still stung. They had suffered a bit of a falling out, and then time had slowly and completely unwound their bond of friendship. Hector's obituary had hit Manny so hard because of all the new details he learned about Hector's life. Manny was surprised to learn that Hector had married before him and even had two gorgeous little girls.

Hector had also sent Manny a friend request on social media, which was still pending. Manny accepted it. Hector's loved ones and friends had turned his account and wall into a loving tribute. Manny recognized a post from Hector's mom and his older brother, but didn't know most of the other folks. They posted touching stories. Manny felt compelled to write something, but too many ideas buzzed around his head.

Manny recalled a poem in Spanish by Rocamour. It was about a trip Rocamour and a female friend, Catarina, made during *Semana Santa* to a national park in Ushuaia, Argentina. She died two weeks later in a car crash near the Plaza Serrano in Buenos Aires. The poet and Catarina had taken a picture of themselves standing in front of a sign at a national park in Ushuaia that proclaimed: "The End of the World." Five lines echoed in Manny's head:

> *"Nos paramos frente a un cartel*
> *Que nos advirtió del 'Fin del Mundo'*
> *Pero no hicimos caso*
> *Como tontos nos reímos*
> *Y tu mundo pronto acabaría."*

Manny thought back to one of his last face-to-face encounters with Hector. The night before he left San Francisco, he had attended a party at Hector's new apartment. He had desperately needed to buy or at least borrow Hector's car to make the return trip to Brownsville. A long bus trip for an undocumented immigrant would have been too risky. Hector had easily acquiesced, but also told him a secret about the year he served in Iraq. Hector had only shared the secret with one other person before telling Manny.

Manny had been too young and immature to grasp the weight of Hector's burden. Certain details rubbed him the wrong way. In his adolescent brain, Manny had gone to Hector because he

161

needed Hector's car to get home ASAP. All other information and communications were superfluous. Looking back, Manny wished he'd listened to Hector more attentively. He wished their friendship had endured.

Manny got up and walked around the house. He had bought this house for his mom as a symbol of his love, but the place had been filled with sad memories of a tortured and confused woman who had ceased to be his mother years ago. The bathroom reminded him of the commode his mother needed. The couch reminded him of every time his mother stood up and insisted that a dead brother was coming to pick her up. It was all too much. He and Fher had packed up some boxes and talked about moving, but not set a date.

Tomorrow, Manny promised himself, he would finally call a realtor and list the house for sale.

# Chapter 32

The rented moving truck was parked in front of the house. Its presence reminded Manny that he had to move and quickly. Inside the house, Manny and Fher sat on the floor and were exhausted; they had loaded boxes and furniture for the better part of the day. At around 2:30 pm, Manny had caved and hired a company to finish loading and also sweep, mop, and dust the house. He knew his mom would roll in her grave at the thought of a stranger cleaning her home, but Manny and Fher were running on fumes.

Manny had already signed the closing papers with the realtor in advance and reserved a room for a week at an extended stay in Northeast Houston. He took one last tour of the house, but felt little attachment. He regretted most having spent so much of his life far from his mom when she was healthy, and only appearing in her hour of need when she couldn't appreciate it.

Still, they were not leaving the Valley just yet. Manny had made one last promise to himself and Fher. They left the house, got in Manny's minivan, and headed to a relatively small hotel on the Northern half of South Padre Island. They dropped off their luggage in the room and then went to a small outdoor burger joint and bar on the inside-facing bay. They ordered fried fish and then rented and rode jet skis for a few hours. When they got back to the hotel around 8:00 pm, a small crowd of teenagers had gathered near the pool. Manny could see in Fher's eyes that his son wanted to check things out.

Manny gave his son a copy of the room key and permission to go hang out by the pool. His son, beaming a smile from ear-to-ear, entered the bathroom and changed. However, when he came out, he was shocked to see his dad also dressed in swimming trunks. Fher assumed this meant some form of parental supervision and prepared to throw a fit.

Manny preempted the theatrics and explained: he was going to walk along the beach and maybe swim.

The sun had set by the time Manny started to walk Northward along the white sand beach. He enjoyed the quiet and didn't see a soul. He smiled as he passed by the barbecue pits among the sand dunes. Once, he and Hector had almost gotten in a fight with some other boys that centered around a barbecue pit. He walked about two miles and stopped. He looked out onto the sea. The clouds covered the sky like a blanket. Stars hid in fear and not even the Moon showed her face.

"Did the *Isla Esmeralda* even exist?" Manny asked himself. Was it just some confused fragment of a childhood memory and embellished by his imagination? He scanned the blurry horizon where ocean met sky. Then, for a moment, he saw a faint green light. He closed his eyes. He took a deep breath. He opened them again. The light was still there. He took off his shirt and sandals, and left them in a pile on the sand.

He slowly waded out into the water. He thought back to his days at the YMCA pool with Bryce. He even recalled a few pool dates with *Catracha*. The warm Gulf water felt amazing. He relaxed, took a deep breath, and then tossed himself into the waves. Kick. Stroke. Air. Kick. Stroke. Air. He pumped his arms and violently thrashed his legs.

This time, he would reach the *Isla Esmeralda*. And he would do it himself; no whistle, no float, and no father waiting behind on the sand.

# Chapter 33

Manny stepped onto the elevator and pressed the down button. He had just met with his financial advisor, and things sounded okay. During the meeting, the young man had spoken to Manny about "annuities" and "bonds" and "dividends", but he might as well have spoken in Chinese. Nevertheless, the young man's confidence in speaking this foreign language of finance assured Manny. Manny knew that he had more money than when he started investing, and this quantity grew most years.

After about ten floors of descent, the elevator stopped. In stepped a six-foot tall, middle-aged blonde woman with an athletic figure. She donned a black suit jacket and knee-length skirt. She smiled at Manny as she entered the elevator before pressing the first-floor button and politely turning to face the door.

He thought back to his mom, who had encouraged him to keep dating despite his divorce and advancing age. In fact, before the dementia took over, Manny's mom had been desperately worried that her son had become *"volteado"*, or "gay." Her prejudice did not stem from moral condemnation, but rather empathy for the single women of the world. One more gay man meant one less man for single heterosexual women everywhere.

She often saw an effeminate man and muttered under her breath: *"¡Tantas mujeres solteras y el mundo lleno de maricas!"* Still, at other times, she would extend an uncertain olive branch to Manny. *"¿Pero si amas a un hombre, quién soy yo para juzgarte? Yo tambien los he amado."*

Manny recalled a fight in the Valley just after Mass between his mom and Hector's mom, which he heard about from Phoebe about a year after the fact. Apparently, despite Hector's precautions, word of the boys' debauchery in San Antonio and in San Francisco had reached the Valley. One Sunday after Mass, Manny's mom had gone to Hector's mom to greet her, and Hector's mom refused to even make eye contact. Manny's mom grew angry and demanded an explanation. Hector's mom pointed a finger at her and shouted for all to hear: "*¡Tu hijo corrompiste al mio!*"  Phoebe had had to separate the two before any blows landed.

Manny laughed at his mom's energy levels then and even over a decade later, when her mind started to go but her body and heart remained active. After Manny moved back to Brownsville, she made him and Fher escort her to the Friday-night dances for old folks at the *pulga*. Fher ate *elote*, Manny downed five-dollar pitchers of Miller Lite, and his mom danced *boleros* with a never-ending carousel of *viejos verdes* in cowboy boots and *sombreros*. Every one of those old dudes dressed like Vicente Fernandez. His mom would occasionally take a break to drink water and wink at her son and grandson. "*¡Quizás éste tenga una hija o una nietecita!*"

Before dementia robbed her memory, she implored Manny to go on dates, to talk to single women, and to forget his messy divorce. In Manny's head, his natural timidness divided the female of the species into two categories: the unapproachable Beatrices or the impossible-to-attain Lolitas. He would find himself staring at a beautiful woman while he was out on a walk or at the store. He dared not approach, but would think about her for days on end afterwards. When Fher asked Manny once how to ask a girl out, he replied honestly: "I don't even know anymore. I'm not sure I *ever* knew."

Now, back in Houston, Manny brimmed with the confidence of a restart. He had finished his online degree, gotten a teaching certificate, and would start a new job teaching at Houston ISD come August. Naively, he viewed becoming a high school teacher as entering the life of the mind. He imagined Socratic dialogues and articulate debates. In reality, he had stood up to millionaire coaches and billionaire owners, but was about to get his ass kicked by a group of 25 high schoolers.

On some evenings, Manny gathered the courage to pull out and peruse his old diary. The notebooks were out of order and a mess, and, when reading the scribbled text, he barely recognized his adolescent voice. Still, the notebooks helped him to finally face a past and certain moments he had tried to forget. The red binder with folded edges contained entries from his time in San Francisco, and he needed a whiskey on the rocks to stomach certain parts. The green one was about family histories and contained some happier moments from his time with *Catracha*. He could handle that sober.

Manny forgot about the notebooks, pulled himself to the present, and glanced at the woman on the elevator in the mirror. Of course, no lady could match his nostalgic embellishments of *Catracha*, he thought. But surely many if not most women were better people than Albertine. He owed it to himself to try and find out. The much taller woman caught view of his wandering eyes through the elevator mirror, and again she smiled.

A younger Manny would have stared at the gringa up-and-down. He would have appraised her figure, clothes, and hair. Now, though, Manny wondered where the woman was from, who she was. Did she have a zest for life like his own mom during her Golden Years? Did she herself have children? What was she reading, if she read? What was her sense of humor, if any? Manny desired to converse with her, and at length. Maybe even all night. Manny cleared his throat. The elevator stopped on the second-floor, his exit point.

He looked down and took a few steps, but then halted in the threshold of the elevator door. He turned, looked up, made eye contact with her, smiled, and opened his mouth to speak.

Elliott Turner

# PART THREE

*"You can't get away from yourself by moving from one place to another. There's nothing to that."*

Ernest Hemingway, *The Sun Also Rises*

Elliott Turner

Hector's hands trembled as he carefully used a knife to slice an avocado into lengthwise pieces. The weight of the upcoming social engagement loomed large and complicated even simple tasks. Hector and Matt were hosting a party that evening at their apartment in Oakland. They had invited a collection of co-workers, friends, friends of friends, and interesting acquaintances. Of course, they had hosted parties before countless times. However, this was the first time they were doing so *as a couple*.

Hector would be introducing Matt as his boyfriend to everybody, which meant Hector *was gay*. Hector would even introduce Matt as his boyfriend *to Manny* and Manny's friends, if Manny showed up that is. Hector had eventually accepted himself for who he was after some confusing years, but he feared the coming collision between his past and present. He felt like a bystander on a beach who stares at an approaching Tsunami.

Hector lowered his gaze and tried to bury himself in minutia. He just wanted to focus and prepare food, but he could not stop sweating.

-Where's the salt?

-I think it's in the pantry.

-You think or you know?

-Oh, sorry, here it is.

-Could you try to stand less by the sink? I'm doing something.

-Whoa, are you menstruating or what?

-...

-Come on. Relax. We're throwing a party. Try to have fun.

-Keep your sexist comments to yourself and stay out of my way.

-Come on. Everything is turning out perfect, Hectorín. Don't give me that face.

Unlike Hector, Matt Morrison had been gay since exiting his mother's womb. He often joked that the doctor performed the c-section, popped the placenta, and said "Congrats, it's a fag!" As a young boy, Matt played with dolls, spoke with a slight lisp, and avoided sports like the plague. He played cello in high school and only went to one dance in all four years: when a female friend asked him. Upon hearing of his son's homosexuality, his indifferent father, an executive who drove a fancy car and worked long hours, merely remarked: "Well that will make a good college admissions essay."

Matt was half Hispanic, but friends joked that nobody knew which half. His mother was from Mexico City, but had skin as fair as snow. Her blue eyes shined like diamonds, and nobody blinked when she gave birth to a pasty white baby. Her husband only spoke English and Matt grew up in an affluent neighborhood. Thus, Matt's mother only half-heartedly taught Matt the most basic of Spanish. He knew that Mexicans say *"bueno"* when answering a phone and *"ándale"* when hanging up. That was pretty much it.

-What size cooler did you get?

-I don't know, big? It's the blue thing over there.

-...

-Again with the face? Come on, that's big.

-...

-Hectorín you're killing me. If I'd have known throwing a party with you could be this little fun, I'd have dumped you ages ago.

-Lots of people are coming. They will want cold beverages. You really think that's big enough? The fridge is already packed I remind you.

-That cooler is so big it even has wheels and one of those plastic things to pull it!

-How many beers will fit in that, with ice? Tell me. What do you think?

-...

-...

-I'm guesstimating twenty, twenty-five tops.

-That's a good number if, say, everybody only drinks one beer. Most people will drink more than a single beer.

Hector had always been the laid-back one in the relationship, so his sudden change in temperament annoyed Matt. Matt himself had never made a secret of his own sexual orientation, so he struggled to feel pity for closeted members of his own caste. He viewed the process of coming out as simple, like pulling off a bandaid.

As a Catholic Mexican-American from Texas, Hector in fact feared the Earth would open up and literally swallow him whole. Hector easily could think of at least thirty friends and relatives who would cut off all ties with him upon learning that he was gay. Those still on speaking terms would call him "*marica*" both behind his back and to his face.

-Oh *Dios Mio*, this guac is delicious! I can't believe you made this.

-Hey, it's not even six. Did you open a bag of chips *already*?

-We are throwing the party. As in, you and me. Who else cares if the chips go bad early or whatever? Besides, with this guac, these things will get eaten in no time.

-...

-Come on, try one.

-...

-Just take a minute and have one.

-I know what my own damn guac tastes like!

-...

-Sorry, sorry.

Matt also took things easy because he had always felt like an outcast, a babe excommunicated from the Hispanic world before baptism. As a child and even in the present day, most of his friends assumed he was white. His poor Spanish only cemented this perception. Part of what attracted him to Hector was, in his mind, Hector's *authenticity*. Matt loved to listen in on Hector's conversations over the phone; he would try to pick out words or phrases as Hector spoke in rapid-fire Spanish.

Despite a hot start, Hector's passion for Matt had cooled considerably over the last month. As the two had gotten to know one another, certain tics and habits of Matt had started to annoy him. Matt was deeply jealous of any male or female whom Matt perceived may have attracted Hector's interest. This bothered Hector to no end.

Still, Hector took Matt to Mexican places in the Mission and taught him how to order *tacos al pastor* in Spanish. He peppered him with anecdotes from Mexican history and even talked Liga MX to him. Matt only watched the soccer games to practice listening to the Univision announcers and stare at athletic men in tight shorts.

-What wine did we get?

-...

-Please tell me you got wine last night. Not just beer.

-...

-Okay, it's my turn to get angry. Well, what liquor do we have?

-Some vodka. Some whiskey, I think.

-Hectorcito, this party is not just for *your* friends. Our mutual friends prefer wine and liquor to natty old Miller Lite. Please tell me you at least got some Corona.

-Your friends only like talking about wine, not actually drinking it.

-...

174

-...

-This is why I said we should go shopping together or make a list.

-You never said that!

Their first big fight had happened in May. As Matt often remarked, Hector was a man of few words, but many texts. Behind his quiet demeanor, Matt suspected and probed for hidden reserves of emotions in his beloved Hectorín. For example, he had never seen Hector cry. If Matt wanted to know Hector's thoughts, the best avenue was a text message. Thus, Matt came to see Hector's phone as the only gateway to Hector himself.

This created friction. Hector refused to give Matt his cell phone password. A classic debate ensued. If Hector was without sin, what could he have to hide from Matt? On the other hand, if Hector was presumed innocent, then why should he have to produce evidence to that effect? At the time of the fight, the two still lived in different neighborhoods, so Matt abruptly left and threatened to cut off communication with Hector.

What Hector did not know is that Matt had secretly reviewed the image files on Hector's old laptop. Matt stumbled upon a folder labeled "Monterrey" and another which said "Tijuana" but a more accurate name would have been "red light district." The pictures were not graphic or anything: just images of Hector with men in various states of undress. What most worried Matt was that not one of those men looked like him.

During that heated first fight, he immediately thought of confronting Hector about his *polvillos* in Mexico. Instead, he bit his tongue and caved hard. He texted Hector at 11:14 pm the same night, returned to Hector's place and begged for a second chance. Hector smiled and accepted. However, whenever Hector left his phone unattended and it vibrated, Matt liked to grab it and see if Hector had gotten a call or message or email. And *from whom*.

They had only had one other kinda serious fight: Matt had found a picture on Hector's phone of some weird, buff white dude wearing the type of white sunglasses you can only obtain and overpay for at the mall. The white sunglasses even had a strap on the back; this look was normally reserved for the truck-driving crowd. Matt already knew about Hector's eclectic tastes, but rural, white *and poor*?

Still, he again failed to put up a fight and accepted Hector's word that the bro was just a buddy from the army; all the guys from the base had shirtless pictures of one another flexing tattooed arms.

-What time is it Hectorín? I still need to *ducharme*.

-About five o'clock.

-Five? Fuck. And the evites told people to arrive at six!

-Nobody shows up to a party on time.

-You don't know that. I'm going to grab a quick shower - you okay with clean up and organizing?

-...

-Okay, I'll set up the table and appetizer trays before showering.

-...

-Okay, I'll also put away the dishes like I said I would. But I need to jump in that shower in ten minutes.

-...

-...

-*Órale*.

While Matt bathed, Hector finished the guacamole and put the beers on ice. Matt's feathers were easily ruffled in love, but he was a very cold and disciplined student. He studied English full time at

San Francisco State and lived the orderly existence of privilege. Classes started on time, school loans disbursed twice a year, and his parents filled his bank account with supplemental funds upon request.

Hector viewed himself as bringing balance to Matt's life when, after getting a B on an exam and flipping out, Hector would calm Matt down and shift the conversation away from the least painful method of suicide.

Matt appreciated Hector in those moments, but deep down still kinda thought that Hector was ignorant. Grades were important. They led to important things.

As he organized the alcoholic drinks, Hector again worried about the guest list. The eclectic group would include some of Matt's SFSU friends, a heavy dose from their gay brigade, and Manny and some Gales players. *Maybe*. Hector was preoccupied by the clashing of these two worlds; he erroneously assumed that Manny and his athlete buddies did not have their own gay friends.

He didn't realize that, in fact, one of the Gales players was openly gay and nobody cared because the man could head a free-kick.

-Hey aren't you going to change?

-What? What's wrong?

-Oh nothing. You just always wear that shirt.

-What do you mean, *always*?

-Hector, I met you when you were wearing that shirt. It's a great shirt. But, like, all threads fade, you know?

-...

-Forget I said anything.

-...

While Hector changed, Matt pushed the couch in the living room up against the wall. He then set up a card table in the middle of the room and draped a white tablecloth over it. Matt harbored one worry: Manny. Was he a threat?

Hector had shielded Matt from his past, subtly but obstinately redirecting all conversations about his childhood in Texas. This void created a blank slate upon which Matt imagined at times preposterously jealous ideas. From Facebook stalking and Hector's own descriptions, Matt thought this Manny character looked a bit too similar to himself. Matt had pushed Hector to invite Manny to the party in part because Matt trusted his gaydar more than his other five senses combined.

After finally meeting Manny in person, he and Hector could talk.

+++

The first two guests arrived shortly after 6:30. The male - a pale, tall, blonde American - was accompanied by a female, named Philipa, who had curly red locks and was short and pudgy. Matt answered the door and immediately recognized them: they were paralegals at a downtown law firm where he had interned last summer. The guy stumbled as he walked into the apartment and slurred his speech.

-Pedro, Philipa, so great to see you. Come here, girl!

-Matt, the place looks great. How have you been? Long-time no see.

-Issss there a chair somewhere?

-Whoa partner. Somebody pre-gamed!

-Well, brunch turned into a noon Bloody Mary into an early happy hour. We both could use a glass of water.

-And you guys remember Hector?

-...

-Nice to see you again.

-Hectorin please get a chair or something. So, may I inquire just how things are at Lock & Rubenstein?

As Matt talked up the guests, his voice took on a shrill tone. Hector still harbored a deep-rooted distrust of flamboyantly gay men, including his own boyfriend. Hector sometimes uttered such Spanish pejoratives for gay men like "*marica*" in Matt's presence from time-to-time. He never taught Matt the Mexican word "*joto*" because it was reserved for really dainty queens that nobody respected. Hector couldn't watch a house-flipping reality TV show without thinking "*joto*" at least a hundred times.

Pedro struck Hector as the most dangerous guest in terms of upsetting the party's social equilibrium. Pedro was an aggressive advocate that all men were in fact gay, most just didn't know it yet. He relentlessly hit on straight guys and reminded Hector of his older and creepy uncles back in the Valley who glared inappropriately at middle school girls and mumbled about "*virgencitas.*"

Hector was glad Pedro had arrived first, in the belief that meant Pedro would also leave early, perhaps even before Manny showed up.

-Hector, stop hopping between songs. It hurts my head! And what is this crap? Didn't we talk about this?

-Crap? *Crap?* This is Don Omar.

-I told you none of this stuff. The production hurts my ears.

-That was Daddy Yankee. Totally different. One is Puerto Rican. The other is Dominican.

-I kinda like reggaeton.

-Really Philipa?

-Well, it's easy to dance to.

-...

-Isn't this that Don Omar song: *"Ayer Lápiz"*?

-...

-Well, if Pedro and Philipa are okay with it, a few songs won't hurt.

-Isn't it: *"Ayer la ví"*?

-You'd have to ask Hector. Hector, please turn down the volume at least.

Philipa Konieczny was a first generation Polish-American immigrant. She had studied Spanish since grade school and it was her major in college. In her last semester, she had completed two advanced seminars, one on Lope de Vega and the other a queer reading of *Don Quijote*. She had even defended an honor's thesis on the political fiction of Mario Vargas Llosa. This meant, of course, that she spoke very little *actual* Spanish. She constantly mispronounced basic words and asked native speakers for the accurate lyrics to popular songs.

The nice ones indulged her. The mean ones misled her.

Hector brought out a large plate with appetizers and placed it on the folding table in the center of the living room. Pedro stumbled to the couch and laid down. Philipa, Matt, and Hector stood around and continued to chat. At the time, a recent incident had captured the media's attention: an undocumented immigrant, twice deported, had gotten drunk, ran over a high school valedictorian and fled the scene of the crime. He was arrested two days later, and the incident was referred to as "The Gonzalez case."

Everybody had an opinion. These opinions were freely offered sans solicitation.

-So, you guys hear about the plea in the Gonzalez case?

-No.

-Not guilty, right?

-Yes.

-Not guilty to what?

-A partner at the firm said he was charged with second degree homicide.

-Which partner?

-Homicide? But it was a car accident?

-Langley. The older bald guy with the goatee.

-Oh.

-A lot of people are up in arms about it.

Hector associated the Gonzalez case with politics and cared so little for politics that he could not even name a single senator. His parents had taught him that all politicians were crooks. He had no formed opinion on the Gonzalez case, and he was also a bit intimidated by some of Matt's friends. In the past, he could talk about intellectual stuff with Manny and Maribel without fear of being mocked, but Matt's friends viewed all conversation as competitive debate. They often laced their observations with sarcasm and condescension.

Matt changed topics to the law firm and backstabbing associates, but the office gossip lulled Hector into a daze. Before Hector knew it, he'd finished his second beer and felt way too tipsy. He then excused himself to the bathroom.

In hushed tones, Philipa complimented Hector's physical features to Matt and was excited to learn that Hector spoke fluent Spanish. She asked where Hector went to college. Matt leaned in and informed Philipa vaguely that Hector did not finish college and was sore on the topic of formal education.

When Hector returned to the living room, Philipa excused herself to freshen up in the now vacant bathroom. As soon as the door closed, Matt's face turned serious.

-So Hector, nice skirt Philipa is wearing tonight, right?

-Huh?

-You think I didn't see you? There are only four people here, Hector.

-What?

-You speak with your eyes, Hectorin. I would have thought her skirt was see-through, not black.

-You're tripping.

-Tonight is about us. You. Me. Control yourself. Be mature. I'm speaking in a controlled tone and giving you a warning. Do not ruin tonight for me.

-...

Philipa came out of the bathroom a few minutes later and insisted on a mini-tour of the entire apartment. First, they showed her the bedroom with its brown wooden desk in the corner, black leather office chair with wheels, queen-sized bed, and long black curtains that covered the three windows on the west side of the room. Hector and Matt had not hung up any framed couple pictures *yet*; only a few vintage Mexican film posters dotted the wall, along with an image of the Virgin of Guadalupe.

Matt explained that he was agnostic, but Hector still felt reverence for the saints of his Catholic upbringing. Hector even refused to face the wall with the poster of the Virgin when being penetrated, but he kept that fact to himself.

-What? Drinking an aquarium? Who changed the music?

-This is Wilco, Hector. It's kinda classic. People like this. What do you think, Philipa?

-This is a party. Not a wake. This is crap.

-Philipa, please tell Hector this is real music.

-...

-Maybe later in the night we can play this crap.

-...

-I like the image of the Virgin. I actually go to Spanish-language mass sometimes, you know, to practice the language.

To Hector's dismay, Matt had surreptitiously selected an iTunes playlist full of melodic if melancholic tunes. For Hector, the terms "indie" and "emo" were four-letter words, not genres of music. A salsa singer could pour his heart out and Hector would feel the beat, but an acoustic guitar and a male singing falsetto made his stomach churn. He switched the music to a Pandora channel.

-So, Hector, Matt tells me you work at a five-star hotel. That must be rad. Which one?

-The Grand Hotel.

-Is that near the wharf?

-It's only actually four-stars I think.

-Hey, also, you speak Spanish, right? *Cuál es la trabajo de usted?*

-*Soy botones.*

-*Botones? Que? No entiendo.* As in, "buttons?"

-It means "bellhop."

-Hectorin don't be modest. He's more than a bellhop. He is a wiz in customer service and even supervises a modest-sized staff.

-So *botones* means "bellhop." Cool.

-What about you? You work part-time at that law firm, right?

-This is *"Demasiada romántico"*, but which Eddie sings it – Herrera or Santiago?

Back in the living room, the voice of Eddie Herrera stirred Pedro back to life. He got up from the couch, took one wobbly step, turned around, took another wobbly step, and then sat back down on the couch. He then fell over to his side. Philipa and Matt decided that Pedro should be moved to the bedroom.

Hector thought otherwise, but, before he could speak, the doorbell rang.

+++

Hector did not know any of the second wave of guests. All of them were clean-cut twenty-somethings who wore their ambition, or pretention, on the sleeves of their designer clothes. They were a pack of eight or so, but only a few stood out. A black guy wore a navy blue polo shirt with gray cargo shorts, white tennis shoes, and had a buzz cut. His forehead protruded like a second-story balcony on the front of a house. Another guy - olive-skinned and presumably Mexican or Hispanic - had long black hair parted in the middle, and a five o'clock shade. He wore a purple, long-sleeved dress-shirt, black slacks, and dress shoes. A girl, a *guerita*, was thin as a stick and had curly, salt-and pepper brown hair. She wore a pink blouse and blue jeans. She had paid twenty-dollars extra for her jeans to be torn at the knees before purchase.

-Thomas, Askary, Andy, you guys made it!

-Of course we made it. We had to see your pad and your new bae.

-Oh yeah, guys, this is Hector.

-Nice to meet you Hector, I'm Askary. We all go to school with Matt.

-Nice to meet you too. Cool.

-Andy, guess what: Hector *habla mucho* of the old *Español!*

-*Que padre. De donde eres?*

-*De bien lejos. Tejas.*

-Hey guys, very funny. Thomas and me don't speak ye old *Español.* Flirt in English, *por favor.*

-...

-...

-*Hola. Yo soy Philipa.*

The new guests devoured the chips and guacamole like a pack of wolves. Some even paid compliments to Hector and tried to put him at ease. Hector was naturally shy - which Matt had never noticed - but the guests immediately picked up on this quirk. They balanced a respect for Hector's social reticence with genuine attempts to include him in conversation as much as possible.

Hector did not know that Matt actually had a few decent human beings as friends, and was pleasantly surprised.

As the number of guests increased, smaller groups formed, dispersed throughout the apartment, and conversations varied in topic and length. The apartment's entryway, living room, and kitchen gave ample space for talking heads to hop between social circles, but was still small enough where everybody could hear what everybody else was talking about.

-So, this is really weird, but, Konieczny, is that name Polish?

-Why yes. Nostradamus!

-Okay, here's a harder one: your curly red hair, I think it's, it's...just magnificent.

-...

-Thank you.

-Now, this may sound odd, but...do you have Jewish ancestry?

-...

Matt checked on Pedro and Hector played with the music. Thomas and Askary sat on the couch with their eyes glued to their phones. Other guests stood around, drank, and talked. Philipa had hoped to corner Andy, practice her Spanish, and, if things went well, probe into his sexual orientation and perhaps his relationship status. Life at the law firm was part-time but still hectic, so she was hoping Andy could help her body emit endorphins later that night in private.

-I'm only asking because I've recently gotten in touch with my own Jewish ancestry.

-Oh, really?

-Yeah. I paid for one of those online family lineage reports, and my family immigrated to Mexico from Spain around the time of the *Santa Inquisición*. I don't think it's a coincidence.

-...

- I think we're *conversos*, which is the term for Jews that converted to Catholicism to avoid the rack. We've been Catholic for a few hundred years, but it's nice to know where we came from.

-...

The room felt ten degrees hotter for Andy. He rolled up his shirtsleeves, revealing muscular but hairy forearms. He mistook Philipa's silence, smile, and nodding for disinterest. In reality, Philipa was saying to herself and in her head the terms: "*Santa Inquisición*" and "*converso*."

-Don't let him fool you. He just wants a free birthright trip to Israel or Spanish citizenship. The man's a grifter.

-Well look who put down his cell phone. *Que milagro!*

-So Matt said you worked at a law firm. What's that like?

-It's pretty intense. Lots of long hours, but the pay is nice.

-I'm thinking of going to law school after I graduate. Did you take the LSAT?

-Well, to be honest, *don't* work in a law firm. I actually took the LSAT last Spring, but am having second thoughts.

-...

-Returning to the more pressing topic: my family's proud lineage from Israel....

Philipa was pretty sure that Thomas was gay. His tone of voice fluctuated greatly and, when he spoke, he overstressed vowels in verbs and subjects. His posture and manner of walking brought to mind a curious peacock. Andy, though, was sending mixed signals. He puffed out his chest and frequently matted his hair with his hand. However, he also had a slight lisp when pronouncing the letter "s" and a more pronounced lisp when saying words that started or ended with "th." Andy's lisp disappeared when he spoke Spanish, which struck Philipa as odd. And excited her greatly.

Back in the bedroom, Pedro remained asleep and his snores were only audible when Matt briefly opened the door to return to the living room. Matt looked at the table and realized there were too few nacho chips and Hector's guacamole was already half-eaten. The beer supply was also dwindling. Very soon, either he or Hector would have to go to the store. Hector would volunteer because he felt uncomfortable among big groups of people, but Matt would want Hector at the apartment to greet any new arrivals.

Hector stood beside the speakers and looked down, his back to the rest of the living room. He was holding something. Matt pounced.

-Who were you texting with?

-What?

-Just now. Who was it? One of our future guests?

-I wasn't texting.

-Yes you were.

-Our wifi is messing up. I was trying to see about a hotspot app.

-Bullshit. Your thumb doesn't move like that when you download an app.

-Look at my phone.

-...

-..

-...

-But yeah, one of our guests texted for directions. That was awhile ago.

-...

-...

-Okay. I believe you. But let's leave the phone and laptop alone for a spell. *Intégrate,* Hectorin!

Askary heard every word spoken between the couple, but stared at her phone and pretended not to. She briefly looked up from her phone, imagined what Philipa would look like with cropped hair, and then returned to staring at her phone. Askary was playing a multiplayer civilization-war game. She was also intermittently checking her voluminous social media profiles. Upon seeing a topic, article, or image of interest, she would press the appropriate touchscreen button with her thumb. Or make a sliding motion.

This continued for some time.

Matt's friends from the law firm gently prodded Hector about the Gonzalez case. Matt's friends from school were also interested in the topic and paid close attention.

-So Hector, what are folks like from Texas? How would they handle a Gonzalez situation?

-...

-Seriously, give us your two cents.

-..

-They'd ….they'd probably give him the chair and then deport the remains back to old *México*!

-Shut up, Tom. Not funny. Let Hector speak. I'm interested in how a red state thinks.

-Well, here's the weird thing. Folks can be really friendly in Texas - Mexican, white, black, whatever. Like, folks are cool to your face, very warm. But once you say certain words like "illegal" or "abortion", their eyes glaze over.

-So what you're saying is there's a lot of hate in the abstract, but in person, not so much.

-I guess.

-But don't cops pick on Mexicans errrr Hispanics? I know white cops mess with black folk all the time. I have friends from Dallas.

-To be honest, the Valley, where I'm from, is like all Hispanic. Like, when you see a white person, you feel like you should take a picture with your cell phone.

Philipa finally succeeded in getting Hector and Andy to speak Spanish with her. Matt understood roughly twenty-percent of the conversation, but smiled and nodded at what he thought were appropriate moments. Thomas returned to accompany Askary in cellphone purgatory on the couch.

-So, like, right before Communion, when they pause to share the "*Pez de Cristo*," I always smirk and think of that candy.

-What game are you playing? Do you have the wifi password?

-Here's a Catholic Spanish-language joke: who is the Patron Saint of Costa Rica?

-Is it too late to switch to multi-player mode? What's our strat?

-Pedro.

-Ahhhh, sorry. Fucking resources. I suck at this. I'll leave you alone.

-That's why *Ticos* always say *"Símon."*

Andy's bilingual pun flew over Philipa's head but she laughed politely. On his phone, Thomas left the same multiplayer game as Askary, but remained seated next to her on the couch.

Philipa attempted to test the waters with Andy by asking him questions to which she knew the answer. First, she asked why Spanish speakers always ended emails with *"besos"*, which meant "kisses." Then, she asked him if he ever ended emails in that way. Andy replied that he preferred to end emails with *"un abrazo,"* which means "a hug." Philipa's eyes glimmered with optimism.

Andy noticed that English polluted Hector's Spanish. For example, Hector often ended sentences with prepositions. Andy also occasionally translated for Matt. Still, Andy was bemused by the sight of Matt alongside Hector; Matt had draped his right arm around Hector's shoulders and smiled ear-to-ear.

Pedro entered the living room and Thomas stood up from the couch. He and Pedro awkwardly gave one another half-hearted salutations. A few years earlier, they had dated ever so briefly. So briefly, in fact, you could count the length in hours: the time it takes to meet a guy in a bar, go home, engage in coitus, and then forget to text him the next day.

Pedro had actually quite enjoyed the coitus and had hoped for a text. Still, he felt more uneasy than hurt.

Thomas struggled to recall Pedro's name and forced out awkward sentences with no proper noun object. "How have *you* been?" "What are *you* up to?" Matt intervened.

-Pedro, how do you know Thomas again? I don't recall introducing you.

-Oh you know, I think we chatted it up once at a happy hour or something. It was some time ago.

-It was at Los Rios, May of 2012. I remember because it was *Cinco de Mayo*.

-...

-...

-Cool. Well, Pedro, the lady conveniently seated on the couch next to Tom and just waiting to be sociable is Askary. She studies with us and is a junior as well. Talking to Philipa and Hector over there is Andy.

-Nice to meet you.

-Same.

-Hey Hector, we are running super low on food. I'm going to run to Seven-Eleven. Can you think of anything else we need?

+++

The ingestion of alcohol produced varying results among the guests. After two beers, Askary emerged from her couch cocoon, spread her wings, and started to socialize. Pedro and Philipa both drank *Cuba Libres*, and the rum turned down the volume of their voices. Hector had been nursing the same beer for several hours; he wanted to be sober for when Manny arrived. If Manny arrived, that is.

Several other guests had come and went, but none of them were noteworthy.

Pedro and Tom sat on the couch and spoke. A large group chatted around the table. In the cramped confines, the separate conversations and the music bled into each other. With Matt gone, Hector had changed the playlist to reggaeton with a dash of bachata.

-Yeah I'm sorry I didn't text you. I was such a flake back then.

-What really irks me about the Gonzalez case is how everybody races to condemn all Mexicans because of this one drunk driver. Like, there is so much ignorance of Mexico.

-...

-Well, I'll forgive you, but just this once. Do you still go to Los Rios ever?

-I love this song by *Aventura*!

-Most Americans can't even name one film by Cantinflas. They don't even know about great authors like Octavio Pez.

-...

-I was just there a few weeks ago. They've remodeled the bar area and it's pretty nice.

-Actually, his last name may be pronounced and spelled differently. But I'm not sure.

-Did they just like repaint some walls or what?

-...

-A bit of painting, they also got rid of the TV's. Like, who goes to a bar to watch something you can see at home? Right?

-You are so full of shit. Stop confusing this poor girl. It is "Paz." P-A-Z.

-Wait, which one of you is right? Were you making fun of me?

-...

-What do you mean by saying in Spanish: "pulling my hair"? Is my hair messed up?

Hector heard the doorbell and it couldn't be Matt: he would have just used his keys to enter. A guest opened the door and in walked Manny, wearing a plastic boot, along with three other SF

Gales players. A few other stragglers also entered. One of the Gales players was Bryce, who Hector had already met briefly. Another player was a short, muscular Hispanic with short hair, puffy cheeks, and a huge unibrow. Then there was a white dude with long, wavy blonde hair and very pale skin. Pedro remarked in a low voice to Tom: "fresh meat."

Hector and Manny embraced. Hector then introduced Manny to Pedro and Tom on the couch. Pedro's icy glare would have chilled an Eskimo.

Matt had told Pedro about his suspicions: that Manny was more than an "old friend" of Hector. Tom picked up on Pedro's hostility and mirrored it.

Pedro received the other three players much more warmly. In particular, the blonde white guy caught his eye. Pedro was excited by the way this new entrant stood with his left hand on his hip when he laughed.

Hector and Manny almost immediately broke off from the group and entered the bedroom. Both had something to share and ask. They left the bedroom door ajar but spoke in low whispers. The blonde white guy loitered near the couch. Bryce and the other Gales players nursed *Cuba Libres* and Bryce whispered his grievances to his comrade. The white guy locked eyes with Pedro, approached, and chatted him up.

-Psssttt, this is not an impressive guy-to-girl ratio.

-Nice to meet you. My name is Thad. I'm friends with Manny, who knows Hector. And you are?

-Yeah I know, but Manny needs to talk to Hector. Plus, we can just pregame for free here and jet to a bar at any time.

-Hey, Bart, where did James go?

-I'm Pedro. And this is Tom. So, how do you know Manny?

- Dude, these drinks are weak.

-This is also a great song by *Aventura*!

-We play for the San Francisco Gales. It's a soccer team.

-Oh, cool, a soccer player. I love soccer. I used to play when I was younger. What position do you prefer?

-Which of the two James? The younger one?

-Just relax, Bryce. We'll be out of here in a half-hour, tops.

If Thad played a sport, Pedro assumed, Thad must be straight. However, feminine aspects of Thad's speech and posture indicated otherwise. Pedro's eyes locked onto Thad and Tom became invisible.

Meanwhile, Askary stood uncomfortably close to Philipa. Uncomfortably close for Philipa, that is. Askary hung on Philipa's every word as she tried to speak Spanish. When Philipa said a word that started with a vowel, she puffed her lips. When she said a word that started with a "b", "v", or "p", she would curl her lips inwards. Askary cared little for second languages, but admired the dexterity of Philipa's oral region.

Bryce and the other Gales player, Simon, pounded a few beers and waited patiently for Manny to emerge from the bedroom. Bryce's gaydar was impeccable, but he confused the presence of homosexuals with impending danger. A nervous fear overtook his generally good-natured social skills. He rudely avoided eye contact with any of the possible homosexual males in the room and stared at his phone.

-I've lived in San Francisco for a spell now. Like, two years.

-Cool. I've been here about a decade. I work at a law firm and stuck around after college.

-Wait a second. Why did you just call a girl a "strawberry" in Spanish? *Fresa*? Is it because she's sweet?

-What type of law?

-Oh, so it's more of an insult.

-How long have you been studying Spanish? You really roll your "r" really well!

-It's commercial litigation, so the hours are fucking brutal. I barely have time to get a nightcap after leaving the office some days.

-Ummm, thanks.

Andy exited the table area to go to the bathroom. Philipa was left with Askary. Because Askary was still a student, Philipa assumed she was immature and treated her in a manner that was both condescending and maternal. They spoke about classes, majors, and professors. Askary did not mind being spoken down to, so long as she could watch those lips form words.

Pedro felt a strong bite at the fishing line and struggled to hold his rod in check. He was getting serious "into me" vibes from Thad.

However, his original assumption was flawed: Thad was bisexual and had been for some time. Thad knew of fetishists in the LGBT community who regularly sought to "convert" straight men, and he played the part of the bi-curious heterosexual to bait said persons. He relished the role, in fact.

Pedro, for his part, generally detested male bisexuals as indecisive and lacking standards. If he had known Thad was bisexual, he would have never flirted with him.

-So, what's the deal with Andy?

-What do you mean?

-It must be awesome being an athlete, what with the fans and groupies.

-Well, he's clearly very handsome. You two are friends, right?

-Just got a text. John and Tom will be here shortly.

-Ha. Not a lot of groupies at the lower-tier Gales games. We do have some loyal fans, but nothing to write home about.

-You could say that.

-I remember reading an article once, and this may not be appropriate, saying that soccer players don't have sex during the World Cup. Is that true?

-Well, is Andy seeing anybody?

-I've never been to a World Cup, so I can't answer. I've had sex though. It's pretty enjoyable.

Andy returned before Askary could feed a self-serving lie about him to Philipa. Andy was single and heterosexual, but Askary was jealous of all the attention he had been receiving. Across the room, Tom grew bored by the flirtations between Pedro and Thad, so he stood up and made the acquaintance of Bryce and Simon. In Bryce's worldview, black + male = gay did not compute, just as 2+2 does not = 5. He assumed Tom was straight, so he relaxed and was his normal friendly self. Tom revealed that he was from the Midwest, but had family in Texas. Bryce latched onto their tenuous Southern connection.

The front door rattled and opened. Matt stepped inside, carrying a box of Corona in one hand and a bag of groceries in the other arm. He had forgotten wine. He instantly surveyed the room: lots of new people had arrived he didn't know. No sign of Hector. He locked eyes with Pedro, who mouthed the name "Hector" to him. Pedro then made eyes towards the bedroom door.

+++

The clenched jaw. The wrinkled nose. The furled eyebrow. Hector could tell Matt was upset when he entered the room, but he also knew Matt hated fighting in front of others.

196

Still, Matt shocked Hector by walking straight to Hector and sticking his tongue down his throat.

After batting Hector's uvula from side-to-side like a tetherball for two minutes, he stepped back, took a deep breath, and extended his hand to Manny.

-Sorry, I don't think we've met. You must be Manny, Hector's *friend* from Texas.

-Oh yeah, we go way back. And your name?

-Hector hasn't told you my name?

-I haven't really talked with Hector a lot lately; been rehabbing from an injury.

-I think I saw James in the bathroom. It's kinda packed and tough to keep track of people.

-But, hello, everybody has Facebook. I'm kinda hard to miss on Hector's wall and recent picture folders.

-...

-Not everybody is addicted to Facebook, Matt.

-Whatever. Nice to meet you, finally. Hector has told me all sorts of stories about you. Quite the *amigos*, no?

-Really?

Matt hated the way Manny looked at Hector before answering questions. Matt suspected that he had surprised them in the bedroom and interrupted something important. Still, he did not know exactly what. Regardless, it had been his idea to invite Manny, so Matt made polite small talk through clenched teeth. After a few minutes, though, he asked Manny to step out so that he and Hector could have a moment.

Manny exited the room and headed towards Bryce, Simon, and Tom. He overheard Spanish being spoken, though, and decided to check out the refreshment table. Philipa looked at his plastic boot and inquired as to what happened. She doted attention on him while Askary grinded her teeth. Meanwhile, Thad excused himself and went to the restroom. Pedro swiftly approached Bryce and Simon; he needed answers.

-So, you broke your leg? That sounds awful! How exactly?

-You guys also play for the Gales? Cool.

-Yeah, I was in shock and had to go to the Emergency Room and get surgery and stuff. It sucked.

-So what's up with Thad? Is he seeing anybody? A girlfriend?

-Now that you're injured, how does that work with the Gales?

-Nobody can keep up with Thad. Girlfriend. Boyfriend. It's always one or the other with him.

-The Gales have been pretty good to me. The club still pays me while I rehab, so I can't complain too much. Most contracts are only for six months anyways.

-...

-...

-Six months? That seems like a super short time!

-I'm sorry...are, are you kidding?

-...

Pedro retreated to the couch, angry. The bedroom door opened, and out stepped Hector and Matt; they were smiling and holding hands. They went to the kitchen and unpacked the new beer and finger food. Thad emerged shortly thereafter from the bathroom, and decided to chat up his Gales teammates. Manny basked in the glow of Philipa's attention, but also kinda dug Askary's slim figure and curly brown hair.

Manny did not care much for Andy, though. Manny prided himself on being well read, but felt a tinge of envy and insecurity when confronted by those possessing a respectable, formal education. Conversely, Andy had always prided himself on being athletic, but couldn't compete with a professional soccer player. Philipa sensed the tension between the two, but assumed she was the cause.

Matt approached and set out a new tray of vegetables and a bowl of chips. He glared at Manny the whole time, didn't say a word, and promptly went to the couch. He sat next to Pedro and they spoke in hushed tones. Hector stayed in the kitchen: he knew to stay away from Manny for at least a half-hour. Meanwhile, Bryce began to suspect that Tom was gay and became tense.

-That's awesome you speak Spanish. So does Andy. *Que tal tu estancia en San Francisco hasta ahora?*

-Yeah this seems like a nice, chill spot. We're heading out soon, though. Gotta go spit game at some ladies.

-So your name is Askary? That's a cool name. What do you do?

-Speak for yourself. I'm digging the vibe here and can't afford another fifty-dollar bar tab.

-Oh, so you study with Andy. You also speak Spanish?

-So, Andy, I never got your take on the Gonzalez case. Sorry to be a nuisance, but it's all we talk about at the firm.

-...

-And Manny, being a Texan but also Hispanic, what's your take?

-*Pinche mojado. Depórtalo.*

Andy was taken aback by Manny's language, but Hector had heard and couldn't control his laughter from the kitchen. He was the only person in the room who could fully appreciate the remark's irony. Manny quickly explained that he was joking, and then defined the term "*mojado*" for Philipa. Polite and nervous laughter ensued. Askary closely observed how Philipa's mouth formed a large circle as she struggled to pronounce the second syllable of the offensive term.

Pedro and Matt continued to brood on the couch. They did not realize that the acoustics of the room carried their whispers to the kitchen. Hector grew red in the face from anger at hearing parts of their conversation.

-He even looks like me. Same frame, same eyes, same hair.

-I can't believe that little slut thought he could fool me.

-Why speak in a bedroom? Why close the door? How can a relationship be built on trust when one person hides things from another?

-Like, why do that? Why play with people? As if.

-The jeans he's currently wearing are, like, identical to ones Hector said I looked good in a few weeks ago.

-Part of me just wants to fuck him to teach him a lesson. But it looks like Tom has that covered. Slut meets slut. So perfect.

Andy and Manny eventually warmed to each other; they reminisced about *huevos rancheros* and *chilaquiles*. Philipa felt the urge to break out a notepad: she was learning so many new words and phrases. She barely noticed when Askary retreated to the kitchen to see what Hector was up to.

Tom and Thad were hitting things off quite well, to the not-so-hidden disgust of Bryce. Bryce had known about Thad's orientation for some time, but had never seen him in action.

The doorbell rang, followed by a cautious knock at the door. Matt stood up and walked over to answer it. Inside stepped a single, middle-aged Hispanic man. To Manny's shock, it was his uncle Julio Luis.

+++

Julio immediately walked over to Manny and gave him a bear hug. *Tio Julio* was a celebrity on campus, an accomplished public speaker, and all the students at the party recognized him immediately.

He relished being the center of youthful attention and stood at the refreshment table; he beckoned all to come join him. About twelve or so gathered round the table. Julio reached into his small paper sack and pulled out a bottle of vintage red wine. Some people discussed grapes and cultivation. Bryce and Manny sighed in unison. Hector stealthily crept to the kitchen, retrieved glasses, and returned.

Everybody basked in Julio's glow, except for Pedro, who had once been rebuffed by Julio in a bar and pretended not to recognize him. Pedro made a mental note that Julio was possibly serving alcohol to minors. Tom and Thad also remained aloof. They stood at the far corner of the kitchen and talked.

-That's Professor Julio Luis. He teaches Classics.

-Classics? Like the Greeks and Romans and stuff? Cool.

-Professor Cristobal, I've heard rumours about a complaint against you by a student or something. What's up with that?

-…

-Did you go to a private high school or something?

-Naw. I studied for a year at college before deciding to play soccer.

-I can't comment, but let's not worry. Some just can't accept that you're not just my students, you're my friends. Let's just try to enjoy tonight. Who wants a glass?

-…

-A brain *and* a body! Damn.

-Just imagine if today there were still Caracallan baths. You and your man-servant could take the day off, grab a strigil, and enjoy a nice oil rubdown, relieve some stress.

-...

The front of Tom's pants tightened. Meanwhile, *Tio Julio* poured wine for his friends and talked about famous speakers who had visited the University and who, after giving a talk, had gone out on the town with him. Manny listened with curiosity and awe as his uncle dropped famous academic name after name. Julio had even brought two baguettes to go with the wine.

However, *Tio Julio* messed things up when he mentioned that Hector *and* Manny had once lived with him at the same time. Matt knew this already, but still interjected.

-I didn't know that *both* of them lived with you.

-Oh yes, well, I got this text from my lovely nephew. He and his friend were on their way to San Fran and needed a place to stay. How could I refuse?

-But, wait a second - you have a three-bedroom apartment? That seems like a lot of space.

-So, Hector, how exactly did you meet Matt again?

-I only have a two-bedroom.

-Professor Julio introduced us.

Matt still could not fathom his beloved Hector platonically sharing a bedroom with a person so superficially similar to himself. Manny was shocked; his uncle Julio had somehow spotted the truth about Hector before he did and also played matchmaker. In the kitchen, Thad and Tom spoke in whispers.

-Oh crap, it's already 10:30. Askary and I are going to catch a show at the Principe Castro.

-What's that?

-It's a cabaret-style bar. They do this drag karaoke thing at eleven most nights. It's fun, but not so sure it's your scene.

-Hey, I didn't get your number.

-Here you go. Text me so I have yours. So, Thad, later tonight Askary and I are probably getting a nightcap after the Castro show at this rad lounge in the Hotel Cadogan. Maybe you could join us?

-...

Askary and Tom thanked the hosts for the party, talked briefly to Professor Julio, and then left. Pedro continued his balancing act of glaring at Thad while avoiding eye contact. At the request of Matt, Professor Julio gave his famous end-of-semester "*Teutoberg aquila*" speech. Few paid attention.

-You must never stop looking for your *aquila*. Rome fell not when they lost that *aquila* in the German forest, but when they stopped searching for it.

-But, how do you know what your *aquila* even is?

-You must know yourself. Deep down, we all seek that which we have lost. We can feel it, even if we can never fully describe it.

-Isn't that like Plato's idea of love?

-Exactly. Very good Matt.

Matt then asked to be excused; he dragged Hector by the hand to the bathroom. They shut the door, but Matt's voice was still audible. Manny heard snippets of the conversation.

-You two stayed together in some trailer in San Antonio. You two stayed together in a hotel on the way here. You shared a bedroom for months at Professor Cristobal's pad. How can I *not* think this?

-...

-Don't do that. Look at me when I speak to you, not the ground. Don't check out on me Hectorin.

-...

-No, I'm not saying that. He's been nice and all. Still, why did you two have to lock yourself in our bedroom for so long? Even Pedro noticed!

-...

-This entire party you've been mentally checked out. You've barely spoken to anyone. Are you too good for my friends? Are you too good for me?

-...

-You've just been talking with Manny or jerking off by yourself in the kitchen. Pedro swears he saw you glance at Manny's butt once. And, yes, your eyes have been glued to Philipa's skirt also. Even Askary noticed!

-...

-I can't be the one to move this relationship forward by myself, Hectorin. This party was *my* idea, remember? Inviting Manny was *my* idea, do you recall? If I had known you were going to be like this or Manny was going to bring his skanky little bi blonde friend, I'd have kept my mouth shut.

-...

Manny was confused. Matt sounded eerily like *Catracha*. He heard feet shuffling and hastily retreated from near the door.

At the table, talk had turned to his uncle's forthcoming novel; Manny was hearing about this topic for the first time. He had never imagined his uncle was an author. Manny was intrigued, but still desperately needed to speak to Hector about the car.

Philipa, tipsy, tugged Andy away from the table and they both sat on the couch. She put her hand on his thigh. He smiled at her; he was quite drunk. She was only a bit tipsy. Still, she giggled and leaned forward; her nose was soon only inches from his.

-You know what word I have trouble saying in Spanish?

-*Ní idea. Díme.*

-I'll give you a hint: it means "hairbrush."

-*Cepillo?*

-Well, I've been really, *really* into *Bolaño* as of late.

-Almost. Guess again.

-*Peine?*

-Bingo. But when I say it, it sounds like…

Andy believed her when she said she struggled to pronounce diphthongs in Spanish. However, with lips that looked so sweet, he could care less about what came out of that mouth.

+++

The once-hot embers of the party cooled off around midnight. Thad had spent most of the party glued to his cellphone; he flirted and then somewhat graphically sexted with Tom. He absolutely had to go to the Hotel Cadogan, but Bryce was punch drunk and Simon had escaped to a nearby sports bar when nobody was paying attention. Simon did not answer any texts or calls. This meant a sport was being shown on a television. Thad pondered paying a cab to take Bryce home, but concluded it was too risky. Loyalty came before his seething loins.

*Tio Julio,* with his perceptive eye for personality and discord, had detected the tension between Manny, Matt, and Hector. He immediately deduced the cause, and set about to boast Manny's heterosexual bonafides in Matt's eyes through a series of questions. He asked about Manny's old, long-term girlfriend back in Texas who *Tio Julio* recalled was from Honduras. He inquired as to any California girls that Manny surely had met. Manny got the drift and followed along; he soon talked about women in terms befitting a sailor.

Manny even brought up Hector's habit of always sleeping on the floor. The two talked in detail in front of Julio and Matt about the time they spent in San Antonio; they reminisced about the trailer of Willian Boros. Manny omitted any mention of the *regias,* and any other fact that may arouse suspicion. Hector briefly mentioned Willian's wife, but only to make fun of how terribly she kept house. The theme of her cuckolding was not broached. Matt gradually relaxed, but only a little bit.

-Professor Julio, what's your take on the Gonzalez case?

-What do you mean?

-Well, haven't you seen the news?

-Of course.

-Wait, do you mean *Bolaños as in* the deceased Mexican actor who played *El Chavo* or the author of *The Savage Defectives*?

-And haven't you heard what people are saying?

-More or less.

-Well? What do you think?

-I am a literature and classics professor. Not political science. However, it certainly upsets the stomach how people with agendas will turn a tragedy into support for their cause. People kill one another every day. This was an awful car accident, committed by a drunkard, but I fail to see what it has to do with immigrants in general.

-I hate to butt in, but....you have to admit it looks weird, all these *Hispanics* immediately jumping to support a *Hispanic* immigrant.

-Bryce, you are drunk. Sit back down. Are you about to say something racist?

-...

-Let me talk. Like, if this dude was an Asian immigrant or from Africa, would you still be defending him? He killed that girl, you know. She is dead.

-Bryce, calm down buddy. It's just a debate.

-Relax, brother.

-Well, I think your line of argument is interesting, but confused: I am not defending a drunk driver and killer. I am merely pointing out that said incident is unrelated to immigration or nationality. We could have a solid steel border wall a mile high and there'd still be drunk drivers. And they'd kill young women.

Bryce closed his eyes and sat back down on a chair near the kitchen. Thad eventually helped him stand up and walk to the bathroom. A faint symphony of vomits reverberated and was audible through the gap between the floor and the door. The two left shortly thereafter. Meanwhile, nobody could locate Andy and Philipa, at least until Hector tried to open the bedroom door. It was locked. He shook the handle, but stopped upon hearing a few hushed cries of *"papacito."* He thought it prudent to wait.

Pedro announced that he was going outside to take a smoke break. He was angry at the world. First, Tom had not even asked him for his phone number before leaving. Second, the object of his attentions had turned out to be a fraud. He felt both rejected and swindled. He did not plan on smoking. Instead, he just left.

Eventually, *Tio Julio* gave his thanks to Matt, hugged Manny warmly, and made his exit around 12:30 am. He had just gotten back from a week-long writing conference in Jerusalem, and was tired. Shortly thereafter, Andy and Philipa exited the bedroom. Her unkempt red hair resembled a bush, but she didn't care; her half-smile resembled a sideways crescent moon.

Andy, still quite drunk, stumbled as he escorted Philipa to the door and promised before everyone to make sure that the young lady got home. Postcoital endorphins turned him into a chivalrous if not *machista* Latin male. He insisted on opening the entryway door for her, carried her coat, and wrapped his hairy arm around her shoulder. Philipa was sober and a bit put off, and made hasty plans to ditch him at the earliest opportunity. She would probably give him a bogus phone number as well.

-Well, I didn't see that coming. And you, Hectorin?

-I always thought Andy was gay or something.

-Who was that redhead?

-Philipa.

-Is she a student or something?

-Attraction 'tis a fickle, whimsical Goddess, no?

-She worked with me at a law firm a year or so ago.

-And Manny, who was that blonde guy? Flirt-and-a-half.

-Yeah I don't really know him that well. He's better friends with Bryce.

-What class did you take with my Uncle?

-I thought Pedro was going to flip his shit.

-What happened?

-It was this pretty cool lit seminar based on the ocean: we read parts of *Moby Dick* and *20,000 Leagues under the Sea*.

Matt yawned and stood up from the couch. He kissed Hector on the cheek and announced he was retiring to bed. Of course, he would only sleep after changing the sheets and inspecting the pillows for stains. He then shook Manny's hand and thanked him for coming. He even invited Manny to swing by the apartment some other day for lunch. Touched, Manny thanked him for the invite but announced he was leaving town.

-What? *Why?*

-Big storm just hit Brownsville. Gotta help my family.

-And the Gales? Is there a team down there you can play for? And your recovery? How can *you*, right now in your current state, be of help?

-...

-...

-Seriously, like, what will you do when you get there? Do you have a job lined up?

-...

-Hector says there's like no jobs at all down there. Couldn't you work from here and send money?

-...

-...

-Look, I just have to get down there. My family needs me. I kinda need them.

-Well, good luck. I hope they're okay. You're just as nice and handsome as Hector said. Nice meeting you and safe travels.

-Thanks.

Matt retreated to the bedroom and closed the door softly behind him. Manny sat next to Hector on the couch. They were side-by-side, but looked straight ahead. Neither knew what to say.

Elliott Turner

# PART FOUR

*"[H]ow fragile situations are. But not tenuous. Delicate, but not flimsy, not indulgent. Delicate, that's why they keep breaking, they must break and you must get the pieces together and show it before it breaks again, or put them aside for a moment when something else breaks and turn to that, and all this keeps going on."*

William Gaddis, *The Recognitions*

Elliott Turner

# Close Call
## *16th of July 2013*

"That Mexican actor Cantinflas from back in the day got deported and still was like a major success" I said to myself over and over and over again as I sat patiently in the driver's seat of the Corolla stopped on the side of the highway near the middle of nowhere Colorado. Behind me the police car slowed down and then parked, lights still flashing, and out stepped an old white dude with thinning gray hair, a pot belly, and a thick moustache. I watched him through my rearview mirror and noticed for the first time the two words stuck on the back window of Hector's car: "Semper Fi."

"Semper Fi" meant *"Siempre Fiel"* in Spanish, right? I suspected it has something to do with the Marine Corps. Despite my nerves I looked at the MP3 player stuck to the stereo and held back a smile like WTF Hector he had left two MP3 players behind and his music tastes had changed 180 degrees from like sometimes obscure but usually mainstream but good Latin rock and reggaeton and bachata to kinda old sad white people music like *Ratón Modesto* and *Moog-buey* and *Construidos para Spillear* and *Cucharra* and *Hierro y Vino* and um yeah *Juan Efectivo* was cool but the ballads I could barely stand it but the radio didn't work so blah blah Hector must have been caught in a bad romance or something in which the soundtrack now I was trapped.

The distraction kinda helped 'cause I just had to stay cool you know stay calm so like I knew I should maybe keep my hands on the steering wheel even though I wasn't steering or lower them down to my lap but don't cops like to see your hands right so I decided I'm gonna keep them up then. Man that old dude was waddling and taking his sweet time I knew that the plates were good and stuff even though they were from California I just had to relax I said just gotta breathe.

-Hey there young man, you have any idea why I pulled you over?

Because I'm *mojado*? Because I'm a spic? Naw I didn't say any of that but I kinda thought it but this old white dude was actually kinda chill and relaxed and that helped me to relax and I remembered that when my dad got mad I would talk to him in Spanish and use the "usted" and he would calm down so I decided to speak like real formal and call this old dude "sir" and "officer" and looked him in the eyes as best I could.

I said that I did not know why he had stopped me but I was sorry and in a rush to get back to Texas because of the recent hurricane and I wanted to be sure my mom was okay and help her out and stuff. I kinda sorta rambled and like you know sometimes sentences they can run on and on then you use "then" as a conjunction and you forget the pauses where the Oxford Comma should go and well like what the hell I was nervous. Really fucking nervous.

-Well, young man, I'm sorry to hear about that. But we got ourselves a problem with this here vehicle.

When I heard those words, I could have shit my pants. Did Hector mess up the plates or registration or something? I knew I wasn't speeding but man Hector bought this *carcacha* used and who knew from where it came? Plus half the parts were used ones we got from junkyards near the border between Texas and Mexico this thing was a Frankenstein and maybe it had like a killer history or was part of a drug bust or raid or something.

Still, the cop had not yet asked me for my license or insurance, which was good. I didn't have no license. I had half-thought of a lame excuse for this omission like I lost it and that's why I'm rushing back to Texas to get it but then why are the Corolla's plates now California and not Texas and I kinda wondered why Hector did switch the plates but then I remembered he was planning on staying in San Francisco like maybe forever and the longness of forever dawned on me.

-What's the problem, officer?
-...
-...
-Young man, can I have a look at your driver's license and insurance please?

*Chinga chinga chinga* I thought but I still reached over to the glove compartment as nonchalantly as I could and whew I saw Hector's car insurance paper and I handed it to him and then I explained that I had lost my license while roadtripping to and around California but now I needed to get back to Texas ASAP and I would get one when I could in Texas in person. The old officer took the insurance paper back to his car and sat in his car for a long time.

I didn't know if I could use my cell phone or should use my cell phone or if that would be suspicious but like I wanted to text Hector and also was kinda mad and sad and confused as to why *Catracha* hadn't called or messaged me she knew I was on my way home like shouldn't she be happy or something? I knew that we were technically broken up and maybe I blocked her on Facebook but like I was getting tagged in some pictures that would have flipped her out even though we were on hiatus so I had to be sure I untagged all that stuff before she could see me again. On Facebook. Old officer dude got out of the car and walked back towards me. To my relief, his gun remained holstered.

-Son, I saw the back of your car there. What marine division exactly you in? You get back recently from active duty?

-...

-I just, I saw that sticker on your car. You seem a little frazzled. You know my son served a tour in Iraq *and* Afghanistan. That shit'll fuck up a man's mind. You just get back from Iraq?

-...

I really did not want to lie anymore to this sweet old cop but I was thinking why did I get stopped? I already told him a half-truth in that I did lose my Texas license but like that Texas license was the fake Texas license Hector had bought me at the *pulga* so I could get a job and he told me to never ever show that ID to a cop because they could smell the fakes a mile away and then they'd be sure to call the *migra* to come in their green fatigues and send me to Matamoros or Reynosa or wherever and then I'd have to stay at the *Casa de Migrante* run by the Catholics until some *primo* or *tio* came to get me and let me stay with them while I begged relatives in the US for money to be able to cross again maybe near Piedras Negras I hear it's safer there.

I kept quiet and told him that I didn't really want to talk about that but that like I thanked him for his son's service to our country and asked if his son had joined like a support group when he got back because I remembered that Hector went to one of those for a while but it got disbanded because after meetings they'd all just go out and get drunk and start fights and get arrested and stuff. Like you can't just amp up these young men full of adrenaline and testosterone and drill that stuff into them and not expect them to come back all agitated and rowdy and stuff.

-Well that's a hot good idea young man. Support group. You know, I'm not afraid to say I've been going to A.A. for twenty years, and it's time well spent. Where you heading to in Texas, boy?
-Brownsville, sir.
-Where exactly is that?
-It's South Texas, sir. A few hours South of San Antonio, officer.
-...
-...
-Sounds like a shithole.
-...

I can now look back and chuckle at myself. I was so nervous, so excited, so worried, and this old man just wanted to chat and talk about his own son's military service for a spell. Back then, my neuroses and lack of legal status in the US formed a dangerous cocktail of paranoia and sensibility. I overreacted to the slightest of slights, to any comment about "illegals", a term I detested then and still dislike today. I also perceived danger where little existed.

I can still recall my fifth grade year of school when a police officer came to school during an assembly. Across the great nation of America, such officers often visit grade school children to talk about

217

the dangers of drugs. Not in the Valley. The officers come for one reason: to teach us not to run whenever we see a man in uniform wearing a badge. The children of immigrants and many of us immigrants ourselves, we had internalized the notion that a man in a badge and uniform can only mean trouble. When the officer walked into the auditorium, about ten of us looked around, panicked, and I knew I wasn't the only one thinking *"corre pendejo correle!"*

-Well, son, here's the issue. You got a tail light out. I think you'd best stop at the Autozone up the road and change it.
-...
-Otherwise you might get a ticket for the light and no license. I'm gonna just give you a warning this time, you hear.

Then came the moment of non-truth the old man said he thought I looked like an Iraq veteran and if I was going back he wished me well and maybe I said something random about the word "Fallujah" which I thought was like a town and Hector said that place was fucked up so I mentioned it and the old man got teary-eyed because some neighbor boy got disabled there after stepping on or over an I.E.D. and I didn't even remember what an I.E.D. was or what those letters stood for but I had trouble looking him in the eye I felt really really fucking bad and guilty.

Then came the like weird moment where the old guy looked at me and said "don't you hesitate to pull the trigger and tag one of those camel-fuckers" and then he said "it's either them or us" and I was like alarm bells alarm bells I'd never heard no white person speak like that except for Bryce but even he who hated the burning of Atlanta and that Sherman dude had never said a word like that or

218

anything remotely similar but I just looked at this old cop and stoically nodded and then I went on my way and after a few miles I stopped at an Autozone and changed the tail light and looked at the *Semper Fi* on the back of the Corolla and made the Sign of the Cross my guardian angel must be work'in overtime.

I stopped to sleep in like New Mexico and then the second day I was fucking amped especially when I crossed that *rio rojo* and entered Texas. I laughed and thought of all the things I had missed about Texas like weird shit like seeing Mexican flags on one truck and Confederate flags on another and Texas flags on another Bryce had said California changed my English so I spoke like a "fucking carpetbagger" but now back in Texas I could say "plain and dry" at the hamburgeria and they'd know what was up. I could even get jalapenos on my hamburger without going to some expensive place.

After driving through Austin I finally reached San Antonio where I could get a good taco and the RGV beckoned to me calling my name suddenly a million things and memories infected my mind and sent shivers up my body like when you are rolling (I have heard) like things about the RGV that I hated I now loved like those signs for "puppys libres" on the side of the road and people mowing lawns at night while holding flashlights and like that single native species of palm tree of the RGV the *gordita* and *chaparra* that sabal Mexicana so stout so leafless yet so proud and defiant I always glared at those *flacucha* palm trees in Cali imported from Spain with serious distrust like why aren't you eating better?

Nostalgia grabbed hold of me and I missed that little vertical finger trigger pull that means "yes" and even get this those folding tables with gently used clothing that sprout up every morning like a flower opening its petals to embrace the sun's light and and are everywhere clothes in good shape and negotiable prices even better than Ross and near Falfurrias I turned off the car's a/c and rolled down the windows and could feel the air's warmth and humidity wrapping me like a blanket and I knew I was home almost.

I didn't even stop at the bathroom just North of the *garrita* in Falfurrias I knew it was a big step maybe backwards but my right foot was made of lead even if the left leg ached a bit I did flick off the *garrita* camera which takes pictures of southward bound motorists fuck them but at the same time I was elated I was the returning prodigal son with tales to tell and shit.

I assumed everything in Brownsville was as I had left it. The concepts of time and change did not enter my thoughts. I also didn't realize that time marches at different rhythms for different people and in different situations. Mostly happy and occupied, I felt the past several months pass in the blink of an eye. For *Catracha*, who truly loved me and missed me, each single day had passed really slow and felt like a month. She had cracked, but I couldn't hear or sense it from afar. Or maybe I didn't want to. Instead, I thought life in the RGV would freeze-frame exactly as I had left things, family and friends included.

I looked in the dash mirror at myself and smiled as I passed Edinburg. I didn't know the girl who I'd first loved was about to irreparably break my heart. I had no clue how much my mother had suffered in my absence to keep things together. I didn't even know the storms had trashed her car - she didn't want to tell me or upset me while I was away. The darkness and suffering awaiting me must have hidden on the other side of the white clouds in the sky above as I sped past Weslaco and remembered that blissful feeling of locking lips with *Catracha*.

### Al Diablo, Padre
### *4th of July, Year Unknown*

Even back then when I was like sixteen-years-old or whatever I remember looking at my dad's grinning face the day of that Fourth of July barbecue, the last time I ever saw him, and thinking "What the fuck is so funny?" I probably didn't think the exact word "fuck" but like the sixteen-year old equivalent because I didn't use that word then but I was really angry like he had just fought with my mom nuclear war-style with shouts and he even punched a hole in the damn wall. Now, one hour later, he was joking with his brother.

Everything started with a cell phone, like a small, black, really simple old school cheap one that you have to pay for cards to get minutes on and send messages. The day of the Fourth my mom woke up early and decided to clean my dad's *troca* and what did she find hidden underneath the driver's seat but this old crummy cell like pre-password era cell and just the existence of this second cell cast a dark shadow on my dad's already shady *mujeriego* character but like the messages holy shit the messages. !!!!!

My mom had put up with some shit before. My dad used the family laptop and had no clue about browser history or that crap and my mom did so sometimes he'd get home from work and my mom would set him up by asking if he'd used the computer yesterday and he'd say yes and then bam she'd lay the smack down and he'd get mad about her "spying" as if but then finally, secretly, I started to get on the computer and delete my dad's offending website visits and man that shit was gross even by twenty-first century perv'in out tonight standards just seeing the page titles and clicking delete on the mouse made me feel queasy.

So like this Fourth of July epic fight happens because in addition to reading terribly misspelled Spanglish sexts like *"Yo kiero tu kunt"* mom calls a few numbers and a few go to voicemail and lo and behold she hears recorded female voices but then this one gal answers and says off the bat *"Hola Papy"* and my mom got pissed and insulted this little trick and said *"Esta es mamy, zorra de mierda, y quien te crees tu?"*

The biggest dilemma, though, was that the parental fighting was always followed by this smooth power play by Papy whereby he actually *liked* to get kicked out of the house because that meant *rienda suelta* like he could go meet up with his *cuates* and pals and kick back some beers and watch Liga MX or the NFL or whatever no kids no wife no bullshit was kinda the prevailing attitude. This pissed off my mom even more because like she worked part-time and earned her own money but she needed Papy's *lana* to be able to pay that *renta* in a week and she knew that he knew that she knew this.

After this particular shout match though my mom got an idea she decided hey if you are going to just leave take Manny with you and look after him. This pissed off my dad because unless he was taking me to soccer or something he himself liked he viewed time spent with kids as time wasted. Yes, we could run to the fridge to then bring him another cold Miller Lite but aside from that we made noise and got into trouble and had to be fed three times a day. I really did not want to go with Papy because I was sure he was going to my *tio's*.

Looking back today, my first instinct after my dad split was to assume he had abandoned us. I was angry at him. As the years passed without a word, I started to construct a different narrative. I heard terrifying stories about folks getting deported and then being murdered. I read tales about people trying to cross and dying in the desert. I envisioned my dad heroically trying to return to us, only to be murdered by undesirables or Mother Nature. In large part, I fabricated this story as a means of self-preservation. I couldn't bear the thought of him having just left us, as if we were of no value.

When I found out the truth while living in Mexico decades later, I grew angry and spiteful. My initial and harsh judgment had been correct. I was mad, but less at my dad and more at myself for the years of lies. I was also unnecessarily curt and cold to my half-sisters when I met them. After all, they didn't create that monster, they just took advantage of the situation as best they could. Deep down, another doubt lingered and festered and grew. How many other childhood memories had I slanted in my head to suit my own ego? Was it too late to correct this? Could I act as a painter and use a knife to chip away at my own canvas of superficial memories to reveal even more unsettling truths?

So like yeah the *asado* we went to was at my *tio's* and I just remember how fat this *tio* was and also his wife and kids like they just drank *gaseosa* like water and I laughed because whenever my family had a birthday party or something my mom would hide the Coca-cola before this *tio's* family came over like she would place two liter containers under the sink and she called him *esponja* behind his back and she also hated how when this *tio* fought with his wife he would come over to chill on our couch for a week or so and he would complain about the corn tortillas she used as if *maiz azul* was below him but not us.

My dad and the *tio* are taking turns grilling the *cabrito* and knocking back some piss-beer and my *primos* are all inside watching TV because it's the afternoon and it's hot as hell outside like your clothes are drenched in your own sweat and sticking to your skin even if you stand perfectly still in the shade there ain't no breeze and I half-expected Sir Brunetto to appear and shake my hand.

I avoided my cousins like the plague because we didn't have anything in common and they always got into stupid trouble and then blamed me and then my dad would always blame me saying *"Que pena"* and about how he could never take me anywhere but truth is if he had taken me anywhere but my *tio*'s I would have been happy and much better behaved. It was so frickin hot but I didn't want to go inside because they were all watching some stupid *telenovela* or some trashy family dispute TV show so I just stood outside and sweated and smelled the goat meat getting grilled.

Then papy tried to pull a fast one. His cell phone hummed and he answered, speaking briefly and curtly so that my curious ears picked up nothing. Then he said to me and his brother that his work had called and he had to go in for a few hours. My *tio* tried to suppress a smile and I was pissed but then I realized and suggested hey my Dad can just take me to the jobsite and I can escape from this boring and lame place. A barrage of comments followed I told Dad I should go along since Mom told him to spend the day with me and watch me and he said the jobsite was dangerous or something and I said fine I would just call Mom to let her know and to pick me up and then my dad's eyes narrowed like a serpent's and his pupils grew darker and larger, like a pit.

My dad unleashed a verbal barrage from point blank range akin to a hairdryer set to hyperdrive but I just kept my cool and repeated my dual demands which were I either got to spend time with him at *tio*'s or work or I could go home to be with my siblings dad kept trying to say that my *primos* were my family but I said if he left I would borrow somebody's cell to call mom and even if I couldn't I would just fill her in on the loop and what had transpired after the fact like when we got home. I did not know dad was not going home then or ever. This threat seemed to fall upon him like the heated tip of a spear; his face turned red and writhed in agony from his own fury.

Decades later, my *tio* Julio shared with me a brief conversation he had one night at a party with my Gales roommate Bryce. Basically, Bryce revealed to him that while I was in the hospital and on drugs, I suffered from two recurring hallucinations. In the first, I spoke Spanglish in a soft tone and cried. Bryce deduced I saw a little girl standing beside me and I kept saying "No, not right now, *no quiero Takis.*" He had asked Julio what Takis were. In the second recurring hallucination, I got angry and yelled pejoratives at a man standing at the foot of my bed. Luckily, Bryce already knew a fair number of swear words in Spanish. Still, he had wanted to know who "Juan Joaquin" was.

So like yeah my last memory of my dad was him shooing me into his car, him driving me back to our apartment, him shooing me out of the car in the parking lot and driving off pissed as hell. I cried. At the time, I didn't know exactly what was up like part of me thought maybe my dad really did have to go to work at a place that's not safe for children but overall my impression then was really fucking accurate and to this day has only been affirmed: he didn't love me.

At least not then. Maybe ever. I never learned the exact reason(s) as to why he left us for good or any related details. Maribel said he could not stand the RGV - everything, including us, reminded him of his dead daughter Gemma and drove him crazy. Moms thought he got sick of America, of being poor, and ran off to be with his wife in Mexico who was kinda loaded but spent money like it was nothing.

Maybe both were right but, still, as a twenty-something, I still imagined that my dad must have died and this must be the only explanation during my adolescence every now and then the truly delusional part of me would imagine a future where he shows up out of thin air and asks for forgiveness and maybe he's in A.A or has cancer or some other legit reason to stop being a prick and for me to stop being a prick and I am able to like forgive him and maybe even get along but nope did not happen. The closest we came was me hallucinating and shouting at the specter of his *hijo de puta* ass in the tenth-floor room of a hospital in San Francisco with Bryce getting spooked and then the C.N.A. and maybe the resident nurse frantically ran down the hall to see what the fuck was going on.

# Unmasked Again
## *14th and 15th of July 2013*

Sometimes two conversations with the same person will just sorta fuse and melt into one another in your head and trying to sort out your memory like separating one *plática* from another is a waste of time because they are scrambled and will stay that way and that is what happened the last couple times I spoke with Hector in San Francisco. The last two times we spoke in person, to be precise. Like I look back and try to separate the two but well when cooking you sprinkle sea salt into water to make it boil faster well the first *plática* was the not-quite boiling water and the second *plática* was the sea salt.

So that night I went with my boys to Hector's party and I kinda knew that something was up because before Hector had blocked me on Facebook for reasons unknown there had been some tagged pics showing him canoodling with his roommate thus I suspected that they were more than roommates which was and is and will be okay so long as I'm not like you know excluded from the conversation like ever since he got that job as *botones* at a hotel we started to grow different and he started to act different.

So my Gales buddies and I go to the party and a quick survey of the location shows not a whole lotta lovely girls to hit on in fact most of them looked like they also preferred the company of women and the men appeared of the type to prefer the company of men again okay but like my boys came ready for the hunt and looked at me like WTF but I was like WTF this is the 21st century my friend Hector invited me via text and said it was important and I also kinda needed to beg grovel cry for a car so this is what it was. We arrived and then Hector said that me and him needed to talk about something and I thought

I already knew what it was but then we went inside the bedroom and he kinda half-closed the door.

Words flowed and random questions and thoughts entered my head, but I chose not to voice them in front of Hector. I feared being labeled ignorant and immature. Upon retrospection, my fears were very well-founded.

*Have you ever fantasized about me naked? If yes, gross. If no, why the fuck not?*

So like Hector starts off with the truth and that is that he turned like maybe about two years ago and he met this dude this white dude Garrett while in the army in Iraq but he said he had always kinda known but this part kinda bugged me because like we grew up together and had talked about girls a lot and like one of us couldn't get to second-base with a girl without telling the other all the glorious details a few hours later but I bit my lip and listened. I was and am still a bit fuzzy on how and when Hector turned but I also figured that none of those details were important like Hector was Hector.

Then the conversation changed and changed in a big way like I was still dealing with Hector coming out you know *declarandose* and then he kept talking about Garrett from the military base like Garrett sounded like a total prick he played sports in high school probably football the fake *futbol* with concussions and pigskin whatever and Garrett had like black hair with blonde frosted tips and he even drove a fucking red Jeep wrangler like the kind you can pull off the roof and sides or whatever.

229

Hector and I had totally mocked the fuck out of Garrett-types all throughout our youth and like Garrett rolled with other dumb-as-sin football players in high school prob'ly and had a *chapa* and had tattooed on his bicep two small letters "H" and "B" which stood for "Hot Boys" because that's what his crew called themselves. Like for real. At the time I thought "that's pretty *gay*" but I caught myself said "this guy was *gay* so it's okay" but like no not even I meant to think and say "that's pathetic." "Gay is not a synonym of pathetic by any means or a negative adjective. Duh." Beyond semantics, you can ink your love of mom, God, Jesus, a bae, your child, and cool foreign languages and it's all good but "HB" for "Hot Boys" is a no no no.

*Latinas don't give head, ergo, I assume Latinos, such as you, do not either.*

So like Garrett and Hector met and Hector was really confused like "who the fuck am I" in-a-general-sense confused but also like "why am I into *this dude* of all the dudes" serious questions and doubts and stuff. Garrett was super friendly and always talking about life back in Arizona with his parents and sister and he was also like into hugs and like didn't always respect people's physical space as in he stood really close sometimes Hector would catch Garrett staring at his *boca* during a *plática* and Hector would stop talking and expect Garrett to reply but he didn't that dude would keep staring at Hector's mouth and it was awkward but also kinda excited Hector.

Hector thought like "Is this dude into me?" and also writ large "am I even into dudes?" and then one day late at night after playing cards for what seemed like forever after lights out when everybody else had lost their money and left to sleep Garrett kissed Hector and Hector felt like this surge you know every hair on your body stands-on-end like serious gigawattage charge of current it coursed through took over his body and he knew the answer to all his questions was yes Yes YES *YES*.

*Bucket list and relationship goals: anal. Check.*

I know for a fact that Hector had like tons of free time while on tour at that base in Iraq because that mofo was always online he sat glued to the computer all the time like always plugged into gchat and with all that free time we hatched our website AnchorBabes grew and became popular and got pageviewed and we had fun making fun of the "anchor baby" bullshit we always heard on the radio and in the news in Texas. This site got crazy mad popular and then *Catracha* saw like the emails we'd get like girls and guys who were kids of immigrants sending us their pic they wanted to be on the site but some of the pics were you know too racy so *Catracha* got jealous of me getting them emails so Hector was in charge.

We chatted at length about the goals of the site and the need for *infrarrealismo* which was this old school of thought that said that we have to like look at reality super close to try and find universal truths so we decided that like the pics of AnchorBabes had to be raw, realistic, no filter no models no fakes heck no makeup like come as you are and you are beautiful as God made you. The comments section was pretty cool like it opened our eyes to you know people's sensibilities like some of the girls and even guys would say stuff about people and even a few discussions on E.D. like you know some prick dude would say something about a chubby gal on the site and other girls would shame him but then things got too nasty too often and we had to switch to Tumblr to get rid of comments. Folks were

231

pissed. Like, hundreds of emails a day for a few weeks pissed. *Pobre* Hector.

*If you bring a white boy home, your parents are going to kill you.*

So I knew that Hector had lots of free time in the military even while on a tour and now I know just what else who else he was doing he and Garrett would always steal kisses when they could and started to like really heavily text message a lot when apart and like it was still not cool to be turned and in the army and both had to hide it but then Garrett's tour ended and it was a big moment they said they would try to do the whole distance thing. And that shit's hard.

Hector came back for an extended vacation once and I remember it was weird because he was barely back in Brownsville for a day before he jetted off in the Corolla at the time he like told us that he was meeting up with some military buddies in Ruidoso, New Mexico to go hiking but now he told me the truth he met up with Garrett and they rented a room together at some cheap mountain resort and folks in New Mexico didn't like care they had turned and even the Indians or Native Americans or whatever were cool they you know Hector and Garrett could walk out in public down the main drag holding hands.

Sometime during the *plática* Hector's boyfriend err roommate err *novio* Matt came back and entered the bedroom and gave me the eye and Hector totally changed subjects away from Garrett but then like a few hours later when the party was ending his boyfriend was pretty cool and nice and went to bed Hector and I started talking again. Hector returned to our earlier talk and said that he thought

232

distance was going well but then fucking shit Garrett got in a car accident like shit this dude leaves Iraq unscathed and a drunk motherfucker t-bones him one night at an intersection. He suffered a broken leg but the worst part was there was a fire like shit and he got some burns on the face and arms and he couldn't work and he because the injury was not related to Iraq ain't no way the V.A. was gonna foot no plastic surgery bill.

For the first time in my life I saw a single tear roll down Hector's cheek I thought "hey do I like hug him or what" but I didn't because I was fucking stupid and Hector was gay and had hid it from me his best friend for what seemed like a long ass time so like Hector was worried and shit about Garrett but like then Garrett got real depressed and started drinking and like the Skype chats got all boring and pissy and stuff again boom Hector came back and again went to Arizona this time and revealed he visited Garrett but Garrett had like this nasty scar on his neck and a few on his face and Hector felt like shit. He felt like hey I thought I loved this dude but where's the dude I loved and what is wrong with me for like feeling this am I too shallow or superficial?

*A catcher who also pitches? Call Major League Beisbol!*

Looking back, I wish I'd hugged Hector. I wish I could take a pair of scissors and cut out the cobwebs of prejudice and immature thoughts that had infected my mind. Often, our closest relationships don't end with a bang, but rather a whimper. Indifference appears and gets multiplied by each passing day until entropy consumes the connection. I can imagine a world where I stay in San Francisco and am also a better person and can chill with Hector and we grow old as friends. I can imagine a world where I return to the Valley but get over being blocked on Facebook and call Hector at least once a month to touch base. I can imagine a world where I was the friend Hector deserved and needed; it's just a shame I'll never get a chance to live in it.

So like yeah finally I realize that shit it's like three o'clock in the morning and I feed Hector some stock reassuring friend words that he's not a monster and people change and blah blah blah and then he asks me if I'm going to the Valley and I say yeah and he asks how and I say I'm not sure if I go by bus the *Migra* will pop my ass and he nods and he knows my mind man he still knew my mind and he says he was looking to sell the Corolla because parking is so expensive and I can have it. I didn't even ask man Hector and me were so tight even then I said quite a few *muchas gracias* and wished him luck you know and then I left and then we met later that morning and I got the car and left town.

Well no that's not all not quite. Hector gave me the car and stuff but then he wanted to like talk about his current boyfriend Matt who was jealous and I was like thankful but tired and exhausted and ready to leave and I kinda sorta maybe said "Yo, I know you're a *joto* now and that's okay, but don't rub my nose in it. My family needs me" I'd never seen Hector fully, straight on cry before and he did both eyes open tears flowing like I couldn't handle it and I had got the car so like nothing holding me back and yeah I left. Pretty predictably, after that *despedida* I never saw Hector again in person. I just exited the place, got in the car, and drove off. Didn't look back. Until now.

In the RGV living with mom and my family and working doing shitty jobs I could have called him, messaged him, but I kinda sorta waited for him to make the move for reconciliation. A few years after I got back to the RGV, I heard from from a friend that Hector was coming back and people asked me if I was going to see him but I didn't have the courage to ask him for forgiveness, to confess my sins. When I finally realized he was gay that night, I was mad because I felt like he'd kept a secret from me, his best friend. I should have been the first to know, not that jealous as fuck Matt dude who was stuck up along with his college-educated asshole friends.

I'd often wondered just exactly why Hector went with me to San Antonio and then California; he'd been a big brother and that's how I saw it, but then I suddenly saw through the lies or thought I did. Was he really a night security guard? A bellhop at a hotel? Or did he just make that shit up and come along with me to go fuck dudes late at night and far away from the prying eyes of the RGV? He had ran off to Ruidoso to fuck that white trash dude, so like was going with me and helping me play soccer and get past that *garrita* even that important to him?

You never realize just how fucked up your thoughts are until you hear yourself speak or see them written down. I read these July entries decades too late.

# Órale, Mojado
## *6th of March 2007*

One might get the overarching impression that my dad was a *borracho* and a *mujeriego* and my childhood sucked but like you gotta understand there were good moments and even little glimpses of humanity from time-to-time. My mom was brilliant with reading and words and prose but really struggled with math so like my dad after coming home late at night would pound a brew and help me with Algebra homework as best he could and I remember thinking that in an alternate life maybe my dad would be like an engineer or something and drink less but in truth I was just happy to get help and like you know see him.

When you grow up bilingual you always use and observe language as an indicator of emotion beyond mere superficial volume level. When my mom got angry, she spoke rapidfire in Spanish and sometimes she would even say to her kids *"malcriado"* which means "ill-bred" and I would say *"pero tú me criaste"* which translates to "but *you* raised me" and then she'd call me *"hijo de puta"* and I would shut up. My dad, though, got pissed and started to speak in really broken English. Once at a grade school parent-teacher conference he refused to believe it was my fault I did not do homework. He yelled at the teacher and said "You must 'spire them!" Only a few days later did we realize he meant "inspire."

So like before I realized or even knew anything about immigration or the law or how those things worked all I can recall is being super super pissed and confused when I was in middle school and my soccer club traveled one weekend to San Antonio and all the parents went with their kids like the club rented a chartered bus but neither my mom nor my dad went with me. I now know they couldn't pass that *garrita* in Falfurrias but then I was mad and I sat on the bus with a friend I think his name was James he was shorter than me and a bit chubby with a buzzed black haircut and also darker skinned his mom and dad were super nice.

We played all day Saturday and came back late at night I scored like four goals in three games and we got a fourth-place medal we won two games and lost one but like I just remember how odd it felt to like hear silence at games normally my dad would patrol the sidelines like a wolf he would curse at everybody who impeded me such as linesmen with the audacity to think I was offsides he got kicked out of so many games and I pretended to be embarrassed but I guess deep down I knew he cared.

The long bus ride home was a trap because like the bus stopped at a gas station slash diner but I didn't have any money or nothing my mom had made me a sack lunch with only two sandwiches my stomach growled but if I had learned anything from moms and dad it was pride comes first whenever we went out to another person's house we never *ever* could admit we were hungry or liked food these people would implore us to eat sometimes but we had to stand strong. Otherwise we got the eye from mom, and back home we'd get a hiding.

So like I sat on the bus while every single kid and their family got off to go eat and I pretended to be asleep so that nobody would bug me about going because I know that if I went down off the bus I'd be invited to eat and then some parent would maybe mention it non-maliciously to my parents and then my butt would be sore from getting spanked by plastic flip-flops so I closed my eyes, leaned back and tried to ignore the rumblings of my stomach. After about twenty minutes, the groans and audible shakes stopped and I started to doze off. Then my friends and their family got back on the bus, snacks in hand. A few kids smelled like roasted hot dogs and the odor made me wince but not out of disgust.

I caved and accepted some snacks and basically anything a teammate offered me something to eat I ate and I ate with hunger and careless abandon. My friends laughed and called me *comelón* and one gave me a small bag of Cheetos to see if I could finish it within two minutes and I did and we like laughed as kids do not really thinking but then I saw the parents watching us and friendly and laughing and I thought "Oh, crap" like somebody is gonna tell my parents about this later then I said my stomach hurt and I left to sit in the bathroom at the back of the bus for a while.

My mom found out a few days later and called me *malcriado* and *comelón* and *hijo de puta* as she spanked me with her plastic flip-flops but like here's the problem I was in middle school I'd inherited a bit of flesh on that rear-end so like getting spanked was not the corporal capital punishment it once was. In fact, I tried to hide it but deep down it made me laugh and that laughter formed in my tummy and grew it strengthened rose and I laughed out loud. *Chingado.* My dad got home, spoke two minutes with my mom alone in their room, and came out like a disgruntled bull and I was dressed in all red.

My dad yanked me by the arm and walked me out the apartment and then lifted me physically into his truck, then drove me up to the very last place you can park before crossing the old international bridge into Matamoros, Mexico he said in Spanish quite clearly that "in Texas a father could only spank his child but that once in Mexico

I could count on getting my ass whooped so which was it gonna be" was I gonna respect my mom or were we going to take a little trip South? I was petrified and picked option A and then he took me to Sonic for some cheddar peppers to celebrate all my goals it was as if nothing had happened.

A few years later when I was like bigger and even more unruly he again drove me to the old international bridge but now I knew about immigration and that like he couldn't go back to Mexico because if he did it would be tough to come back so I myself got all pissed and said "Órale mojado" which is embarrassing I feel bad I said that and used that word and disrespected him even though he was a prick he was still my father you know that term means "go ahead wetback" and he slapped my face not too hard but enough to shut me up. He told me I could talk to him like that because he was a man and I was becoming a man and it means shit to him because I knew shit but to never talk to my mom like that or he would beat the shit out of me and then I could call CPS and get his ass deported because like nobody talks to their mom like that nobody.

A few years later when dad was gone and money was tight and food felt scarce my mom just kinda laughed I'd be hungry and think of that trip back from San Antonio by myself or when I was little and went out for walks with Gemma man I miss those walks but my mom told us about her childhood and how her family didn't even have an apartment like they did the *posadas* like lived at people's houses as long as they would put up with them.

I thought that sounded pretty bad and then she kinda told me just a little bit about what happened during the war before they came here like some *campesinos* called themselves Zapatistas and started shooting cops and the army and said they were "liberating" territory and then more army soldiers came in and if you knew somebody who was a suspected "Zapatista" then you were on a black list folks got forced to pick sides my Uncle Julio got recruited into the military he had to like burn the bodies of killed enemies and like the nerves would still be alive and the fucking bodies would jump and bounce and move muscles aflame and he is still a vegetarian to this day for a decade he couldn't smell meat grilling without wanting to throw up.

My mom told me this story to like impart on me that life was rough but could be rougher however I knew I was hungry and wanted food and should be eating food even if the bodies of blackened and flaming cadavers danced circles in my head.

# Unmasked
## *31st of October 2012*

Before I really for sure one-hundred percent knew that Hector had turned we went out for Halloween in San Francisco and that's probably my last really happy memory from those times with Hec like my leg wasn't broken and we were still a bit close and we just kinda fucked around you know well at least early on in the night. Hector was on this "I am Hispanic and from Texas" kick so I followed his lead and we had decided that we would dress as *charros* and all night we were going to pretend to be some *pinche* band like the *Tucanes de Tijuana* you know that *música regional* shit.

Hector took me to some odd corners of San Francisco in search of authentic cowboy costumes. Like the city didn't have a Cavender's or real boot store so we went to like costume stores one called Camille's and also some like I don't know how to say it but like LGBT-friendly and LGBT-populated corners but like I was cool with that even if in regards to attire I insisted on some authenticity like no way I was wearing some pink cowboy hat or tight leather cowboy shirt and like in all honesty actually finding real boots in that town was the hardest part.

After like eight fucking hours of canvassing the city proper and even riding BART all around and back we finally got our stuff in order and went to Tio Julio's to change. We got dressed and swore to one another that we would remain in character all night no matter what and that with each new person we met one of us would invent some shit and the other would follow along no exceptions. Hector wore black boots, blue jeans, a black long-sleeved cowboy shirt and a black cowboy hat. I had brown boots, blue jeans, a white t-shirt and a tan cowboy hat.

We both had found and wore huge Texas belt buckles that kicked serious ass. I painted on a fake moustache and stubble. Hector may or may not have had a beard at the time I can't remember. Throughout the night we kept changing the name of our band the trick was thinking of a type of bird in Spanish and then like a city or town or region in Mexico whose name started with the same letter.

*Damos la bienvenida a los Búhos de Rio Bravo!*

We went to this kinda ratty dive bar to start the night near my Tio Julio's place and like my cell phone kept exploding because me and *Catracha* were kinda on the mend u know texting n stuff and but like I'd met this rad *chilanga* chick at a coffee shop rather she accosted me I was in my training gear and she came up to me in line and said in rapid fire rat-a-tat Spanish *"Tu hablas Espanol, verdad?"* And I kinda coyly answered back *"Tal vez"* And and she thought it was *chido* that I played soccer and we sat and sipped on some mochas and promised to meet up later this was three days ago maybe four.

The *chilanga* had dyed her gorgeous, shiny black hair green near the tips which normally I detest like why ruin that darkness with purple and red but like on her hair it looked authentic like 100% *Mexicana* this girl was for real she spoke Spanish real fast and and always conjugated verbs and used verbs I'd never heard of like who the hell says *"obsequiar"* instead of *"regalar"*?? While I texted with *Catracha* words of assurance and fidelity and seriousness, this *chilanga* and I sorta coyly flirted and man did the thought of me with her get me hot like I was on fire underneath that white shirt I really wanted her to show up already and to toss some dogs.

Hector and me still playfully mistranslated Spanish phrases to one another like he would pretend to get angry and ask *"Cual es tu carne conmigo?"* then I would respond in mistranslated English "There is a fart between you and me!" nobody else really got the jokes but that was okay and also kind of the point and actually a small, select handful got the jokes of which half did not think they were that funny. I had never done shots before, but Hector ordered us some shots of Tequila to get the night started. We were traveling by Uber and/or cab that night so no need for a d.d.

*Damos la bienvenida a los Zopilotes de Zacatecas!*

I wasn't the only one sitting and pining away and awaiting the presence of another. Hector had like invited a friend he had met through a friend at work the guy's name was Ricardo and he was Cuban or Cuban-American or something and Hector thought we would all get along swimmingly but like what struck me as odd at the time was who cared if a friend showed up or didn't at the same spot that night? We did about two rounds of shots and then decided to calm things down by sipping on beers for a spell I drank Miller Lite while Hector ordered a Corona Extra.

A group of *gueras* approached and Hector informed them he played the moog and I played the trombone for our band. Another group of ladies flocked and this time I played the lead trumpet and Hector played the drums. We had actually gone on a few smaller tours of unheard of regions of Mexico with *La Banda El Re-tacaño* not to be confused with the more well-known and illustrious *Banda El Recodo*. We were in San Francisco recording our first studio album. We were unsure if they knew we were joking. So were they.

243

We finished our drinks and left for a slightly more upscale bar near the Marina. *Catracha* kept putting the pressure on me for us to video call but I knew that if she saw me out with Hector dressed up and even if she heard the background noise of the bar on a phone call I would be dead-in-the-water like no way she'd believe I'd matured and we could revert to our status as an item despite being apart. I kept texting and saying my reception in S.F. sucked but that we'd be sure to maybe Skype on the computer tomorrow afternoon she was not buying what I was saying I eventually turned off the vibrate on my phone and even put it on silence.

*Damos la bienvenida a las Gallinas de Guadalajara!*

The *chilanga* showed up she was dressed as a vampire but not like a skanky costume vampire rather a pretty well-covered vampire with those thin dimpled cheeks and her already pale skin I was quite infatuated like she didn't need to advertise what she got. In addition to a fly body and cute face this girl had brains to spare and was real sharp-witted like she held her own Hector was impressed and a bit tipsy said to me "Damn Manny, I thought you only liked dumb and skanky *gueras*" and I'm sure my face got bright red and I know that this gal heard Hector and then looked at me like checking me out like could this gross truth be true but I did my best to brush off the insult even if deep down it stung because it rung true.

The *chilanga* and I made our way to the quasi-dance floor near the bar and kinda danced *pegaditos* for a spell she knew how to move her body and in my body the blood sprinted South from my head to the boneless appendage just below the waist. During one of the romantic songs I pulled her close and we locked lips and then she said whispered into my ear that she had to tell me a secret and had to tell me it now and a million possibilities entered my head all of them bad well most of like them but I still followed her outside to the rooftop bar.

*Damos la bienvenida a los Chocoyos de Chihuahua!*

She didn't immediately tell me instead we waxed for a bit on literature and caught some air San Francisco also was cold for me and even colder at night I told her I loved and had just finished *The Alchemist* she said I gotta read it in Spanish though 'cause that's more like Portuguese and and she recommended *On the Road* and I made a mental note then she suddenly leaned in and whispered again in my ear that she "was here illegally." I was kinda dazed but she had like really cute eyes and looked really sincere and I told her that was okay and nothing to be ashamed of and like I knew other people who were in the same situation. Then she got pissy. Like in the snap of a finger quick.

Turns out she meant she was not even eighteen she had used a fake ID to get into the club and then came the total suckerpunch she started tossin around the word "*mojado*" and was like offended that I could have assumed she could have been an "illegal immigrant." The girl was fine but by this time the blood had exited my boneless appendage and returned to my brain, where it burned. I had no use for this gal not even in the single-night sense of the word she realized that she may have offended me and then she started speaking fast and all hyperactive and tried to change subjects but I stayed strong and stared back with cold, reptilian eyes.

*Damos la bienvenida a los Colibríes de Cuzcatlan!*

Girl got the picture and found an excuse to part ways so I headed back inside and found Hector at the bar sitting beside this olive-skinned Latin dude with dark, immaculately styled black hair and dressed in a pretty tight black dress shirt and also kinda tight gray dress pants. His shoes had been polished recently, his eyebrows plucked by a careful hand. The dude was Ricardo and he and Hector spoke in stage whispers apparently some quasi-famous writer dude had just entered the bar the guy was white and pretty well-built but Hector and Ricardo were passing bets as to ahem his sexual orientation I was kinda bored so I texted a bit at *Catracha* and Ricardo ordered us several rounds of shots he seemed a bit off but nice enough.

Next thing I recall is waking up in my room I shared with Hector at *Tio Julio*'s place but there were like two pretty big differences first we had ditched the old single mattress ages ago we had two single beds mine on the far side and Hector's near the door and in Hector's bed there was also Ricardo like they weren't cuddling or anything but like this was a first at the time I still didn't suspect anything maybe Ricardo got drunk and needed to crash here which was cool but like the second thing really bugged me: I was not wearing my clothes from last night. I was wearing Hector's athletic shorts and one of my old white t-shirts.

I fucking flipped like got super angry and even shouted and said expletives Ricardo tried to be this mature calm down figure but his tone struck me as paternalistic and condescending so the Spanish expletives started to flow from my lips Hector said that night before I had gotten hammered thrown up and even thrown up on my clothes so he changed me no big deal but I was like really fucking pissed. In my head a thousand possibilities floated like what else happened what else was done to me but like in reality I was sore at lots of external things that *chilanga* girl turned out to be stuck up and a minor and *Catracha* was not texting back and like even then I could smell the change in the air and feel Hector and I's friendship slowly unraveling.

I didn't calm down or even stop shaking instead I quickly changed my clothes and left the apartment to go on a walk I called friends and teammates from the Gales and within weeks I planned to move out after Christmas and in the meantime resolved to never go out with Hector again.

I can barely stand to look back at this moment. With the passing of decades, I can clearly imagine that night and fill in the black spots left by an imperfect memory: Hector my caring friend holding back my head as I lurched over a toilet and vomited my guts out. Hector helping me to get my clothes off with the utmost privacy before lending me his own and also helping me dress. Yet none of those visions entered my head at the time.

I look back on my own past as we all do, seeing a fork in the road and shouting at myself to turn right and not left. Yet I still turn left, no matter how many times the memory plays again and again in my head. A world exists where Hector and I remain friends, where Hector and I grow old and watch ourselves age with grace and humor and happiness. Rather than worsen our estrangement, time solidifies our bonds of friendship. On a subconscious level, I now know that even then I must have known about Hector being gay and that's why I was a colossal prick. I shudder. Hector had stood up for me and to me so many times, like that one night in Sharyland, yet I couldn't stand up to myself and confront my own darkest prejudices for him.

Life tosses shit in your path like you spend enough days with your eyes open and awake and alive and some form of adversity will come up and slap you in the face when a couple a pair lovers significant others is close and tight and loving and supportive they cling together and hurdle over shit but for my parents who barely spoke never spent much time together and were more roommates than married couple well shit really hit the fan one summer in I think grade school. That's when my older sis Gemma got real sick.

I can still smell the immaculately clean back seats of the cab in my dad's red *troca* like it always had that new car smell even when it was years old and we sped down the highway heading West because finally we were going on a family trip to Falcon Lake kinda near Laredo and some dude even agreed to loan us a boat we were going on a boat I was stoked and curious and excited. I barely noticed that my older sister Gemma had like been sick and stayed behind with the *madrina* all I could think about was boat boat boat and water water water.

Gemma and me were petty tight from what I can recall like these little slivers of memory an appetizer brief moments like I recall we went on walks a lot when mom and dad were at work and we were home from school and bored. Out in the Valley there are tons of open fields and even like these grapefruit fields and orange groves were close enough to visit and if it was not like too hot we'd walk and walk and find these fields and play hide-and-seek and stuff like that. One field had like a drainage canal or something and we even went swimming in that thing no parental supervision no lifeguard no life jacket just two grade school kids in waist-high water splashing and laughing and messing around.

Gemma died before being confirmed as an adult in the Church and I remember when I like studied *catecismo* this seemed like a big deal and I thought of 2 Macabees 12:46 alot like us all needing to pray for the dead so that we can cleanse their soul and they can go to Heaven and to be honest it bothered me to think that an almighty God maybe just sent my older sister to like burn a bit you know 1 Cor 3:15 before going to Heaven like the thought of Gemma suffering made me really sad and angry because I knew a secret about her I knew sins that not even Mammy y Papi knew about *nunca si dieron cuenta* so like I alone could really pray for her.

*Heavenly Father, in union with the merits of Jesus and Mary, I offer to You for the sake of the poor souls all the satisfactory value of my works during life, as well as all that will be done for me after death.*

We got to Falcon Lake and set up like tents and as we drove around the camp area we saw some really truly dope RV's like they had silver rims and huge TV antennas on top and they were mostly driven by elderly white people but we also saw a few *raza* out there you know grilling *cabrito* or something. It was really hot and muggy and the air suffocated me with each breath but the worst was the *pinche* mosquitos especially around the evening they swarmed and feasted on our exposed skin so we had two tents and me and my brother were in one we zipped it up as best we could.

Night descended the *zancudos* departed and we all sat around a campfire it was pretty cool and we even started to make s'mores sandwiches and all that traditional American-camping-in-America stuff like if you want to go without running water or electricity in

Mexico you can just wait for the next *apagón* but then things got really heated really intense really fast my mom got a call from the *madrina* and allegedly Gemma was found lying in a bathroom stiff as a mannequin my mom was super livid she had been against the trip because of Gemma but my dad had pushed and pushed and pushed and like we were all packed up and back in the car within twenty minutes flying East on the highway towards Brownsville.

I was really pissed about not getting to see or even sit on the promised boat. I had no clue how serious Gemma was sick in fact I like barely had started to have a concept of death itself like sometimes I'd feel this panic realizing that one day my eyes wouldn't open but I couldn't yet project that same fear and unease onto the prospect of other people dying. When we rolled up to the hospital we waited in the car for hours while my mom went in and then my dad eventually herded us to the waiting room he and mom were not talking like silence boom the kiss of death ten times worse than a shoutfest maybe he felt bad on the inside I don't know.

*I give You my all through the hands of the Immaculate Virgin Mary that she may set free whatever souls she pleases, according to her heavenly wisdom and mother's love for them.*

At around three in the morning an uncle came to take me and my bro and sis back to our apartment my dad and mom stayed with Gemma on the drive back I saw the 7-11 where Gemma and I would walk and sometimes I won't lie we were hungry like not just stomach churnin hungry but like vision blurry desperate for food so Gemma got this plan I would go inside and pretend that I was looking for my dad while she, a bit older and more coy, would go and lift some items and we did it she coughed and that was my cue to start crying while she stole and it worked and she lifted a bag of Takis the Mexican spicy potato chips but I felt really bad next time I said we shouldn't but she just got mad and went inside by herself and lifted some and I felt bad for not helping and bad the Takis were lifted but damn I was hungry.

Gemma died and I can't really remember her funeral all I recall is dad and mom calling every relative to beg and plead for money to bury her right with a tombstone maybe a little statue *si había lana* and of course everybody who could come did come and afterwards here's the odd part my dad just stopped sleeping at the house for days at a time he would disappear he may have been drinking but like my mom still made dinner each night as best she could and she still served food on a plate and set out silverware and even *a plate of food for Gemma* so like we all sat and ate and looked at those two plates and those empty chairs for like lots of months. Food was scarce but those two plates were served like wtf.

At night after everybody was asleep I would sneak out and eat Dad's food and even Gemma's food and even bring some back to my room for Pablo but one night I heard this odd low sound like a squeaking and I saw the door to my parents' bedroom was slightly ajar I tiptoed near and my dad was sitting on the bed, hands covering his face, crying, he told my mom that he would be outside like near downtown Brownsville and see Gemma standing there and then he would blink and she'd be gone and this had happened to him like several times a week scratch that like all day every day and all over the place.

"Wow," I thought to myself, "the beast eats, the beast sleeps, and now we see that the beast has actual feelings. Maybe." My mom was none too impressed she sat next to him on the bed but had her arms crossed and a serious look on the face like a "where-the-hell-you-been" kinda glare I retreated cautiously and carefully and returned to my bedroom. On one mattress in the corner Pablo slept on his side facing the wall and on the other mattress Phoebe was curled up into the tiniest little ball.

*Recieve this offering, O God, and grant me in return an increase of Your grace. Amen.*

## More Regrets
### *22nd of June 2012*

Goddamn these skanky *gueras* and my lust for them. I blame Western literature I see skin that is white and think white is a metaphor means innocent and good but that is not always the case. Like Pavlov's dogs when they heard a bell ring and started to drool well if when I was and am ever in a bar or establishment of ill repute of that sort well if a lady with vanilla skin and a short skirt or a sassy gait strolls in well my tongue and mouth take a life of their own like how did this happen nature nurture genetics sheesh I am as hopeless as I am clueless. It could be the foreign element like you know different some got that red hair bright as a flame others more mellow almost orange like leaves before they drop off trees in the fall then you got that almost scratch not quite brown not quite black and of course blonde but I liked that dirty blonde seems more real even though I know it's fake.

I was pissed and angry and felt betrayed when Hector, Maribel and I rolled up to *El Toro*'s trailer after our night out in San Antonio. I was most definitely not speaking to at or even in the general direction of Hector aka Brutus aka Benedict Arnold aka dude who instead of being my wingman had totally macked on those fine *regias* and all but yanked them out from under my nose. At that time I had no clue Hector had turned was turning was starting to turn so he was like my *carnal* but also like the competition for voluptuous young vixens. And he had gotten laid before meandI had not gotten laid *ever* and this was a very big deal for me even though in the grand scheme of life and the universe this that meant less than jackshit.

Hector and Maribel headed towards the bedroom as I sat by Esme on the couch, she was watching TV, and I really didn't want to see Hector for a spell. I sat at the opposite end of the sofa and she was like watching really *really* old TV shows we are talking *I Love Lucy* and *The Dick Van Dyke Show* and all sorts of other old stuff that made me think of those black-and-white Cantinflas films my mom adored. Esme kept looking at me out of the corner of her eyes and had this really weird posture like her legs were crossed but her arms were open and her chest kinda pointed in my direction and she was acting weird like kinda laughing too hard at jokes and something kinda smelled like a skunk faintly her eyes were also bloodshot.

*Oh glorious apostle St. Jude, faithful servant and friend of Jesus, the name of the traitor who delivered thy beloved Master into the hands of His enemies has caused thee to be forgotten by many, but...*

My body has always been my own but like some parts of it at that time were getting a life of their own you know I'd be chilling in a class and suddenly an appendage filled with blood popped up and started to throb I wasn't no Mr. experience like *Catracha* didn't believe in sex before marriage or at least with me that's what she said and I respected her so we just kinda messed around whereas Hector man he had been around the block and told me every detail like hell even I felt dirty after some of that stuff like I needed to wash my own *pinches oidos*.

Dread and excitement and anticipation are powerful forces in the human body when they mix you can literally feel yourself split in two or like you have an out-of-body experience like I can still feel my soul or whatever lift up out of my body and see my shallow husk seated on the couch like oh shit Esme just scooted over towards my shallow husk and uh oh she is all giggles and looking at my shallow husk face and aww dam she just put her hand on my shallow husk

255

left thigh and that shallow husk of mine was still all *caliente* from them *regia* girls earlier look out!

Warmth heat *calor* explosion hair standing on end skin shaking and stretching lips lock hands explore north then south then north again clothing removed removed awkwardly damn *sosten* warmth and more warmth whoa like whoa hands traveling south under pants belt off boxer fly open whoa as in *ayy santo cielo ayyyyyy santo cieloooooooo*. The shallow husk descends into a dark place to the chagrin of my soul that floats overhead and would be texting SMH to myself if it were possible.

Like every ounce of my moral fiber told me this girl was wrong and doing this to the girl of a guy letting me sleep in his trailer who was helping me reach my dream as a soccer player was wrong but damn I couldn't breathe this girl played my body like a piano she'd touch a note with a finger and I'd fight to hold back a shriek and when she covered my mouth to keep me from moaning too audibly I bit her a bit just 'cause you know and then she bit me a bit just 'cause you know. Then like boom alert what the fuck was that did I just see a head around the corner was somebody watching us like who Hector *El Toro* Maribel?

I lightly pushed her off and pulled up my pants lickety split then I put my finger over my lips for her to be quiet then gestured with my hand for her to wait I tip-toed around the trailer I could hear *El Toro* snoring whew not him and then I lightly opened the door to the other room Hector was lying on the floor and Maribel was on her side on the mattress did my mind just play tricks on me?

256

Seeing Maribel there reminded me of this time at the library when I was in middle school and well Maribel wanted me to read literature and "serious fiction" but like I would hide from her in remote corners to read none other than Danielle Steel I craved consumed that stuff but Maribel said that all those stories were the same somebody fell in love somebody got laid the end but but like Danielle taught my mom how to read my mom had all those books in English and the stack of books in our apartment always included mom's handwritten translations of words she didn't know in the margins.

Reading something written with love and that included love was like a security blanket but like here's the deal blankets are really cool they blanket you when you are cold and alone and yes the narrator is weak and there-but-not-really-there and you get confused by changing perspectives but love you read about love and you know there is love and consummation somewhere in there it will happen just keep turning those pages not like that Cervantes' tome where two stags hit the road and just meet people and and and Danielle plays your heart like a fiddle but…still…maybe…well…

*Pray for me who am so miserable; make use, I implore thee, of that particular privilege accorded thee of bringing visible and speedy help where help is almost despaired of. Come to my assistance in this great need…*

Standing by the door, I soon forgot about Maribel and Danielle and thought of Esme and I felt disgusted like my heart was racing I'd never done nothing like that either in terms of body logistics and stuff but also like moral-wise and I was afraid but that also kinda like excited me because I was an idiot I didn't know what to do though because like if we continued we could get caught but if I didn't like

257

finish the job could she get mad and needy and say something? My dick had gotten me in a deep mess and my head was spinning and like a thousand thoughts passed between those ears but not one of them was sensical.

Everything was wrong hell everything about everything was wrong this was sinful *flagrante delicto* stuff and I was tempted and I had started to cave I could have said no or pretended to be asleep or tried to de-escalate the situation but instead my mouth and my hands and my appendage got all greedy at the sight and smell of that vanilla white skin and Esme had freckles like those little brown dots white people sometimes get on their skin and they felt good and also tasted good sorta like regular skin but different.

I was a lost cause like if at eighteen I was doing this shit and not able to keep my dick in my pants what hope was there for me later when things got serious and I had a real job and real money and like had learned how to *echar perros* and carry real conversations with girls. I'd dated *Catracha* for years but we were so comfortable with one another she was like my sister and a friend. Weirder shit entered my head like my spirit floated over my body again and I swear I could see dark patches like the sin staining my husk and I thought if Judas had like asked for forgiveness instead of hanging himself would he have passed through St. Peter's gate as in the Sodomites' bigger sin was being unrepentant not like the whole sodomy thing right? I walked back to the couch and shook my head Esme like enough was enough this needed to end. I turned and slowly walked away my mind a mess and my body ablaze.

I knew from CCE that feeling guilt was not enough and confession was important and like shit my soul thought as it floated over my stained, dark body you got yourself in a right mess and then I was standing by the bedroom door for Maribel and Hector's room I was maybe gonna open it and try to crash with Maribel but still thinking and Esme appeared beside me she touched my hand I turned saw her blouse unbuttoned I could see her black bra and her bare pale skin she stepped towards me I could smell my sweat on her sweat this drove me crazy she smiled and nodded towards the bathroom door my soul shouted "HELL NO" and guilt entered my mind pre-sinful deed but I still walked into that bathroom and we like you know.

*I promise thee, O blessed St. Jude, to be ever mindful of this great favor, and I will never cease to honor thee as my special and powerful patron, and to do all in my power to encourage devotion to thee. Amen*

259

## Trapped
### *20th of August 2011*

    That summer before my senior year of high school I could smell a change in the salty air that floats into Brownsville from the nearby Gulf of Mexico *Catracha* and me were probably as happy together as we'd ever be and Hector and I was tight so we decided one hot, muggy August day to drive all the way to McAllen well really Sharyland to attend some rave-type thing in an old and unused orange grove it was thrown by some really *really* rich *regias* who had recently fled Mexico to escape the violence and had cash to burn.

My older half-sister had agreed to watch the younger siblings so I could attend said "rave" like things had changed so much and so fast after *Gemma* passed away and later dad left moms stopped seeing Maribel as this little spawn of a witch and actually remembered her birthday and invited her over to our house it helped that Maribel's mom had turned and like wore jeans and t-shirts she had cut her hair short and was no longer a temptress of dad and and my dad left and my mom even insisted on like helping throw Maribel a *quinceanera* she didn't call her *"mi'ja"* or nothing but did say *"mi queridita"*.

The rave event was pretty poorly attended but like we didn't care yes we kinda took delight in the rich and snobby sufferings of the *regia* throwing the party but like the DJ think his name was "Vintage ILL" kicked butt and yes oh yes glowsticks proliferated but like no oh no we did not partake in any drug use I was still in high school and obsessed with soccer my body was a temple so no ecstasy and also *Catracha* only allowed the occasional visit to third base man I was so pure and kinda innocent back then.

The DJ played a song I loved like I found out later looking online he had remixed some older song from DJ Shadow and this song ebbed and flowed between nervous melancholic and upbeat giddiness and *Catracha* and I danced so close our bodies touching swaying shaking moving in unison feeling the same beat this girl did it all for me from the first time I saw her at Church it was a *flechazo* that's why it hurt to hear all the time folks tell me even Maribel that we were just young kids that we didn't know what love was that it was just adolescent hormones.

Even now when I hear a version of that song, I mentally check out of my current body and return to that hot, humid August day in an orange grove in Sharyland. I can feel the mosquitoes amass and swarm. I can see the glow sticks flying all around in the night. I can smell the sweat on *Catracha*'s neck. I'm still blown away whenever a song or story or album can transport me so far away so quickly.

Unseasoned, my adolescent heart told me that *Catracha* was the one, the only one, and that we would love each other forever. I had no fucking clue how royally I could screw things up. I let doubt seep into my heart from my mind, but mainly due to my ears. The whole world told me that high school sweethearts had to break up, that a boy needed to get laid to become a man, and a host of other lies. Even Maribel, so fond of *Catracha*, told me that everything would change once I went to college. Assuming I went to college.

So like the feeling of immediacy dominated me 'cause like *Catracha* was close to turning 18 and she had this plan basically she was sick of living in poor and way-too-hot Brownsville and had friends in Houston so she planned on leaving the Valley ASAP she knew somebody that knew somebody who could get her past the *garrita* in Falfurrias. I had this royally fucked up *machista* idea belief worry that like hey *Catracha* was my girlfriend first and longest and like we should do the deed first you know with-one-another it wasn't even like romantic the notions that floated around in the dark recesses of my head.

I'd been getting better like since my dad left after a half a year or something this white dude who worked as an engineer started to spit game at my mom but like I'd never seen this style of game he would come over and just sip coffee with her and listen like my mom would talk for fifteen minutes and then he would interject with a brief remark of incredulousness "really" or an interrogatory "and how did you feel" like they had real life conversations without shouting. Dude even tried to work a number on us kids he was nice and respectful I was reticent at first but hell he even tried to heat tortillas on a wet paper towel in the microwave to make us tacos he got an A for effort even if he had never heard of a *comal*.

I stole his tricks like I would talk with *Catracha* but like bite my tongue and wait for her to stop talking before I would ask her you know how she was feeling or what was next that shit worked we got closer and this Polish I think dude sent my mom flowers so I scraped some funds together and once got *Catracha* a bouquet of Texas blue bonnets she melted in my arms. Then shit fell apart. This guy got a job in Houston and proposed to my mom and wanted to take us to Houston with him but my mom said no and he asked again and she said no and then she was sad like in a dark place she stopped putting on her face each morning like before she stopped dying her hair and you could see the *canas* grow in number and start to dominate her scalp after work she'd just sit on the couch, smoke, cough a bit, and watch *telenovelas*.

I felt a huge crushing weight because then I believed that like this Polish dude could marry her and get her papers in order and then, hey, guess what not so fast what about me Mr. fucking *mojado* me the anchor baby who couldn't also get papers who was stuck in the RGV who mom can't leave behind the *bebé* born in San Cristóbal who hangs like a millstone around his mom's neck and siphons off her happiness. I was fucking mad at myself but like shit to be honest I was pissy with everyone even my mom even though like I was wrong so wrong and I was even pissy with *Catracha* and even Hector who was back from Iraq on some sort of leave and acting a bit weird but hey we still decided to roll over to Sharyland for that rave for a bit of escapism Lord I needed it.

You can't have a group of *raza* in one large, open place without some folks grilling meat even at a rave so like lots of folks around midnight started to cook that *cabrito*. Then I saw this little kid standing near a grill and holy shit he was cooking a pack of hotdogs on top *and they were still in the package* and I recognized this kid his name was Tofino he was in sixth grade I also knew his older brother David and you say his name like Mexicans say it "Dahhhh veeed" not like white people say it well I started laughing and then Tofino looked pissed and lo and behold Dah-veed appeared to snarl his ugly ass face.

As background Dah-veed had dropped out of high school a few years back he and his family lived off his dad's bogus monthly S.S.I. check or something his dad sat around and drank all day and I am pretty sure they are a drug family they live in a notorious *colonia* so they probably stash bricks of *mota* in or under their double-wide trailer every few months to make some cash still they are dirty as sin but arrogant as fuck even though this bro couldn't get any ass he has to wait for Spring Break every March to prey on drunken *gueras* he couldn't get any ass during *Semana Santa* when the rich Mexican girls come up to invade Padre Island because they can smell a poor, worthless, ambitionless spic a mile away.

David steps up to me and of course launches the first verbal blow with a classic "ignore these *mojados* Tofy" and *Catracha* wants us to walk away she spoke to me in her broken English that was as cute as a toddler's first steps but nobody is getting the last word on me not in any context especially some worthless fucking *papelado* who could go to Houston anyday of the week he wanted and get a real job but like doesn't so I shout to David "teach your fucking *pocho* bro how to cook like a Mexican, not some ignorant ass *gringo*" and whoa did that open up David's eyes they brightened like Christmas lights then they went black as an abyss and I knew he wanted to fight and I knew his crew they did drugs and were lanky and Hector and me coulda fucking pawned those clowns one arm tied behind our backs.

In my mind Hector uses his military training and goes berserk beating the crap out of these worthless *pochos* in my imagination Hector holds down this Dah-veed and I pummel his face in with my two fists but in reality Hector the wise holds me back, he restrains me, he calms me, he soothes me, he forces reason to enter my overworked brain and the instincts for hatred and violence dissipate and exit. I regain my composure and we turn to go away but then David calls Hector a coward and it's on again but Hector steps up to him and nose-to-nose says "I know and respect the law, unlike you and your family. Hit me first, that way I can pummel your ass in self-defence." David's tongue tied itself in knots. His gaze fell to the ground, and after about a minute of silence he walked away.

I was still amped from that possible fight but like other things man damn testosterone scrambled my brain my girlfriend was great but like as a stupid teenager I wanted sex and society said that males wanted sex and *Catracha* wasn't giving me sex so that confused and angered me and now this druggy *papelado* who could leave the Valley and make a life anywhere in the US and get a real job get paid in check not cash under the table was talking shit and Hector shut him up good but man the world was out to get me.

I wanted out. I needed out. I remained on edge for days after that rave, I even fought pretty seriously with *Catracha* and went to one of those convenient store drive-thrus *con chavas enbikiniadas* and she heard and got madder but like in that time we were in love so we patched things up lickedy-split still I surveyed my surroundings the RGV felt everyday more and more like a tarpit and I was the trapped, sinking mammoth in the back of my head I thought "I need to get the fuck outta here" but how?

## Nuevo Amanecer
### *9th of April 2012*

A few white clouds temporarily blocked the pulsating sun and I saw some *colibries* buzz around the bushes as I stood before the Shrine in San Juan, Texas like the place had a really big basilica, a kinda run-down two-story hotel for pilgrims and an old folks home and gift shop and lots of big green spaces and sidewalks including spots to do the Stations of the Cross come Easter what blew my mind though were the spigots over a fountain that spewed out holy water the idea was for pilgrims to take home a bottle but like locals showed up every few minutes and filled up huge five-gallon jugs.

Stopping at the Shrine for an early Mass before heading Westwards and then North to Falfurrias was Maribel's idea she was kinda superstitious in a Catholic sorta way. On tap was a sermon from none other than *Padre* Gerald Mapple, this aging white and bald Great Lakes transplant whose skin in the summer turned as pink as a little girl's bedroom he was originally an Episcopalian and had had a wife and son but his wife had died from some illness in Spain decades ago and his son had committed suicide in New York and had been an artist *Padre* Mapple was of course a Jesuit he had landed in the RGV because he enjoyed the sauce quite too much and was one of those faux-communists that would be killed if transferred to a non-democratic English-speaking country.

He was light years better than the pedo-priests normally foisted and flung into the RGV by bishops you know the off-color-dudes who are too eager for youth camps and retreats and lock-ins they were normally awaiting extradition or prosecution or both so why not do a pit-stop near an international border where they can drive away from an arrest warrant in ten minutes if need be. Just makes sense.

The Shrine had been around forever a few decades ago some pilot crashed into the building but like only the pilot died and some *padre* saved a statue of Our Lady and that's that there was also a monument to immigrants and along the sidewalks folks would make those little side-of-the-road remembrance boxes with images of the Virgin and maybe a candle and a pic of a family member who had gotten lost in either the *cruzada* from Mexico or trying to sneak past Falfurrias in the surrounding woods. Hector man he could be an asshole he had convinced me that I was going to have to get out of his car and walk around the checkpoint so like I saw these little mini-homages to the dead with eyes wide open and a sense of both reverence and dread.

*Padre* Mapple's politics and faux-communism bored me to tears but when he spoke about immigrants he had so much passion in his heart that veins on his forehead bulged and his face got red he spoke this broken-ass dialect of Spanish like really fluent but at the same time *mocho* I wouldn't call it "Tex-Mex" well yeah maybe I would he tried to pronounce the "v" and "s" like Spaniards really overdoing the "th" sound and also used the vosotros for third-person plural which sounded like an off-key note to our Mexican ears oh oh and he also said Tamaulipas like "Tom" "all" "leap" "us."

> *Den gracias al SEÑOR, porque él es bueno;*
> *su gran amor perdura para siempre.*
> *Que lo digan los redimidos del SEÑOR,*
> *a quienes redimió del poder del adversario...*

I had been against going to the Mass because none of us were dressed very nice and looking around the beautiful basilica not a lot of people

267

were present this was a weekday early Mass you know only for the die-hards still they were all dressed to the nines while we rocked t-shirts and jeans and stuck out like sore thumbs Hector was bored as Hell he was spacing but Maribel paid attention and I kinda sorta dug that Bible Verse Father Mapple was trying to wrap his tongue around.

> *...Vagaban perdidos por parajes desiertos,*
> *sin dar con el camino a una ciudad habitable.*
> *Hambrientos y sedientos,*
> *la vida se les iba consumiendo...*

Like we had made plans to go to San Antonio and Hector knew this former pro and I was going to get a tryout and I was stoked and excited but I also felt like terrified I was scared of the *garrita* in Falfurrias but also like what else was going to happen I'd never lived alone like I was happy Maribel would be coming along she had lived by herself three years in college way over in Edinburg like she had her own apartment and stuff and I know that Hector had served abroad but Hell he lived on a base they cooked his meals for him and told him what to do every day that's not exactly independence.

I know Hector was kinda like in a confused state re: the military he was getting paid some serious bank but he also probably saw some serious shit and a few times he'd start to talk to me about military titles like the codes with a letter and number combo and it flew over my head like a jet you know B5 mechanized airborne that kinda talk and I know he made some good friends over there I saw his phone and he had a lot of pics of this white dude from Tucson or something but Hector had done this trick to get out of his tour they had tried to change his contract so he wrote a five page rambling letter to HR and on page four he said if you don't let me out treat this as a FOIA request and nobody read page four so boom he looked online and lawyered up and threatened a FOIA lawsuit and the army I guess cared about their reputation he got out early for like compassionate leave or something.

*...En su angustia clamaron al SEÑOR,*
*y él los sacó de su aflicción.*
*Cambió la tempestad en suave brisa:*
*se sosegaron las olas del mar...*

After the Mass we walked around for a bit and then we got some tacos *machado con huevo* at Stripes and had a brief talk about itinerary Maribel was pushing hard for at least the idea of turning around and going through Corpus she wanted to visit Selena's grave and we knew her feelings on the matter and respected them but this topic had already been raised and like Hector said lied fronted that we had to go through Falfurrias so I could sneak around in the woods but then he mentioned a friend or two working the oil fields near Laredo and Maribel laughed she said nobody would want to go there like those towns were now nothing but bars and man-camps where dudes packed into trailers like way too much testosterone and Hector's blank expression to me looked like boredom and indifference at least at the time.

Looking back, I can see how easily I misread Hector's facial expression and reaction. Like a clumsy scientist, I had already concluded the man-camps would disinterest Hector and this clouded my later observations. The wrinkle-less forehead. The clenched jaw.

269

The narrowed eyes. The look off into space. I assumed these meant disinterest in the current topic, but now I can clearly see the face of a man lost in imagination, a mind humming on the inside at the specter of possibility.

Twenty minutes later after hearing the term "man-camp", only the prospect of passing through a second *garrita* convinced him to ditch the idea of a detour and pit stop near Laredo.

> *...Pero si merman y son humillados,*
> *es por la opresión, la maldad y la aflicción.*
> *Dios desdeña a los nobles*
> *y los hace vagar por desiertos sin senderos.*

I texted *Catracha* while I sat in the front seat of Hector's car and we zipped past Pharr and then headed North and passed Edinburg and the *garrita* was only an hour away she did not reply no shocker the conversation with her last night was like super painful I loved that girl with every molecule of my body even the atoms and shit but I had to leave the RGV the 956 was just too much for me I couldn't see any future worth having down there I told her I was gonna make it big earn that money then find a way to bring her to be with me but she couldn't even look at me she couldn't promise to be true to me she said she needed to see me everyday she said she loved me for who I was not what I might become I loved her for saying that but like you know neither of us was sure about anything and like why not we would maybe try distance or whatever.

I was sad for like what I might be *chingando* with *Catracha* like us it felt right I was happy the pics of me with her like fuck son talk about a goofy ass full-toothed grin even later I could think back to me skipping class getting in the baby blue Honda Civic her bro loaned us and us driving to sneak into some gated apartment complex to chill at a pool her in that fine fine green bikini and seeing her body move in water like so smooth and graceful and holding her close catching some rays and knowing that some school text message was going out to my mom "ALERTA: SU HIJO EMMANUEL HERNÁNDEZ NO LLEGÓ HOY A LA ESCUELA" and there'd be hell to pay later but for now enjoying that simple joy of the presence of another you know sometimes *más vale perdon que permiso*.

I was pissed at my mom I felt betrayed like she'd been my rock she'd kicked my ass when I needed it both before and after my dad had left she'd been both my parents my inspiration and then like this Polish dude came around and things were on the up then he left and boom the crash was immense and immediate suddenly I'm the one cleaning the bathrooms and scrubbing floors and making sure Pablo and Phoebe do their homework at night and bathe and like get up and get ready for school I wasn't even eighteen yet I didn't even need more shit to deal with and like why didn't I know the truth about me and my birthplace like that stuff until way late in the game I didn't ask to come to this country I was set up and then letdown.

A million images entered my head like logistical as in how on said day and as a recently-born child did I get across the *Rio Bravo* back then like sounds kinda sorta irresponsible on the part of my mom *muchas gracias* right? Every few weeks friends in Brownsville had a story about a family member dying lots drowned crossing the *Rio Bravo* which is known as the Rio Grande to most white people in America what happens is when it rains the current gets strong and folks get feet stuck in roots and branches and no way a *pollero* is going to save you law of pirates shit and getting around Falfurrias damn they pack people like sardines into sealed beds of 18-wheelers probably bribe some *limón* to get passed that checkpoint but like when they arrive always a few people normally old die from lack of oxygen then they dump the bodies.

I felt safe riding in the car with Hector I had a little backpack made for meals and my phone had great reception and a compass app I was just gonna head north after he dropped me off. We rocketed up 281 and reached Encino just south of Falfurrias Hector slowed down a bit I gulped and Hector had even loaned me his hiking boots and had me put them on he was a sick, sick twisted joker I got ready to walk run hide dodge whatever but then he laughed and sped up again Maribel was not super impressed and barely cracked a grin but clearly had been kinda sorta in on the joke. What else were those two hiding from me?

**Socorro**
*21st of June 1994*

How many of our most powerful childhood memories are nothing more than a collection of lies, a bundle of hearsay, a twisted web of embellishments? I never believed my dad's story about the *Isla Esmeralda* but it came to me in the hardest moments of soccer practice. As I pushed my physical limits and my mind melted and damn that beep test and run run run harder I saw myself on a beach at night with my dad behind me and he would get me ready and toss me into the ocean and I'd swim and the waves scared me but I was safe he was there watching and then beep test done get water. One of the Ten Commandments bans lies because they're a fucking powerful drug.

I heard three different versions of how my mom crossed me and Gemma near Rio Grande City when I was only a few months old and Gemma was super little one version came from my mom when she was about forty and she was always a master of understatement the second version came from Maribel who claimed to have heard it from my mom during one of the rare times my mom had ingested alcohol and the last came from my Tio Julio after my mom's death when I think about it only one version combining all three really seems possibly true but is still kinda crazy.

My dad killed a communist in San Cristóbal and he and the family had to get the hell outta there ASAP the weird part was that my dad and said communist were actually best friends who got way too drunk late one night at the *rancho* and in a heated argument over a fucking game of dominos there was some fisticuffs and then a gun went off accidentally still next morning the news ran and twisted the story and suddenly my dad was some anti-communist hero but like the town was full of communist sympathisers and he knew the story was not true and hell the guy's mom and dad even forgave my dad but my dad and mom knew it was time to leave the D.F. was a polluted shithole at the time so they figured South Texas would do just fine.

Papy left before everybody else but barely got through Piedras Negras like things had changed since he last crossed to the US there were little teenagers with walkie talkies all along the river and they were there to call in the big boys if some migrant tried to cross without paying a toll my dad knew some people from his time with the army and barely got through but he did and made his way to Brownsville and started to work and send us money and he wanted my mom to come and cross before I was born and that was the plan I was going to be a baby boy and thus I was the priority not Gemma. Or my mom. Prick.

When you cross you pick your poisons I had thought that maybe my mom had borrowed some friend's passport with a visa or something but no her and Gemma were going to try to cross the old-fashioned way like on their feet and over well through the river thus the ideal time to do so was at night and importantly when it was raining that was because the border patrol officers absolutely hated to get their shiny nice jeeps dirty and even more so hated to get out of said jeeps and get their own boots dirty still the rain raised the level of the river and the current so it was much more dangerous one misstep or a foot caught in the roots and plants on the bed of the river and lights out *Adiós*.

My dad had paid a four-figure sum in the hopes that the *pollero* aka *guía* aka coyote aka guide who was assisting my pregnant mom and

Gemma would be a solid pro and like not do something sketchy like abandon or injure them in one version of the story my dad went to early morning Mass every day while he was waiting for us but in another version he was living with Maribel's mom and drinking heavily every night and not sure we would make the crossing like we'd get popped by the *limones* and then he'd have to decide to fork over real money to some shady attorney to try and get us out or accept that we were destined to stay in Mexico.

I was born in Mexico because of the rain or rather the lack of it. My mom arrived pregnant in Reynosa with Gemma in tow she stayed with cousins who worked in the *maquiladoras* but after a month of no rain which meant not a good time to cross well my grandma convinced her to return to San Cristóbal the fighting had died down and my mom and Gemma did return and then the doctor told her it was dangerous for my mom to travel and walk too much and thus I was born in the *Hospital de Caridad* in San Cristóbal and then a few months later we were back in Reynosa praying for rain and staying on cramped couches in little tin shacks with only occasional running water and electricity.

Even post-preggers my mom was beautiful she always felt the sting of young men's eyes when she went out in public like that barbaric Latin male gaze akin to a starving coyote seeing a rare steak for the first time I can only imagine the *piropos* back in the day she could go to a Western Union to get some dollars from my dad and not worry as much about getting tagged and followed and robbed there was no war back back then in Tamaulipas small businesses flourished my mom loved this little *reposteria* called *La Espiga* which every morning served super cheap and delicious *conchitas* and also other *cosas de horno*.

Mom had gotten in touch with the *pollero* once it started to rain like a group of her, me, Gemma, the guide and five other migrants would head over to *Ciudad Camargo* just on the other side of Rio Grande City and a popular crossing point sure enough after weeks of waiting the storm clouds gathered and huddled and discussed among themselves via thunderbolts and finally in the afternoon dropped a little and then a lot of rain the *pollero* and the *pollitos* aka us all got in a truck in the truck's bed of the truck and headed West on highway *Dos* which is less of a highway and more of a two-lane paved road my mom and Gemma and me got to sit inside the cab of the truck because we were little and my mom never stopped talking about how my dad was a former army guy who had popped a communist in San Cristóbal.

My mom was kinda freaked out by our *pollero* he had an eye patch over his right eye the dude was dark, tall, and menacing but like his right arm also flopped by his arm he must have been an ex-soldier and my mom thought WTF my guide is *tuerto* and *manco* and like how can he lead them with one good arm but like this was not a run-of-the-mill professional service there was no professional association to call and complain no receipt no refund no regrets or something. What really bugged her was how he smiled and winked at Gemma. His name I think I heard was Rolando or Jude or something it was probably made up.

We hung out in *Ciudad Camargo* until nightfall at some random woman's house my mom prayed and prayed for a safe crossing and tried to will Saint Matthew 21:22 into truth and then Jude counted that toll money and night fell and we got in a truck and we headed up highway *Dos* a bit more like even though the *Rio Bravo* was super close to Rio Grande City you had no chance of crossing there the *migra* would find you so easily thus we were to cross near La Rosita and we parked just off the highway and approached the river banks everybody had a bag with a change of clothes because we were going to get wet crossing and Gemma clasped her St. Christopher medallion like it would protect her but like it was raining so WTF my present self asks still a bigger problem emerged: me. I started to cry and wail and moan and scream was I trying to save my future self from the slings and arrows of a life in the US as a *mojado*?

The *pollero* was pissed but my mom breastfed me a bit and I got full and shut up and after about thirty minutes of waiting our guide got a vibrate on his pager like the old school black ones doctors used to have well it was time to operate the *migra* was changing shifts and we had to move fast the river was not so much a river but mud and mosquitos Gemma said timidly a few times *"No me quiero ir"* so mom ended up carrying Gemma in one arm and me in the other as we waded across the river.

Once we got to the other side of the river the *pollero* told everybody to shut up and lie down like he probably was waiting for another pager buzz when the new shift from the *migra* starts they always like to do a perimeter check first thing before they park at some spot and either doze off or start smoking or joke around on the radio because it was raining it was really unlikely any officer would get out of the truck my mom could hear a few times over the course of an hour a motor vehicle in the distance stop and an engine turn off and then turn on and then the vehicle would drive off.

Then uh oh Mr. Big Mouth yours truly started to get agitated and wailing and everybody knows that the shrieks of a baby can carry for miles if not entire continents the *pollero* got livid and started to make really serious threats as in "toss that baby in the river" he had a dozen other clients there near us buried in the mud but like nobody else looked angry just terrified deer in the headlights I'm sure nobody wanted to see me tossed in the river but *por el otro lado* nobody wanted a date with the United States Customs and Border Patrol my mom tried to hush me then hush the *pollero* she said I just needed some *teta* and tried to breastfeed to shut me up but nope not it.

The *pollero* rolled over to my mom and things got real serious real quick in hushed and angry tones he told her to resolve the situation or he would do it when he reached for me she slapped him bam angry *madre Latina* style he got pissed and grabbed her neck with that left hand and decided to squeeze the life out of the *perra y los cachorros* but then he got stung by a mosquito and pulled his left arm away he realized it was a bug bite and my mom started to sob I was still wailing too and he got even more angry so he grabbed her throat again with that left hand and squeezed harder and harder her chest tightened darkness threatened to force her eyes shut she tried to scream *"ayuda"* but couldn't, she tried to scream *"auxilio"* but couldn't, she then tried to scream "___", but then *the pollero screamed* in agony and pulled his arm away there was one problem: my sister Gemma's like six-year-old teeth were firmly planted in that bastard's forearm she drew blood and wouldn't let go.

All the other migrants flipped out and stood up and started running because they heard this dude screaming bloody hell and they also heard the approach of a motor vehicle even the *pollero* stood up and started to run only my mom stayed behind lying in the mud holding her two babies close Gemma had lost a tooth but I had finally shut up bright lights flashed on and scanned the area near the river a voice in a *mocho* accent announced in Spanish over a loudspeaker for everybody to *"pararse"* which most of them did even though the *pollero* waded back across the river and disappeared into Mexico. The migrants were rounded up, a few more vehicles arrived, and then everybody got loaded up and shipped to detention centers for processing.

Everybody except for Gemma, my mom and me. We laid in the mud and rain and battled mosquitoes in silence for an hour until finally my mom had the strength and nerve to stand up we then wandered for about two hours my mom finally found a small gas station *Bendito Sea Dios* and there was a payphone she had a plastic bag in her underwear with five twenty-dollar bills and eight quarters she had memorized the number for my dad's *primo* in McAllen this was plan B because my dad had crossed a few times himself and knew these things were never executed as efficiently or pleasantly as one would like.

And that was my grand entrance, my first night in the United States of America. Seventeen years later I'd leave the Valley and curse my parents for bringing me there and another twenty years later after that I'd return and I'd wish I'd just been a better son and I'd slowly watch my mother's health crumble before my eyes only then could I finally leave the RGV and leave for good.

## Aquella Noche
### 12<sup>th</sup> *of December 2010*

Juana Inés de la Cruz got a raw deal and this angered me greatly. At least, angered the adolescent me. The girl could write but these stuffy, cloistered old dudes told her not to write. She had to sneak into her *abue*'s library to read as a girl. She read Latin by three. She wrote a eucharist poem by eight. Why couldn't, why *shouldn't* this girl put pen to paper? Why was the world so crazy? All these thoughts stewed in my teenage head and heart as my mom yet again forced me and the fam to go to a special Mass that evening.

I could barely understand the Latin. The little bit I picked up was because some words sounded like Spanish. Mass in Spanish and English was tolerable, but Latin was an invitation to mentally space out for an hour. I didn't want to disrespect God or nothing but like come on how am I gonna stay focused with this Priest facing a wall his back to me and talking in some language I don't get? I didn't fall asleep or fidget I just was there physically but not exactly there.

*Fratres, agnoscámus peccáta nostra...*

We always had to sit in that front row and so I kinda stared for a while at that famous image of the Virgin of Guadalupe which was hung before a few candles because today was her feast day and we were paying her homage but before Mass got started in Latin the Priest spoke to us in his *mocho* Spanish and was pissed as hell. He had found a candle of the *Santísima Muerte* in the chapel of perpetual adoration. This was like a big "no no" because the *Santísima Muerte* was not sanctioned, was not official, did not exist, was pagan idolatry. Did the Virgin de Guadalupe have similar beginnings? Maybe. But tonight we hung an image of her on a wall and the Priest tossed a candle of the *Santa Muerte* into a trash can for all to see.

So like back to that image I was staring at have you ever noticed the Virgin's eyes? Like, stared at them from afar and then up close? Folks think *Mona Lisa* has this charming smirk and coquettish eyes but the Virgin has these fine, delicate cheekbones and her half-closed eyes are staring back at you but not right at you instead she is looking at something low, like is there something near the ground beneath your feet that has captivated her attention or what?

*...ut apti simus ad sacra mystéria celebránda...*

Around the Virgin you see this orange outline and then all that yellow and I know it's supposed to be the rays of the sun but it really looks like she's laying on some bamboo hammock and like if we are worried about pagans and stuff why so many sun rays gleaming behind this Virgin? The day of the week we go to Church in English is still called "Sunday" and that's maybe Celtic for "Sun Day" and in Latin you got *Dies Solis* and we are not supposed to worship the Sun anymore but that's still there so something is up.

But I love that Virgin's shawl. Dark navy blue with a gold trim and those yellow stars, she is draped in the sky at night. I could stare at the image for hours on end but hey no music at this Mass and that's okay means it's actually shorter but we just gotta listen to some Latin and then a bit of *La Palabra*. Then comes the fun part everybody who has not sinned or has confessed their sins can stand up and get communion. I'm not gonna lie I need to cast off this right hand of mine before I go to bed at night it does bad stuff but it don't feel so right to tell a Priest about it so I am staying seated and watching the procession.

*...confíteor Dio omnipoténti....*

During the summer everybody at Mass is a different shade of brown but in the winter a bunch of "Snow Birds" aka old white people come down from up north to fill up Brownsville's RV parks and Wal-mart parking lots. Usually during communion maybe one-third to one-quarter of the brown folks stand up to take communion because everybody's got some little sin tucked away deep inside which means you should not be taking communion. I repeat, you should *not* be taking communion. That all changes when the old white people roll into town and show up; they are convinced that St. Peter's Gates will be tossed open wide for them so they form nice and neat and orderly but really long lines to take communion. They also don't open their mouth and wait for the Priest to put the wafer in their mouth but stick out their hand as if their hands were clean enough to take the bread, the body of Christ.

So I'm sitting drenched in my thoughts as to my own sin while the usher stands by our aisle for folks to stand up and get in line and my mom is glaring at me with laser eyes like *"Qué pasa?"* "What sin happened under my roof?" and I remain seated and I know that later I'll be trying to brush it off telling her *"Se dice la penitencia, no el pecado"* but she'll still be on my case so I'm gonna have to make something up which is another sin and she'll say my made-up sin is not serious and I should have taken communion.

*...mea culpa mea culpa máxima culpa...*

Then She walked by and everything changed and I couldn't just go back to staring at the Virgin. Or my mom. This girl that walked by was *re re re re buena*. Hair black as charcoal and smooth as ice, down to her shoulders and waving in the air. Hips so full and wide I could feel my hands instinctively grabbing for them and a plump rump that I would wager rendered obsolete cushions on chairs. I turned my head and saw her standing in line and she had on these tight black dress pants and heels and a white blouse with a few of the top buttons unbuttoned and I got struck by Cupid's arrow direct hit you know *puro flechazo*.

God creates beauty everyday like a sunrise and most folks don't notice Hell most get up long after the Sun's rays first jump up over that horizon and pierce through the night but then the Good Lord takes his time to sculpt a lovely maiden and tosses her down to Earth and teenage boys like me notice and notice I did. She walked not with sass but Her hips swayed and She put one foot in front of another in front of another and I couldn't help but think *Dios mio Dios mio* and sweat started to cover my palms I forgot about my psalms.

*...Deo grátias...*

Like who is this chick? Like how long has this *muchacha* been on the same planet as me and why am I only just now finding out about her and I's mutual co-existence in space and time and and like how, when do I rectify this? The girl looked straight ahead and wore a superficially somber expression, but I was sure she saw me seeing her and the corner of her eyes darted up and down playfully. She wanted me to see that I could see that she saw me but was not seeing me.

283

So like my mom didn't get up to get communion and instead gave me the *ojo* but now I remember this one thing my dad said about how God works in *maneras misteriosas* and if I saw a cute girl at CCE and she was in my *catecismo* class then that's clever God up there, knowing how to rope a *chamaco*. This girl made me want to confess all my sins, stand up to get in line for communion, and walk behind her and admire that figure up close. I really wanted to know what this Girl smelled like. I *needed* to know what this Girl smelled like.

*...et cum Spíritu tuo...*

Later like a few days later at school I think I talked with a few of my *carnales* 'cause you gotta investigate this stuff before an approach and this Chick was from Honduras or something. Her and her family just arrived in the RGV not F.O.B. like "Fresh Off the Boat" but like more F.O.R.B. like "Fresh Over the Rio Bravo" but even though then I had realized I didn't have no papers and getting with a girl with papers would like maybe make my life easier and I could get *arreglado* I didn't give two shits. I saw this Girl and knew that *Dios* put Her on this Earth and in my path for a reason.

I was sitting there watching then I saw that this Girl was for real because She didn't stick out Her hand for communion She just kept Her hands clasped in front of those tight black pants and opened Her mouth, Her glorious mouth with these pink but succulent lips and then She kinda half stuck out Her tongue and I coulda fainted, I coulda died and gone to Heaven or Hell or wherever *Dios Mio*. I wanted to be a Priest, I wanted to be the one to place the Body on that glorious tongue and in that heavenly mouth.

*...Let him kiss me with the kisses of his mouth...*

I can't help but think of *The Song of Solomon*. I looked at those lips, that tongue, that mouth, and closed my eyes and could feel the warmth of Her breath on my body and the hair on my body stood up on end and I trembled a little bit and then I closed my eyes and could feel Her breath again but this time She was playfully blowing out a little bit of air between those lips and I could feel that hot air on my skin.

Hot heat warmth skin caress rising. I opened my eyes and exhaled. She gulped down the Body in one swallow and then ever so slowly and confidently strutted over to the Eucharistic minister with the chalice of Blood. She passed right in front of me. She did that thing again where She knew I was watching and She knew that I thought She was *buenisisima* and She walked as if to say *mira esto*. And I did.

*...and his fruit was sweet to my taste...*

Looking back, knowing how things turn out, I can't help but laugh at my insecurity and anxiety then. Now, *hoy en dia*, I know that *Catracha* would become my first girlfriend, that we would date for years, that she would ultimately break my heart when I got back from San Francisco. In my head, my current self sits next to my past self in the pew. I smile and I want to prod myself to action, but also calm myself down. Like, this is kinda gonna work out but also not really work out, you know?

For my past self, at that exact moment, this beautiful young woman represented the height of intoxication, the visual and physical stimuli for hormones to take over the body and mind. She embodied a thousand possibilities at once. Every possibility danced a circle in my head. Was she only visiting family for a weekend? Would she only stick around for a few months before trying to head North? Would she be kind or rude to my approaches? Would she speak Spanish with an accent like me? Did she even speak Spanish? Where was she even from? Could we date? Be friends? *Amigos con derecho?*

It's pretty to think that maybe our adolescent love could have united us forever as in forever-ever, but I know now how that it all us me her ends and most all but one things end and endings that never end hurt the most.

*...I sought him, but found him not...*

When Mass ended I could barely wait for the Priest and altar boys to proceed past us before I shot up like an arrow and scanned the Church for this Temptress. She wasn't sitting anywhere near us and panic grabbed my chest and I had trouble breathing because lots of people just come to Mass like half an hour late, sit for a bit, and take communion and then they leave and what if this Girl and/or Her family was that kinda people I may never see Her again but then I saw Her seated near the back.

She was looking at me but as soon as I looked at her She looked away but then She looked at me again and our eyes connected and uuyyyy uuuyyy *que mirada fija Dios mio* She had these light brown eyes that tasted like caramel. Then I remembered that like I gotta be cool about this and stuff so I pretended sorta to be looking behind Her or for somebody else but I'm sure I didn't fool Her because She kept looking at me and then I turned and the rest of my family stood up to leave and we walked towards the exit in the back of the Church and I kept kinda glancing Her way but She wasn't looking at me anymore.

I lost sight of Her in all the commotion and stuff and then we got near the exit and we said our *buenas noches* to the *Padre* Gwyon 'cause it was late already and Mass was over for us but not for everybody else they were going to the Chapel of Perpetual Adoration to sing that *serenata* to the Virgin and I of course wanted to go and maybe see you-know-who and I begged and pleaded but but my dad had had enough Jesus for 168 hours and would not spend another minute in a Church 'til next Sunday.

I stood just outside the Church exit with my little bro and sis while my parents went to go get the *troca*. Chained hampered restricted tied down I was unable to continue my search efforts and more than a bit frustrated if it had been normal Mass we could have gone to get donuts and juice afterwards but it was not and it was night and it was late but I really wanted to be in or around that building at least a little longer just to you know get another glimpse of that Gal maybe make an approach.

The red *troca* pulled up and my dad got out and opened the doors to the back cab and said *"Hijo, órale! Qué te pasa?"* but I kinda dragged my feet and then my little bro said he had to go pee and I grew ecstatic and my dad got angry but my mom glared at dad and I got to take my little bro back inside while mom, dad, and Phoebe waited in the truck. We stepped inside and I surveyed the surroundings and lots of girls still loitered about, a few of them young, *morena*, and kinda cute, but not the One I had seen earlier. My little bro entered the restroom *solito* and I stood around in the lobby to continue my surveillance efforts under the pretext of standing guard. He took forever and after a few minutes I got nervous and knocked on the door but no answer and then I felt a tap on my shoulder and I assumed it was my angry *padre* so I grimaced but when I turned I smiled because of course it wasn't him, it was Her, the One I would later call *Catracha*.

And that's how it began.

# About

Elliott has written nonfiction, mostly about soccer, for various online and print publications, including The Guardian, VICE Sports, Fusion, The Blizzard, and Howler Magazine. He lives in Houston with his wife, children, two pet dogs, and a pet turtle named Chapo.

You can join the thousands who follow Elliott on Twitter (@futfanatico) and he also has a GoodReads page. For more information on the creation of this novel, go to http://thenotv.info.